Leather Hinges

By

Maxine Bridgman Isackson

This book is a work of fiction. Places, events, and situations in this story are purely fictional. Any resemblance to actual persons, living or dead, is coincidental.

ISBN: 1-4033-8650-1 (e-book)
ISBN: 1-4033-8651-X (Paperback)

This book is printed on acid free paper.

1stBooks - rev. 01/28/03

I dedicate this book to my husband, Richard, our children and grandchildren who have always been there for me with love and support.

Chapter 1

Hallie lifted her chin to a defiant tilt and forced herself to meet the steely blue eyes of the tall, grim-faced man she had once vowed to love, honor, and obey. Their eyes met in a clamorous silence where words battled to come forth through a stubborn wall of pain and pride. It was no use. Words wouldn't change anything, Hallie concluded once again. There was nothing left but to say goodbye with as much dignity as she could muster. She shifted the sleeping baby in her arms so she might offer a hand in farewell. Will, however, ignored the small, callused hand thrust toward him. Instead, he bent down and with a rough abruptness pulled Hallie and the infant into his arms, crushing them to his chest for one brief moment then wheeled and strode out the open door.

Clutching the now wriggling bundle tightly, Hallie pressed the little forehead to her lips, fighting back tears as she listened to the receding clump of Will's old boots on the plank stairs. Visualizing those worn, run over boots prodded Hallie's bitterness to life. Will wore those boots through his own doings. He had chosen to live like a pauper in this forsaken country, dragging her out here practically against her will. Well, she'd had her fill of it! Maybe some women enjoyed living on dirt floors, battling storms, watching folks die. It might suit some, but not her! She was taking little William back home to Missouri before the prairie claimed his life as well.

The baby began to whimper. He was hungry and in need of changing after the long drive in from the homestead. Hallie looked about the unfamiliar room for a place to put him down. The room was part of the upstairs living quarters of the Huebanks, proprietors of the general store on the ground floor. This kindly couple had offered their hospitality and a ride to the train depot at Prairie Rose when they learned Hallie's proposed trip to Missouri would coincide with their own buying trip to Omaha.

The Huebanks assumed Hallie was just going back to her family for a visit. No one except Will knew she planned to purchase a "one-way" ticket.

The baby changed, Hallie chose a rocker by the window overlooking the street and sat down resting the now fretting infant

1

across her lap while she unbuttoned her dress. With little William settled at her breast, Hallie leaned back against the softness of the padded chair easing the ache in her back acquired from the jolting wagon ride to town. Resting her head on the edge of the chair back she closed her eyes, the tension subsiding as the baby fed contentedly.

Faded streaks of late afternoon sun crept through the lace curtains softly lighting the tired young face framed by clusters of dark curls. A pretty face, finely structured with small straight nose and a rather stubborn chin. Firm skin, pale beneath the shelter of tumbled curls on the high forehead, an unfashionable tan otherwise where the sun and wind had had their way.

Lulled by the warmth of the sunlight and by the nursing child, problems faded, thoughts drifted. Drifted to a happier time. To the carefree days of girlhood…to the old, stone farmhouse.

Hallie was once again age ten, one of three little girls clad in gingham dresses and starched pinafores playing beneath the sheltering branches of the giant oak tree in the Melrose yard.

"Girls! Girls! You're going to get those clean pinafores all mussed up and dirty." This warning came from Ida, next to the oldest of the seven Melrose children who regularly despaired of her three younger sisters; Catherine, Hallie, and Amanda. The three were prone to neglect chores, lose school books, or get a dress torn.

The ringleader of the frolicking trio was Hallie, the middle one in age. Wiry and dark-haired like her Aunt Daphne, Hallie's only regret thus far was that God in his wisdom had seen fit to make her a girl instead of a boy.

"Oh, Ida. We're only playing," Hallie giggled just as Amanda grabbed one of the ties on her pinafore. Hallie felt the stitches give and knew Ida would scold. Ida was more of a stickler about such things than Mama. Mama wouldn't stand for bad manners nor allow a sassy mouth, but smudged stockings or a little rip in a dress didn't upset her all that much. Sometimes, you could even get Mama to see things from a ten-year-olds' point of view.

This was not always the case, however, as Hallie was reminded when she presented a petition to her mother after supper. Martha Melrose was in the process of putting each of her three younger daughters' freshly washed heads of hair up on rags. Rag strips when carefully wound and tied with portions of damp hair would produce

2

the long, uniform curls desired for Sundays and holidays. Hallie was the daughter now seated for her turn on the tall kitchen stool enduring this Saturday evening ritual.

"Mama, why can't I wear britches like the boys?" she began. "If I wore britches I could ride astride and not have to use a silly sidesaddle." And she reasoned with modest righteousness. "And when I climb trees there wouldn't be any worry about showing my bloomers."

Martha Melrose, a plump, pleasant-faced woman, chuckled as she parted off another strip of dark hair then re-dampening it with the comb she dipped into the pan of water sitting on the corner of the table. "My dear, you'll think differently in a few years, mark my word. You'll not want some young man recalling any such scandalous behavior of yours then."

"Oh, Mama! I won't care and it's all so unfair! Girls have to wear skirts and get stuck with dull old housework! The boys never have to do house chores except chop the kindling wood and carry out the ashes. They don't even have to carry water since Papa ran that pipe into the kitchen from the spring."

"Perhaps not, but they do have to do their own chores."

"Yes! Things like milking the cows, currying the horses, and feeding the pigs. Fun things!"

Her mother, winding the last curl, suggested as she knotted the end of the rag strip, "Why don't you run out and walk with you father in the orchard while the bath water is heating?" She nodded toward the window facing the grove of fruit trees. There, her husband could be seen nearing the gate of the white board fence that enclosed the orchard.

Hallie was off like a shot. There was nothing she liked more than a walk with her Papa through the orchard.

August Melrose took great pride in the orchard planted during his own youth by his father when the Melrose family had first made the move to Missouri. The orchard had grown from a few sprigs to the fine grove now covering the land across the lane from the house all the way down from the big barn to the main road. Not only were there a variety of apples, but, there were peach, plum, pear, and cherry trees with bushes of raspberry and gooseberry. Grape vines climbed along the fence next to the lane and strawberries grew in a patch at one corner protected by woven chicken wire.

3

Hallie ran unmindful of the tight projections bouncing on her head as she hurried to catch up with her father just entering the orchard.

"Wait for me, Papa!" she called, and was rewarded by the pleased smile on her father's bearded face. Hallie shared his love of the orchard more than any of the other children and they often took these walks together.

The man and child began their stroll beneath the fragrant boughs of fruit blossoms. A band of sheep permitted to graze the grass beneath the trees, lifted freshly shorn heads to watch as they passed. Down by the main road a horse and buggy trundled along at a slow pace. The driver lifted his hand and August Melrose gave an answering wave.

"Didn't recognize that fellow or his horse. Reckon he might be the new real estate agent been pestering Myrtle Hayes to sell."

Hallie gave scant attention to the passing rig. Folks often took their time driving by this time of year, drinking in their fill of the blooming orchard.

Overhead, in one of the big McIntosh apple trees, a pair of blue jays squabbled causing a cascade of petals to float downward, a delicate cloud of pastel snowflakes.

"It's like a fairyland, isn't it, Papa?" Hallie exclaimed. "It's my very most favorite time of year. Is it yours, Papa?"

"It's hard to beat, but I reckon I like best when the little old nubbins of green fruit have all filled out nice and fat, ripened and ready to eat."

The remembered perfume of ripening fruit and the succulent tastes, juices dripping from eager lips, caused Hallie to grin up at the quizzical eyes looking down at her. She gave a giggle. "That, too. I've got more than one favorite time, but I'll bet that's the very most favorite time of the aunts, and uncles, and cousins. What do you bet?"

"I reckon it just might be," her father gave an answering grin for the orchard's abundance had always been shared. August, as had his father before him, delighted in seeing the young ones leave the orchard munching on a huge apple or pear, pockets bulging with an additional supply while their parents carted off baskets heaped to overflowing.

The Melroses had plenty of family with which to share and no shortage of offspring. First cousins on the Melrose side were non-existent in this generation, however. The Civil War had taken

August's two brothers before they had married and started families. His sister, Aunt Daphne, and her husband who had been crippled in the war didn't have any children.

Hallie adored her Aunt Daphne and Uncle John. Papa said Hallie was the spitting image of his sister when she'd been a girl. Hallie was proud of the comparison. She had decided if she couldn't grow up to be a man, the next best thing would be to turn out a handsome woman like Aunt Daphne who drove a buggy team with such flair and could throw a rock clear across the duck pond when challenged.

A day seldom passed but what there were comings and goings between their farm and Uncle John's for they were neighbors. The other relatives were more apt to be seen on Sundays. After church there was usually a big dinner held at one or another of the relatives. Of course, Papa's only close family besides Aunt Daphne and Uncle John Myer were Grandma and Grandpa Melrose, but Mama's side made up for it.

The grandparents on the Reynold's side had passed away when Hallie was little so she didn't remember them. Mama's two older brothers had married and settled in St. Louis so they didn't see those cousins often. The rest lived close by though. Aunt Susie and her husband, Uncle Tobias, ran the funeral parlor in town. They had a big house on the corner just down from the Methodist Church. They had two daughters, Paulette and Theresa, whose ages jibed closely with those of the Melrose trio. This was about all that did jibe, however, and their visits were not met with enthusiasm.

Uncle Albert was Mama's bachelor brother who lived on the Reynold's old home place and raised blooded horses. Folks said that was where Hallie's brother, Martin, got his love for horses.

Mama had two other sisters who had married a pair of the Lewis brothers south of town. Aunt Rose had four boys and a daughter, Emily. Aunt Meg had three of each and was in the "family way" again. The younger members of the family were not supposed to have this last bit of information, but they did. Secrets were difficult to keep with so many small ears about.

Emily, Aunt Rose's girl, had been born the same fall as Hallie. They were best friends as well as cousins. Emily was a wee bit of a thing, all blond and pink-skinned without a freckle to her name. Hallie had a sprinkle of freckles on her nose. Even when they had first started school, the boys had all stammered and fallen over their feet in

5

Emily's presence. If Emily had been anyone but Emily, Hallie would not have like her one iota. But, Emily went her way seemingly unaware of the affect she had on the opposite gender, content to climb trees with her tomboyish cousin, Hallie. She had even made a vow with Hallie that when they grew up they'd not marry but get them a farm of their own and wear britches if they had a mind to.

"Yes, sir!" Hallie told herself as she kicked at the fluff of a dandelion. "When me and Emily grow up we'll do things to suit ourselves."

"Hallie! Hallie!" It was Ida calling from the back porch. "Mama says come. The bath water's ready."

Chapter 2

The vows Hallie and Emily made at age ten were forgotten in a few short years. The girls grew taller, their bodies filling out in new places and slimming down in others. Boy's activities they once so envied had lost their appeal. They began to find less fault with ruffles and hair ribbons...were thrilled when allowed to lower their hemlines from mid-calf to ankle. By age sixteen they were on the brink of womanhood.

One sunny Saturday morning in May Hallie stood contemplating herself in the full-length mirror hanging on her closet door. She and her cousin, Emily, would soon be among those finishing the required courses of study taught in the higher grades at the town school. They would be graduating with their class at the end of the month...old enough to be escorted to parties and other social functions according to community custom.

"It won't be a problem for Emily," Hallie told herself as she rubbed a finger along the bridge of her nose as though she might magically wipe away the freckles. "But...I doubt any of the good-looking boys ask a freckled-nosed girl to a party if he can help it! I'll probably end up like Alice Dubody." Alice though quite nice was taller than most of the young men in the community and was as flat of figure and plain of face as the walls she so often adorned at parties.

Hallie had overheard Ida and her friend, Nancy Waller, talking one day. "I feel so sorry for poor Alice," Ida had said. "Why, at the Loffet's party, I just finally told Tom he simply had to go over and ask Alice for a dance." Tom Beckworth was the young man who had been courting Ida for several months.

Recalling her sister's remark, Hallie gave a little shiver. Maybe she should skip this summer's parties. If she bleached her face faithfully a few more months with buttermilk, perhaps she would be presentable by the Christmas season. There was no sign the smelly stuff had had any effect so far, but that article in the Ladies' Journal said it would.

When Martha Melrose heard of this plan of delay, she would have none of it. "Hallie, don't be foolish. Ida and Catherine started going to the young people's doings after they graduated." (Catherine had graduated the previous spring, and lucky Amanda had one more year to wait.) "Now, we'll hear no more about not going," she said firmly. "You can ride along with Ida and Tom to the Spring Social."

Hallie groaned inwardly. She'd probably be tagging along with someone the rest of her life. She trudged up the stairs to the room she shared with Amanda to apply another coat of buttermilk to her hapless nose.

The "Spring Social," was hosted by John and Daphne Myer each year in late May to honor the newest graduates. It was considered the social highlight of the year even surpassing the Christmas parties and the Fourth of July celebration.

No invitations, as such, were sent out for the event. It was simply understood that all the young people were invited, barring the "little kids" who were still school age. Everyone wore their best. There was seldom a girl who didn't manage a new dress for the occasion, and for many a boy it was this event that prompted the ordering of his first tailor-made suit.

No such thing as a debutante ball was held in this modest country community.

A few of the grandmothers, however, had had such affairs in their own youth before moving to the far reaches of Missouri. Therefore it was the Myer's social that launched each new crop of daughters deemed old enough for courting in that particular section of Pettis County.

Hallie was to have her first grown-up party dress with a floor-length skirt. Her mother had made it from shimmering peach-colored taffeta she said set off Hallie's white skin and dark hair perfectly.

The evening of the social Ida and Catherine did their best to be helpful. Ida worked with Hallie's hair, brushing the waves and curls around her wrist forming a huge curl she tied with a matching taffeta ribbon at the nape of Hallie's slender neck. Catherine took a moment before dashing downstairs to her waiting escort, Eddy Evart, so skinny he barely parted the wind, but could dance "divinely", to show Hallie how to pinch pink into her cheeks. Martha Melrose did not allow her girls to use even a hint of rouge.

"Bite your lips every now and again," was her parting exhortation. "It will give them color, too.

Ida added more sisterly advice by warning Hallie not to be a chatterbox while dancing, but to smile prettily. "Limit your conversation to an occasional question that will lead your partner into a subject he can talk about," she advised.

"Like what for example?" Hallie wanted to know as she gave another pinch to a cheek. But, Ida, hearing Tom's voice below, only answered. "Oh, for heavens sake! It depends on the boy!" And disappeared down the stairs without further enlightenment.

Amanda who would have to stay home with Mama and Papa, settling for a game of Old Maid with her younger brothers, Troy and Frank, dejectedly worked at a row of tiny buttons on the back of Hallie's dress. After every fourth button or so, she would give a gusty sigh and mourn, "A whole year. I have to wait another whole year!"

Hallie took a last look in the mirror after the dejected Amanda had gone downstairs. Why, she did look rather nice. The rice powder Ida had patted on her nose nearly hid the freckles. A mischievous twinkle lit Hallie's eyes and as was often her habit, she spoke to God with friendly familiarity. "Well, Lord, when you decided to make me a girl, maybe it wasn't such a bad idea after all." She gave a nervous but happy little laugh then lifting her chin high and straightening her shoulders, Mama always stressed posture, Hallie went forth to face the evening.

Dutifully, she attempted to put into practice Ida's instructions pertaining to conversation. Smiling came easily enough, and the leading questions worked for the most part. Henry Bowman was crazy about baseball and was pitcher for the town team. He was more than willing to fill her in on the prospects of the upcoming season. Everett Middleton launched into the fine art of squirrel hunting with only a slight nudge. But, Morris Rookstool produced no more than a timid, "Y-e-yes or N-n-no," regardless of the questions put to him. However, Morris never did say much, Hallie consoled herself as she took a quick peek at her program to see who her next partner would be.

Hallie, having escaped being a dreaded "wallflower", would be pleased to recall that there really hadn't been any that evening. Aunt Daphne had seen to that with just the right word spoken here and there, no one was left out.

The jolly laugh of Birdy Halsop who was more than a little plump, or as the Melrose boys put it, "right down hefty", had been heard from the dance floor throughout the evening.

Uncle John had introduced Delbert Jenkins, a relative newcomer to the community whose eyes and teeth protruded slightly more than usual, to Alice Dubody of past wallflower reputation. It was common knowledge Delbert asked to see her home after the social. By the time Ida and Tom had their wedding in late June, Alice and Delbert had a date set for one of their own.

Ida and Tom had a lovely wedding. Everyone said so. There was a crowd at the reception held at the Melrose farm after the ceremony in the Methodist Church. Friends and family fairly caused the old house to bulge.

Hallie, coming down the stairs from the room where the bride was changing into her going away costume, paused to watch the assembly below. Bits and pieces of conversation floated upward from little groups, friend and neighbor chatting of spring crops, last week's heavy rain, new babies, and the like.

Spread below her were those who peopled her world. Faces known since childhood, some dear, some not so dear, but all of them a part of her life. Her eyes checked out the groups, seeking those closest to her heart. There were Catherine and Amanda flirting with those boys over by the punch bowl. Mama was talking to Parson Beddelridge. The parson was getting hard of hearing, and Mama nearly had to shout.

Papa came passing among the guests, stopping a moment for a few words with this one and then that one. He always looked so handsome when he was dressed up. Papa wasn't tall, but he had broad shoulders with just a hint of a paunch pushing at the bottom buttons of his suit coat.

Her brother, Martin, was visiting with Uncle Albert, probably horse talk, while his Mary Lou danced with one of the McCain boys.

There was no sign of Frank or Troy. They were no doubt outside playing tag or hide-and-seek with other children. She smiled recalling how just a year or two ago she, too, would have escaped the confines of the house to join in such games.

Time certainly brought changes, Hallie reflected. Papa's hair was thinner on top, she noted from her vantage point on the stairs. She hadn't noticed before. Now, Ida was married, leaving the family to live in a home of her own. Catherine was going off to normal school for the summer so she could get her teaching certificate. Martin was seeing a lot of Mary Lou Long. He was talking about wanting to build a house over on the other side of the orchard.

How must Mama and Papa feel, she wondered, with their children growing up and leaving, one by one? When they were all little it had seemed as though life would always be the same with the house full of laughing children, bumps and tears, toys, schoolbooks, only the seasons bringing change.

A feeling of sadness crept over Hallie to be quickly put aside by a reassuring thought. The Melrose children might grow up and marry with homes of their own, but they would always be near one another. They would still be one big family getting together for Sunday dinners and holidays.

Comforted, Hallie went on down the stairs and joined those who were filling their hands and pockets with rice to be thrown at the bride and groom as they departed presently for the train depot. Tom and Ida were going to St. Louis for a short honeymoon. Tom had planned to take his bride down the Mississippi by steamboat as far as New Orleans. His mother, however, had put a damper on such an idea.

"Why, Tom can't leave the farm that long with just his poor mother to manage," she'd said. Everyone knew Mrs. Beckworth could have managed an army had she been so inclined, and the Beckworth's had two hired men. No, she just wasn't going to let Ida get Tom off to herself any longer than she had to. Ida Melrose was marrying a young man with a fine farm and a big house. But...the house had to be shared with his mother...no slight cross to bear, was the general consensus of the community which then conceded, "If anyone can handle such a mother-in-law, it will be a no-nonsense girl like Ida."

Later, after the last guest had departed, and the house had been set to rights, at least to some extent, the remaining Melrose girls gathered in the room Catherine and Ida had shared to discuss the day's happenings.

"Wasn't it just heavenly?" Amanda chirped as she climbed to the middle of the bed and tucked small, bare feet beneath her night-gowned bottom. "I can't wait to get married!"

"It might be wise if you waited a year or two," Catherine responded in a tone Martha Melrose was prone to use when commenting on a silly notion of one of her children. "After all, you are only fourteen."

"Well, one of Bertie Regus' girls got married, and she was just fourteen. And...she's even got a baby! I saw her in the store a couple of weeks ago, and it was just as cute a baby as could be!"

11

Catherine, assuming Ida's role, used an even firmer tone as she informed both her younger sisters…Hallie's ears had perked up at this last news…that nice girls did not talk about "going's-on" of the Regus family.

Hallie made a mental note to question Amanda further when Catherine was occupied elsewhere. This was worth pursuing for she knew it had been around January when Ruby Regus had stopped coming to school, not that she had ever come very often. Bertie had passed out a story of how her Ruby was marrying some traveling man. So how did that all fit together? Mama said it took nine months to get a baby? Mama ought to know having had seven of her own. Maybe, it didn't take all women that long. Mama was such a stickler for doing things right she might figure if six or seven months would do a good job, nine months would do better.

This line of thought was dropped in order to join her sisters in a fascinating debate as to whether or not Ida would allow Tom to see her in her nightgown.

"Ida would never…not in a million years!" Hallie prophesied.

"Well, Zella Middleton said her sister came home from her honeymoon after just one day, crying her eyes out, and her mother took her into the parlor and shut the door!"

Intrigued, Hallie demanded to know if Zella had had sense enough to listen at the keyhole?

"Of course she did!" Amanda indignantly defended her friend. "She couldn't hear much, but she did hear Sally say something about how awful something was. And her mother sounded really provoked, and said it was expected of married women."

The three sisters sat silently in the center of the big, soft, feather bed thinking solemn thoughts. At last, Catherine as the eldest spoke. "As a married woman no doubt Ida will let Tom see her in her nightgown."

Hallie, not to be outdone, nodded wisely. "That's why Ida and Mama embroidered all those pretty flowers on the yokes and put such nice lace on the collars."

At this point, Martha Melrose tapped on the door to suggest firmly that it was time to get some sleep.

Ida made no teary flight back from a blighted honeymoon. Instead, she and Tom returned from the week in St. Louis even more in love than when they had left. At least, Hallie sensed a bond between the newlyweds that had not existed before. Could train rides and the sight of pretty nighties have such an effect, Hallie wondered to herself?

Positive there was much more to the marriage relationship than she had previously supposed, Hallie pestered her mother for more information until in exasperation she was given the guarded details with the stipulation she not share them with her less inquisitive sisters.

Hallie found her new knowledge difficult to digest. Surely not, Mama and Papa?

Ida and Tom? Aunt Susie and Uncle Tobias???

Chapter 3

It was mid-October. Hallie and her cousin, Emily, would be having their seventeenth birthdays before the month was out. Hallie, peeling pears and keeping a watchful eye on a kettle of jam bubbling on the kitchen range, was trying to recall the last social event she had attended.

It must have been when Clifton Maxwell had taken her to the Sunday School picnic. Why, that was way back before school started! There hadn't been a gathering since. With all the fall work everyone had gotten into a rut. The other young people in the community are probably as tired of harvesting, all this preserving…peeling…shucking, and all, as I am.

"Mama, do you think I and Emily could have a party for our birthdays?" Hallie, filled with sudden inspiration, asked her mother who was dipping freshly washed canning jars from a pan of hot water at the kitchen sink with a long-handled fork.

Martha Melrose gingerly placed a steaming jar upside down on a towel spread on the cupboard counter then glanced at the jam kettle. "Hallie, is that jam scorching?"

Hallie dropped the knife and a half-peeled pear in the dishpan of peelings and stepped quickly to the stove. A few deft turns of the wooden spoon whose long handle poked up from the fragrant kettle contents proved the jam to be stuck only slightly to the bottom of the kettle. There was no sign of scorch when Hallie lifted the spoon to wipe off a taste of jam with the tip of her finger. She licked the jam from her finger.

"Uum. This batch is spicier than the last. Did you add more cinnamon?"

Her mother nodded. "Yes, it's Rose's recipe. She always goes heavy on the spices in whatever she makes. Now, what were you saying about a party?"

"Well, Emily and I haven't had one, not a birthday party together, since…when was it…when we were eleven? You remember. Kelvin Brooster ate too much ice cream and was sick all over the front steps and Paulette and Theresa had a fuss and started yanking each other's hair."

14

"Lands, yes! How could I forget? That's no doubt why we've put off having another one."

Hallie and her mother laughed then Hallie urged, "But, do you think we might, Mama? Papa said just last night they would finish picking the field corn in another day or two. It would be such fun. We could have dancing and everything!"

"I don't know. I'd have to ask your father and Aunt Rose. If the party is to be for Emily, too, Rose will want to help."

August Melrose took only a small amount of persuasion, and Aunt Rose had never been one to say no to a party. Emily was ecstatic at the idea so a date was set…the last Saturday evening of the month. It would be at the Melrose house where the hardwood floors were ideal for dancing.

A general cleaning was expedited, fitted around meal preparations and the last of the canning. Amanda and the younger boys were pressed into service as soon as they arrived home from school in the late afternoons.

Woodwork and windows must be washed, curtains done up, rugs beaten and draperies aired. Frank and Troy raked the yard and swept the porches. Lanterns were gathered up to be filled with kerosene, globes washed, and wicks trimmed so the yard and porches might be lighted on the party night. There was cooking and baking, starching and ironing, countless tasks to be completed during the ensuing days.

At last the designated Saturday arrived. Bright and clear. "A good day for a doings," Aunt Rose declared when the Lewis family arrived at mid-morning. They had brought their dress clothes carefully wrapped in clean sheeting so there would be no need to make the journey back to their farm before the evening festivities.

"Now, just put us to work," Aunt Rose commanded as the husbands unhitched the team and led it off to the barn. "I've brought dinner so you won't have to cook at noon, Martha." And a huge picnic hamper was hefted out of the back of the wagon which was handed over to the Lewis twins to carry, with the warning, "Now, don't you go dropping that, you two!"

Of course, Martha Melrose wouldn't hear of anyone starting work until they had all sat down for a cup of coffee and a piece of fresh coffee cake. The work started in earnest after that.

All the boys were dispatched to the wooded hills back of the barn to gather armloads of colorful foliage while the parlor rug was rolled up and put on the back porch. Ladders and baskets were located for the decorating. By the time the boys returned with laden arms, it was noon.

The fried chicken, potato salad and apple pies Aunt Rose had brought were served on the picnic table in the back yard. This was a hurried affair with the girls fretting that the decorating would never be done on time, but of course it was. It was late afternoon though, before the house was pronounce, "ready".

Everyone, including Catherine who was home for the weekend from the school where she taught, stood back with pride to admire their handiwork. Paper streamers of gold and russet were draped above doorways and windows with crisscross strips looped across the ceilings of dining room and parlor. Baskets of assorted sizes had been filled with the arrangements of bright autumn leaves and placed throughout the downstairs rooms and porches.

The dining room table, shoved against the wall, was covered with a white lace tablecloth. There was a large bowl filled with chrysanthemums and late daisies in the center flanked by fat white candles in matching holders ready for lighting. A cut glass punch bowl sat regally at one end while a pair of cake plates stood proudly on tall stems at the other displaying the birthday cakes arrayed in candles and swirls of seven minute frosting.

All was in readiness. Nine-year-old Frank spoke for them all when he exclaimed. "Now, I'd say the whole works looks mighty fine!"

By seven-thirty, buggies and horsebackers began to make their way up the tree-lined lane toward the bright windows and the glowing lanterns. The relatives usually came before others arrived. This evening was no exception. Grandpa and Grandma Melrose came first, driving sedately behind their old roan mare. Uncle Albert was not far behind with a pair of high-stepping bays. Aunt Daphne and Uncle John came next followed by Aunt Meg and Uncle Bob with their brood.

They had gathered in the parlor by the time Aunt Susie, accompanied by her daughters, made their entrance with a chorus of complaints. "Tobias had to drive clear out to the Dryback place. He'll be late if he gets here at all." And shedding her wraps, Aunt Susie continued.

"Wouldn't you know, after teetering on the edge of death for six months, old man Dryback would succeed the night of a party!"

"Well, we are sorry Tobias was called out, but his is a demanding profession." Martha Melrose consoled as she gave Aunt Rose one of those looks they so often shared. It was not the first time their sister had complained of those who were inconsiderate enough to die at her inconvenience.

Meanwhile, Paulette and Theresa were busily fluffing out masses of ruffled tiers and trailing sashes of identical yellow organdy dresses. Yellow bows, like giant butterflies, perched at the back of their heads of tightly curled blond hair.

"Don't my girls look lovely?" Aunt Susie pressed, indicating her two preening canaries.

"Yes, just lovely," assured her sisters, exchanging yet another of those looks.

Susie Elworth and her girls were certain they set the style for the community. Unfortunately, they had no sense of color or line. They simply chose what was pleasing to their eyes some folks had been heard to say must be near a state of blindness.

Other guests began to arrive. Clifton Maxwell came, and before long had gravitated to Hallie's side where he was to be found quite frequently throughout the evening. Clifton was the son of the town's banker. Tall and slender, he was a young man whose fair-haired good looks were much admired by many a young lady. To their chagrin, however, he appeared to have eyes only for Miss Hallie Melrose. Since early summer he had been squiring her about.

Hallie, in her birthday dress of rose-colored velvet couldn't help but feel a bit smug having captured the attentions of the most eligible man in the community. However, she had discovered that this achievement, though not actively sought, was not as satisfying as one might suppose.

The evening progressed with Fiddler Jones and two of his offspring supplying the music. There were square dances, waltzes, and two-steps…whatever folks asked for, interrupted by such games as charades and apple bobbing.

At midnight, the candles were lit on the cakes. Hallie and Emily were brought forward to stand in the glow of the candles while everyone sang "Happy Birthday".

The two stood, arms about one another's waist, smiling happily out at their guests. Perky, little Emily all soft and golden with her elfin smile and darting dimples…Hallie straight and slender, dark hair gleaming in the light, eyes dancing gaily.

"What a pretty pair," folks murmured, and August Melrose was seen to wipe moisture from his eye with unabashed pride.

As Hallie's gaze traveled over the room she found her eyes drawn to a pair of cool, blue ones looking steadily at her. One of these gave a slow, mischievous wink as though it's owner and Hallie were aware of something no one else knew. She felt her cheeks flush, and she quickly looked away. That Will McCain! Whatever did he mean by that wink? Why, he hadn't even asked her to dance, preferring, it would seem, to stand back and watch the proceedings. She had seen him dancing once though with one of the Anderson girls…the pretty one who liked to flirt.

William McCain was older…one of Martin's friends. The McCains lived several miles east on a small farm. There were five sons in the family though only Will and Rueben were present that evening. Rueben had brought Agnes York this evening. He had taken one of the Anderson girls home from church last Sunday, and it would more than likely be someone else next week.

Will had been the same way, but this past summer had brought noticeable changes in his habits. Hallie had heard Martin remark to another friend that Will was slowing down, getting tired of the chase. The friend had chuckled and replied it was no wonder for the pace he'd been keeping would have killed off a lesser man.

Martha Melrose announced it was time for birthday cake. There was laughter and joking as couples paired up to go through the serving line. Hallie and Emily were given the task of cutting and serving their cakes. While Aunt Rose served punch August Melrose and Uncle Seth Lewis, Emily's father, dipped ice cream from the big freezers the boys had cranked that afternoon.

"Happy birthday, Hallie. You've gone and turned into a mighty pretty woman."

Hallie placed a large slice of cake on the plate Will McCain extended toward her. She smiled and replied with a casual, "Why, thank you, Will. What a nice thing to say." But she could feel the flush coloring her cheeks as their eyes met. Her hands were trembling when she reached for the next plate. Woman…. Will McCain had called her a woman! Was that how he thought of her? She glanced quickly to see if Will was watching her. No, he had made his way to the other side of the room and was already in conversation with Martin and Mary Lou.

"He probably didn't mean a thing by it," she told herself. "He probably talks to all the girls that way. Besides, a man of Will's age, he must be at least twenty-three, maybe even twenty-four, wouldn't be interested in one of his friend's little sisters."

Clifton Maxwell called for Hallie the next afternoon to take her for a Sunday drive. He had a handsome, new buggy pulled by a thoroughbred trotter he had purchased in Jefferson City. Clifton handed Hallie into the buggy tucking a lap robe carefully around her...there was a bit of a breeze. He asked if she was comfortable and if she needed another robe to keep her feet warm. As Mama said, Clifton was a thoughtful person and very nice looking besides. He would make some lucky girl a wonderful husband.

They drove to town, then on to the south road that wound through the timber and small farm clearings that lay in that direction. About a mile out, he drew the horse to a stand and pointed out over a small stretch of meadow carved from the timber some years before.

"My father owns this," he said. It was not said in a bragging manner, but simply as a statement of fact. "I've always thought it would make a nice place to build a house. What do you think, Hallie?"

Hallie said she thought it would then quickly changed the subject by pointing out a cardinal flashing red in a hickory tree. The meadow was a lovely place, but she hoped Clifton would not pursue the subject further. He was nice...she was flattered by his attention...but she wasn't ready for this talk of houses.

Clifton, however, was not so easily dissuaded. "I've been thinking, Hallie. How it might be. Close enough to drive back and forth to the bank, for shopping and visiting friends. Plenty of space for flower gardens, an orchard even. It would be a wonderful place to raise a family."

So Clifton talked, glancing shyly at her as they drove on beneath the spreading branches of the black walnut trees lining the road, the wheels crunching the nuts and leaves scattered on the roadway. They past down a lane of hackberry and ash, leaves of gold drifting down to flutter about the horse's high-stepping hooves.

Hallie watched the falling leaves her thoughts on last night's party and of Will McCain. What would it be like to ride along beside him?

Her heart quickened at the thought, and her cheeks grew warm. She peeked over at Clifton from beneath her lashes feeling guilty as though he might have read her mind.

"It's getting chilly, Clifton. Do you think we might start back?"

Clifton turned the buggy around at the next side road.

Chapter 4

It was Thursday. Hallie was out in the orchard picking the last few apples from the big McIntosh tree growing near the fence when Will and Rueben McCain came riding up the lane. As they passed, Rueben touched his hat brim in greeting. Will followed suit with a grin and a, "Howdy there, Hallie. Nice day we're having."

Hallie stood watching them ride on toward the horse barn. Will turned in his saddle to look back, catching her staring after them. Hallie wasn't sure, but she would have sworn that grin of his widened. Thoroughly vexed, she bit her lip in agitation.

Carrying the basket of apples, she marched into the house to set it down with a thump on the kitchen table. "Men!" She went to lift a dishpan from its hook and began peeling apples.

Martha Melrose glanced quizzically at her daughter having no doubt noticed the two McCain brothers riding past the window, but she continued kneading her bread dough without comment.

Martin had asked Will and Rueben to help work some of the colts that morning. As was custom, they were asked to stay on for the noon meal. An extra or two was never a problem at the Melrose table. Additional plates were simply set and the generous amounts of food served as usual.

When the men had filed in after washing up at the bench on the back porch, they settled at the table where August Melrose asked the blessing before the food was past. As the meal progressed they spoke of crops and horses. Martha Melrose made a few pleasantries, inquired of Mrs. McCain and the sprained back she had suffered recently.

Hallie contributed little to the conversation for she was kept busy hopping up from the table to fetch more potatoes or corn bread...refilling coffee cups. It wasn't until dinner was over and the men were getting ready to go back outside, that Will came over by the sink where Hallie had taken a tray of dirty dishes. He watched as she set the tray down and donned an apron.

"I thanked your mother for the fine dinner, Hallie, but I wanted to thank you, too. She said you baked that tasty apple pie."

Flustered, Hallie managed a, "I'm glad you liked it."

She stood there at a loss for further words. She was so unsure of herself with Will. He was older, more experienced. He'd courted older girls. There was even a rumor he had been seen a few times with Bertie Regus' daughter, Dixie.

Strangely enough, Will seemed a little uncertain, too, then…"There's a dance Saturday night at the schoolhouse. I'd like to take you if you'd care to go."

"Yes, I'd like that."

"Fine! I'll come by about seven."

Will was out the door, hurrying to catch up with the others before Hallie could gather her wits to say it was a mistake. Clifton would undoubtedly expect to take her. She went as far as the door, but she didn't call Will back. Instead, she listened to the thud of her heart, and watched that lean, rangy form until it disappeared into the dusky shadows of the barn door.

That was the beginning. From that very first evening, Hallie knew she loved Will. Loved the tingle of his touch as he handed her into his aged buggy, the feel of his arms when they danced, not wanting the music to stop for fear someone else might ask for a dance.

Clifton's invitations were kindly but firmly refused. Will was taking Hallie somewhere at least once a week. The self-consciousness that had afflicted them in the beginning had disappeared. They had developed an easy companionship with the drives home under the stars the best part of an evening, or so Hallie thought. There would be the homey clump, clump of the horses' hooves, the whir of the narrow, buggy wheels in the soft dirt of the road. Will would whistle one of the dance tunes from, time to time, between gaps in conversation. They spoke of friends…what had taken place during the evening…plans for the following week…work to be done.

Then came the night Will brought Hallie home after the supper Grace Attletree gave for her St. Louis cousin. He reached up like always to lift her down from the buggy, but somehow forgot to put her down. Her eyes were level with his in the moonlight. Then Will gave one of his lazy little grins pulling Hallie even closer until she could feel the warmth of his breath on her lips. He kissed her then, first just a brush of his lips to hers then closer still, wrapping her in his arms, pressing his mouth to hers in a long lingering kiss. Hallie felt her whole body softening, threatening to melt…ooze right through Will's arms like so much warm butter. .

Will came courting all that winter. He took Hallie to church, to parties, the socials and whatever else came along. If there were evenings he was tempted to sit home by the fire, he never let on. He was well aware that there was a certain young banker eager to step in and take Hallie if he did not. Folks were laying odds as to whether the Melrose girl would settle for a fellow with Will McCain's poor prospects or go for the security Clifton Maxwell could offer.

The McCains, though well respected, were not well to do, by any means. Will's father, Joseph, had come from Ireland as an immigrant to settle in Missouri. He had hired on at the Brighten place for the harvest and ended up marrying one of the daughters of which there were eight. Joseph and Ada had started with just a milk cow and a flock of chickens. A few rented acres had grown into a small farm paid for after years of hard work. They had five sons. The boys were raised to respect God, family and the soil that provided for them. It was understood God and family came first, but only a little before the land.

"Ah, and there's nothin' like a callin' a bit of the earth your own!" Joseph would say as he crumbled a clod of damp soil in his work-worn hands. This love of the soil was instilled in each boy with the understanding the younger ones would have to acquire their own "bit a earth". This had long been the custom of the McCain family over in the old country, and Joseph was strong on the old ways. The home place was left to the eldest son who in turn would provide for the parents in their old age. Thus it was Joseph himself, a younger son, had journeyed to America in search of his own piece of land.

Joseph would provide Will, his second son, with a good team and the loan of farm implements until he could purchase his own. It was with these scant prospects Will proposed one bright, Sunday morning in March on the way home from church. He offered what he had…his love…his willingness to work hard. Hallie found it to be enough. She accepted.

Hallie suspected that along with Clifton, her mother was not pleased with her choice. As mothers will, Martha Melrose no doubt hoped all her daughters would make "comfortable" marriages. But, once Hallie had accepted Will, no one would have ever known Martha was disappointed, if indeed she was.

August Melrose, if he had doubts, also kept them to himself. "I reckon where there's love and faith, a man and woman can make a go of it," he said.

Plans for another Melrose wedding began. Martin and his Mary Lou had been married at Christmas and had moved into their new house. Now, yet another was to leave the old stone house beside the orchard.

On the second Sunday in June, the Melrose and McCain families, along with a church full of well-wishers, gathered for the marriage ceremony of Hallie Melrose and William McCain. The sun shone, the birds sang from the vast branches of the hickory tree sheltering the church. Their chirping melodies seemed to accompany the organ as Aunt Daphne played on its yellow keys.

Will, his red hair burnished by the sunlight, stood tall...shoulders squared, waiting at the alter for his bride. A look of wonder came over his face as he watched Hallie advance down the aisle on the arm of her father. All brides are proclaimed beautiful, but Hallie, her hair shimmering beneath the gauzy lace of her veil, walking so straight and proud was, as a murmured exclamation from the crowd put it, "Just like a queen!" There was a rippling assent throughout the watching guests.

Ida told of how Hallie and Will's wedding was described by one of the guests, a widow named Hettie Bowers, when she came to visit Ida's mother-in-law a few days after the wedding. Mrs. Beckworth who had been indisposed and had missed the affair.

Ida confided that she suspected Tom's mother had simply lost her taste for weddings since "poor Tomas" had his.

"There they was," Hettie Bowers was reported as having said to her hostess, "A standing' in that sunlight. Folks was a holding' their breaths all over the church. Why, it was just like the bride and groom had been dipped in gold. You just never seen nothing like it!" Hettie had assured her far from enchanted listener. "Why, it was just as if God reached down and gave them his blessing. When the pair of them turned and smiled at one another, well...everybody started smiling, too. There wasn't no tears that I saw. Even your mama," Hettie had informed Ida, who was serving coffee, "was all smiles and that isn't always the case. Remember how you took on at Tom and Ida's wedding?" Hettie had reminded Mrs. Beckworth who had been looking sour enough at that point to have curdled milk, or so Ida had finished her story.

There was no honeymoon trip for Hallie and Will. The corn needed cultivating.

Though the corn looked none too promising, the weeds were thriving. Hallie didn't mind the lack of a trip. Just the prospect of being with Will in their home on the farm he had rented, would surely be as heavenly as any honeymoon. And it was. The little frame house with its four rooms was easily cared for. Hallie bustled through out, cooking and cleaning...dark curls in place...a starched apron covering a gay print from her trousseau.

She was never lonely despite Will spending long hours in the field. There were callers. Catherine and Amanda...Emily. Her mother who if she had ever had doubts as to Hallie's choice gave no indication of it, came by, now and again, as did Will's mother.

They might have a recipe to share or a loaf of fresh bread. They were served dainty sugar cookies or tender slices of cake on plates from the new china set, a wedding gift. Tidbits of gossip were exchanged.

There were weighty decisions to make such as how to rid tomato plants of those fat green worms or on a lighter side, what recipe should be used in preparing a special dish to take to the next carry-in supper at the church. The single girls felt it wouldn't hurt to advertise their cooking ability, and the married ladies of the community had been involved for years in a silent tug-of-war at to who was the better cook. Hallie dove into this friendly fray with enthusiasm, ready to show off just a bit, being the newest bride, and according to Will, the prettiest.

Sundays were always full with church and dinners at the various relatives and friends. Saturday nights Will usually stopped work early and they would go to town to shop, chatting with neighbors along the board walkways, ending up at the drugstore for ice cream. Sometimes, there would be a party or gathering at the home of one of the other young couples. And always, there was the drive home through the friendly darkness cuddled close together on the old buggy seat, knowing an even sweeter closeness awaited them within the confines of their own snug walls.

Life seemed very good to Hallie and she assumed Will felt the same way. It was true he was silent, almost brooding at times, but he was just tired, Hallie would tell herself. He worked very hard and it was depressing to see your neighbor's corn stalks standing a good foot taller than your own. The soil in their rented fields was poor. There was nothing Will could do about that.

Will always looked forward to receiving the newspaper from Jefferson City that came on the Friday mail. He would sit at the kitchen table reading after the supper dishes were cleared, puffing on his pipe and studying some article. He would often read a paragraph or two out loud to Hallie as she sat opposite doing a bit of mending or some embroidering.

Usually, these articles pertained to land or cattle prices, immigration or homestead laws...things men talked about. Hallie would nod or shake her head in accord with her husband's comments. Truth to tell her mind was apt to wander. Had she put enough salt on the pot roast at supper? Should she use this shade of blue for the forget-me-nots on this pillowslip or should it be the darker shade?

Hallie was proud Will was so interested in the affairs of the country, though they had little to do with their own small world. Or so Hallie thought until the day Will came home from a trip to town with a raft of pamphlets and his head chock full of a crazy notion of their going out west to...homestead!

Will wanted to give up the farm with its fields he vowed would never produce much more than weeds and rocks. To Hallie's pleas that some day they would own a farm of their own with better soil, Will responded the chance of their owning land in Missouri was mighty slim. In order to save enough money for a down payment on a good farm they would have to grub and do without for half a lifetime. No, Will had better plans for them.

Out in the state of Nebraska was free land with virgin soil for the asking. All you had to do was file on a piece of the land and work it. At the end of five years it was yours! What more could a man ask?

To Hallie's tears and protests, Will assured her the railroad went nearly all the way so they could make visits back to Missouri. People would be flocking to Nebraska. There were folks from Missouri who had already moved there such as his cousin, Sam. Sam was settled on a fine place. And there would be neighbors...she wouldn't get one bit lonely.

"But, what about this farm? You can't just go off and leave it," Hallie had further protested.

"I've already asked Rueben. He said he'd take it over, harvest the crops if there are any. Now, Hallie, don't fret. Why in a few years we'll have us a farm of our own," Will promised. "As fine as any here in Missouri! Just you wait and see!"

August Melrose said, "It's a wonderful opportunity for young folks." But his eyes were sad, and Hallie didn't really think he had his heart in what he said.

Joseph McCain was elated at his son's plans. "If I was a few years younger, I'd give it a try myself!" he declared.

Hallie's mother wiped a tear from her eye with the corner of her apron when she heard. Her thoughts do doubt on the far prairie…the miles of separation…of babies to be born…of sickness without a doctor.

If these were her thoughts, however, Martha Melrose did not speak of them. Instead, she spoke of what was needed for the journey, of fragile and bulky wedding gifts best left behind and stored until some future time, and of what would be the most practical for life on a homestead.

There were so many plans to make. Things to sell and things to buy. There were farewell parties and dinners where some discouraged, such as Aunt Susie who swore she'd never allow one of her girls to go traipsing off to the wilderness. Will had muttered into Hallie's ear that no one would ask them to go. Then there were those such as Emily and Aunt Daphne who declared they'd miss her terribly, but they just knew she'd have all kinds of exciting adventures.

The hours and days sped by. At times, Hallie felt filled with excitement. But mostly, she found herself dreading this forced change with all her heart, wishing the departure date was months away, seeing it draw closer and closer on the calendar.

All was in readiness at last. It was the final night before they were to leave. This last night would be spent with the Melroses. Martha Melrose and her daughters were getting a supper ready to which Will's family was invited.

August Melrose came in from chores and stood just inside the doorway watching the kitchen bustle. His wife noticed and perhaps sensing his hidden sorrow, suggested he and Hallie go for a walk.

"Why don't you two take a little walk through the orchard while we finish up?"

They had gone, August walking slowly, pausing beneath a tree, here and there, examining the hanging fruit, speaking of the taste and size it had produced the last season. They grew silent as they neared the creek, listening to its merry gurgle, looking down at its rushing freshness.

"I pray you find good water there," her father spoke with a catch in his voice. "Good water and a good life."

"We'll try, Papa," Hallie assured.

"Sometimes, it takes more than trying, honey. Sometimes, life asks more of us than we've got. Just remember, when you're at the end of your rope to ask God for a few more feet."

"I'll remember, Papa. I'll remember." Hallie put her arms around her father and hugged him close. Arms around one another they stood by the stream. Did August Melrose perhaps wonder if he might be bidding goodbye for the last time to this daughter of the kindred soul? Was he thinking of the miles and years that would separate them…change them?

August smiled down at his daughter. "We best be getting up to the house. That looks like the McCains driving up the road."

As they walked back through the orchard, he spoke of the young fruit trees he would send later so Hallie and Will could start their own orchard.

"Oh, do you think we could?" Hallie brightened. "Do you think fruit trees would grow there?"

"Don't see why not? I reckon you'll be filling Will up on apple pie before you know it."

That night when the McCains had gone home, and the family was in bed, Hallie couldn't fall asleep. Will was snoring gently at her side, but her head was full of whirling thoughts. Such a combination of thoughts…some sad…some anticipation. This was to be her first train ride…first journey from the community except for one short trip to Jefferson City.

Hallie must have finally slept for Will was waking her. The aroma of fresh coffee and frying sausage was ascending the stairs.

August Melrose asked the blessing as they all gathered around the table then asked the Lord to watch over and guide the young couple starting out on their journey into a new life. Hallie felt a lump rising in her throat. She could eat but a few bites of her favorite, biscuits and sausage gravy, her mother had prepared.

28

The old kitchen with its well-worn furnishings had never seemed so dear. The metal sink in the corner, the varnished oak cupboards whose shelves held the familiar dishes, the windows so wide and sunny with their ruffled curtains and cherry-red geraniums setting in pots on the sills. The big round table where as a toddler she had began eating her meals aided by a stack of pillows on her chair. When would she be seated here again?

This sad reverie was brought to a halt by the announcement that the train would be at the station in one hour. Dishes were stacked in the sink, and the trip into town was made with the teams at a brisk trot.

There was quite a gathering to see them off. A good many of the Melrose and McCain relatives came, plus a goodly measure of friends. There was a continuous round of hugs and kisses. A chorus of well wishes followed Will and Hallie as they climbed the steps to board.

The train began to move with much huffing and chuffing from the impatient engine up ahead. Will and Hallie turned and faced the crowd. Hallie kept her chin high and waved bravely. She was determined to appear as the brave young woman going off with her man to the wild frontier. There was no way anyone was going to know their adventurous Hallie, was doing her best to control an urge to jump from the train and run for home.

With a big smile and Will's arm around her, Hallie gave a last gay wave then turned with eyes more than a little blurred by tears to enter the passenger car.

Chapter 5

Will and Hallie found seats near the rear of the car and attempted to settle themselves comfortably. They placed their folded lap robes on the seats and pushed their satchels and food basket beneath. Some of the windows were open allowing the already warm August morning air, laden with dust and grit, to circulate throughout the car. It did little to alleviate the odor of stale food, soiled baby diapers, and sweat. The train clattered and whistled. A baby toward the front cried a fretful solo above the chorus of voices.

Seated, Hallie looked about with interest. Never had she seen such a variety of people. Two women her mother would have declared "painted" sat in the two seats facing theirs. The women's cheeks were rouged, and if Hallie was not mistaken, their hair was dyed. At least Hallie had never seen hair of those hues before.

"Where you folks headed?" One of them asked in a friendly voice.

"Prairie Rose, Nebraska is where we get off the train," Will answered though Hallie noted he did not ask the woman her destination.

"Pretty name, but I never heard of it," she said. "Me and Fern, here, are goin' to Omaha. You ever been there?"

Will said they had not.

The one named Fern said from what she'd heard, they hadn't missed much. "Just another town, bigger than some."

The car was crowded. Many of the passengers proved to be prospective homesteaders like themselves, Will and Hallie would discover as the miles passed, and some of the passengers moved about visiting. Others were simply going west, bent on making their fortunes by taking a trade or talent with them that would be in demand on the developing frontier. The majority of the travelers were men. There were young, single fellows seeking adventure, but many were married, hoping to build homes for families that would follow.

A great many of the men smoked cigars and pipes or chewed industriously at tobacco cuds. The chewers appeared to spit indiscriminately at spittoon or floor, where children escaping the confines of their seats scrambled about. Hallie felt sorry for the harassed mothers.

Across the aisle, filling both sets of seats and some adjoining, as well, was a large Swedish family. The parents looked to be in their early forties. Their children ranged in age from a babe in arms to a sturdy youth of perhaps twenty. The eldest daughter, seated by her mother, had blond braids and sparkling blue eyes. Hallie guessed her to be near her own age. The girl glanced shyly at Hallie's dress, still crisp and neat, no doubt comparing it to her own travel-stained apparel. Hallie smiled back.

The mother seemed overly cautious not allowing any of the smaller children farther than the reach of her hand. Fern took it upon herself to explain the unease the mother apparently suffered.

"She had herself a scare." Fern indicated the Swedish woman. "The conductor told me what happened to her back in Chicago. Seems it was real crowded like it is, when they was changing trains. Somehow, her and the two littlest ones got separated from the rest. There she was in one car, the rest of 'em in another...not knowin' even if the others had got on or not. She wasn't carryin' any money...didn't have food or any changes for the baby. Guess she was some upset. The conductor said her man got it across to somebody usin' that translation book they keep passin' back and forth betwixt them what had happened. The conductor hunted around till he found her just two cars down, but could a just as well been another train with her not knowin' what to do nor how to talk American."

Will and Hallie agreed it would have been quite a predicament to find oneself in.

During their journey, they became acquainted with the family. The Andreasons proved to be a friendly, close-knit group with the older children helping with the younger, and all of them solicitous of their parents. It was a mystery to Hallie how Mrs. Andreason had become separated from the rest.

Communication was possible with the aid of the translation book, already the worse for wear, that the Andreasons carried. Using the book and an odd assortment of sign language it was amazing the information they were able to share.

Hallie wished that Charlotte and Oskar Andreason with their nice children were traveling on to settle in the area Will had chosen, but this was not to be. Like Fern and Ettie, their destination was Omaha. The Andreasons had relatives, earlier immigrants, working there.

Hallie was relieved to see some of these relatives at the station to meet the new arrivals.

There was a large, wooden building near the depot Will pointed out to Hallie. This was an immigrant house maintained by the railroad. It provided temporary shelter for such families until they were oriented, if they were not as fortunate as the Andreasons. It was comforting to know some thought had been given to the plight of these people. How frightening and confusing it must be to foreign travelers, she thought. It all seemed quite alien to her. What must it seem to them?

Will and Hallie were to change trains in Omaha. During the short layover, Will went to check on their team of horses and milk cow. These animals were being transported in a cattle car along with their other belongings farther back on the train. This car would be switched to the other train they would be taking. What if there was a mix-up, Hallie wondered? But, Will returned all assurance, and while the switching was being done, they enjoyed a hot meal at a nearby restaurant. They then traveled on into the midsection of Nebraska and beyond.

Most of the land in eastern Nebraska was already settled, Will explained to Hallie, as was much of the choice land along the Platte River. The other portions of the state, however, were still open for settlement. It was to an area that lay north of the Platte at the westerly edge of what was described as central Nebraska they were traveling.

Sam McNeil, Will's cousin, was homesteading in that area. Sam was the son of one of Ada McCain's many sisters, one of whom had also married an Irishman. Through letters from his mother, Sam had learned of Will's plans of making the move to Nebraska. Sam had then written inviting Will and Hallie to come out and live with the McNeils until they could get located. The letter had assured that there was plenty of room in their home. The new "Missus" would be comfortable while Will was out scouting the land and picking a homestead.

The last part of their train journey took them to the little train stop called Prairie Rose. Emerging from the train car, and taking a view not blurred by soot-stained windows, Hallie doubted there was this much treeless land anywhere else in the world. No trees. No mountains. No anything! Just grass and more grass on low rolling hills as far as the eye could see.

A hot wind sent cinders and sand hissing across the loading platform splattering them against the pockmarked wood siding of the tiny depot. The only other buildings were a two-storied frame house and a small barn. Both buildings were unpainted and weathered to a dull gray. A sign, the words, "Meals & Rooms" barely visible on its sand-scoured surface, was nailed above the door of the house. Here the station agent, a rather gruff individual, and his wife who Hallie didn't meet, provided hotel accommodations for those who might request such service.

A bewhiskered fellow, a little shabby and none too clean, stepped forward from the shade of the depot. To Hallie's amazement, Will appeared to recognize him. There was backslapping and friendly laughter then Will brought the man over to meet Hallie.

"This here's, Sam," Will informed her. "He figured he'd better come guide us out to his place."

Hallie managed to produce what she hoped was a gracious smile and put her gloved hand forward. It was engulfed by one of Sam's rough, tobacco stained paws.

He grinned and boomed forth, "Mighty glad to meet ya, Hallie! Welcome to Nebraska."

Their belongings were hastily unloaded then the train chugged off. The young team of grays Joseph McCain had given his son, looked about in a bewildered state…questioning solid footing that neither heaved nor whistled. They shook their heads and sidestepped nervously.

The horses were fed and watered then hitched to the heavily built wagon Will had purchased in Missouri. Hallie had asked at the time, why they could afford to ship something as big as the wagon and not her Majestic wood range. The stove had been a wedding present from her parents and was one of the latest models. Will had explained, impatiently, Hallie had thought, that a good team and wagon were necessities. A fancy stove was not!

Hallie stood in the shade of the loading dock while the two men packed other "necessities" into the wagon. There was the plow, tools, the barrels containing among other things, the bags of seed for next spring's planting, and a supply of flour and sugar. The household items consisted of the grub box with its food stores, a small iron topsy stove, the brass bedstead and a solidly built kitchen table with four oak chairs. A huge cedar chest Grandpa Melrose had brought out from Virginia held their clothing and linens. That was it. The rest of their furniture had been sold, the proceeds going into their meager savings. Their savings, the five hundred dollars August Melrose had given them when they married, was greatly diminished once the train expenses were paid.

Buttercup, the little Jersey milk cow, had been conveniently dry for the train trip.

The cow was tied to the tailgate of the wagon. Hallie patted one of the cow's sleek sides and spoke kindly to her. Buttercup switched her tail at the buzzing flies, blinking long, black eyelashes at the annoying dust, wondering no doubt where the familiar terrain of her bovine world had gone.

The small company set out, heading due north, the canvas tarp covering the wagon popping in the wind. Will and Hallie rode on the wagon seat. Sam rode along side on his saddle horse having declined the invitation to tie his horse to the tailgate beside Buttercup and ride on the seat with them.

"Saddle is easier ridin'," he declared. "Dang wagon can about jounce your liver out."

Hallie was in complete agreement after the first mile with the iron-rimmed wheels bouncing over clumps of bunch grass and yucca plants, Sam said the locals called soapweed. Besides her liver, it felt as though there were several other vital organs threatening to "jounce out".

Will, finally noticed her wincing at the jolts, advised, "Relax, Hallie. Let your body sway with the wagon."

After awhile, Hallie got the hang of it. The jolting was much less if she kept her bottom firmly anchored on the seat and allowed her top half to sway.

It had been the middle of the afternoon when they left the train depot. Hallie, realizing this was open country, had not expected to find farmsteads all along the road, but she was surprised to find...no road! Will seemed delighted by the lack.

"Isn't it something, Hallie! Open land everywhere you look! Ready to plow. No trees to cut down. No rocks to haul off." And with a grin splitting his face he called over to Sam. "It's just like you wrote, Sam. It's the answer to a poor man's prayer!"

They had followed a sort of trail away from Prairie Rose. This had gradually faded as dim traces of wagon tracks branched off at various intervals until there were no wheel markings at all. They were moving across one vast sea of grass with seemingly nothing to guide them. Whatever would they have done without Sam, Hallie wondered?

In the distance, low rolling hills appeared, but these too, were covered with the monotonous waving grass. Here and there, were clumps of the soapweed and what Sam pointed out as buffalo skulls bleaching in the sun.

They traveled on for several miles before a tiny cluster of earthen buildings could be seen on the horizon. Hallie perked up, thinking this might be their destination. Sam, however, cut off at an angle to the west aiming for a gap in the hills missing the queer looking structures by at least a half mile.

They passed through the gap in the hills into a valley rimmed by low hills and the endless grass. Was there no other vegetation? Hallie wondered, thinking of home with its hills and fields, the stretches of timber where the wild berry bushes and vines grew thick along rocky creeks with their cool mossy banks. What an empty, lonely country this is!

"How far is it?" Hallie finally inquired.

"Oh, we won't get there today," was Will's reply. "We'll be stopping for the night with some folks Sam knows."

Hallie resigned herself to the inevitable. Hour after hour the horses plodded on. The wind died down, but the sun continued to beat down on the canvas. The heat was stifling. Sweat trickled from beneath Hallie's hat to mingle with the dust on her cheeks. A thick layer of dust covered their clothing. She could feel the grit of sand between her teeth and the chalky taste of dust on her tongue. The water in the jug beneath the seat was tepid and did little to quench their thirst.

Once or twice, what appeared to be a type of habitation could be seen in the distance, more of those squatty earth colored structures, small with roofs of shaggy grass-covered earth. Probably Indian dwellings, Hallie concluded. The only human they saw was a horsebacker who they sighted against the skyline. He waved then passed from view.

It was dark when a feeble light could be seen ahead. The horses lifted their heads and quickened the pace. They must scent water or other horses, Hallie guessed. The wagon halted within the rectangle of light shining through the open door of a low building distinguishable in the dark. A great gawk of a man, all arms and legs and thin as a rail, ambled out of the shadows to meet them.

"Howdy, folks. We been waitin' for ya! Bessie's got supper ready."

The welcoming scarecrow propelled Hallie over to the open door after helping her down from the wagon. He then took his leave along with Will and Sam to care for the weary animals.

Hallie hesitated, not knowing whether to wait at the door or step inside. Her doubts were settled as the figure of a short, very plump woman appeared outlined in the lamplight. One hand clutched a wooden spoon still dripping from a recent stir in a kettle while the other stretched out to clasp one of Hallie's.

"Come in, girl! Come in!" She chortled. "We been expectin' ya. Sam stopped by on his way in and said you'd bunk with us tonight. Mighty glad to have ya, honey. My name's Bessie Dikeman."

Hallie couldn't help but respond to her vivacious hostess. She told Bessie her name and tried to express her appreciation for the hospitality. Bessie brushed this aside with a, "Land's sake. This ain't nothin'."

Bessie then sat about seeing to Hallie's comfort, talking all the while. First off, knowing how long Hallie's ride had been, she directed her to the even smaller house around back. When Hallie returned, Bessie had a pan of warm water poured so she could have a wash. While Hallie scrubbed the accumulation of dust from hands and face, using the bar of homemade lye soap provided, she listened to Bessie's steady discourse.

"Me and Amos, we been livin' here for two years, now. Come up from Kentucky. We done real good, if I do say so myself. Got our own well. Ain't everbody can say that. Lot's a folks have to haul water for years before they can afford to get them a well dug."

Bessie opened the fire door on her cook stove and to her guest's astonishment, pulled a basket of dry cow dung forward from its place beside the stove and proceeded to stuff pieces of the unusual fuel into the stove. Bessie closed the stove door, wiped her hands on her apron, and pushed the basket back to its place with the toe of her shoe.

"If we'd a had to wait till we could a hired a regular well digger, we'd still be without. But Amos, he's seen'em dig water wells plenty of times back home. He said we'd dig ourselves one. Well, we done it. It's not easy diggin' in this here sand. Caves in, that's the danger. Have to shore it up, foot by foot, as you dig.

Bessie was still telling about digging the well when the men came in crowding the single room of the house. The room contained few furnishings. The stove, old but freshly blackened, sat against one mud plastered wall. A bunk type bed covered with a wash-faded quilt, was fitted into one end, a heavy homemade table and benches sat at the other. The water bench was beside the door with the lone window above it. A few boards attached to the wall near the stove served as a cupboard. A metal trunk with dented sides stood at the foot of the bed, undoubtedly used for clothing and extra bedding. Pegs driven into the walls provided hooks for assorted oddments ranging from coiled rope to a flannel nightgown.

The Dikemans must be terribly poor, Hallie decided. She had never seen such a crude dwelling in her life. Was it possible that other white settlers were living in those dirt huts she'd seen earlier? How awful it must be to live like this. Thank goodness, they were to stay in Sam's roomy home until they could get established on their own place.

Bessie was busily stringing five chipped plates, braced by ill-matched silverware, around the bare boards of the tabletop. In the center she then placed a large dented kettle, steaming and giving forth a mouth-watering fragrance.

Supper consisted of prairie chicken stew, corn bread coated with butter and wild plum jelly. Strong coffee was served in tin cups. The hungry guests savored every mouthful of the well cooked though simple meal.

Sleeping arrangements were also simple. The men spread blankets under the wagon and slept there. Hallie and Bessie shared the bed in the house. Hallie drifted off to sleep lulled by the drone of Bessie's voice telling yet another tale of family happenings in Kentucky.

Breakfast was flapjacks and coffee. They were then given the grand tour of the Dikeman homestead. Will and Hallie had their first close view of this type of prairie architecture. The walls of both the house and equally small barn were constructed of what Amos laughingly called, "Nebraska marble." This material was made of large squares of sod, stacked up like huge bricks. Hallie smiled and praised all she saw, but secretly, she pitied these poor souls having to live in such a manner.

Hallie and Bessie bid each other fond goodbyes, promising to get together again sometime soon. Will offered to pay for the meals and accommodations but was firmly refused.

"That's the way it's done out here," Sam explained later as they drove along. "Folks travelin' through are welcome, and you feed'em what you got, plain or fancy. There ain't but a few will take money for it."

All morning they traveled through the treeless, grassy valleys, over and around endless hills that had become more numerous and more pronounced. It was nearing noon when they drove up over a hill, and Sam pulled his horse to a stop, pointing. "There she is! That there is the McNeil spread!"

Chapter 6

Hallie stood up in the wagon for a better view, holding her hat brim, shading her eyes. She looked in vain for the house she had envisioned after reading Sam's letter. There was nothing to see but a corral occupied by a few horses and a couple of cows looking forlornly toward the wagon and its occupants.

Above the corral on the side of a hill was a sort of cellar, fronted with sod blocks like those used at the Dikeman's place. A bellow from Sam caused Hallie to jump and several people to emerge in haste from the hillside cellar.

Hallie was speechless. Even Will seemed taken aback. This was Sam's home? Will gripped Hallie's hand until it hurt, perhaps more in silent warning to watch what she said than for reassurance as the family converged upon them.

Sam swung down from his saddle and began the introductions. "This here is my wife, Mattie. This is her sister, Pearl. This passel a youngun's I reckon you'll get sorted out 'for long." Sam was indicating the five children Hallie judged to range in age from toddlers still wearing diapers to a boy of about ten.

Sam's wife, Mattie, was small and sandy-haired with narrow, stooped shoulders. Tired lines etched a face that still retained traces of prettiness. Now, only the wide set eyes of deep green held a hint of what child bearing and hard work had destroyed.

Mattie smiled revealing a missing front tooth as she offered a small hand crusted with callus and a soft, "Welcome."

"Matt, you got any dinner left for us?" Sam addressed his wife with a wide grin as he gave a toddler with a saggy, wet diaper a toss up to his shoulder where she perched with a delighted giggle.

"Didn't know just when you'd be coming, but we'll get something fixed in no time." Mattie smiled again glancing shyly at Hallie as she spoke.

Pearl, the sister-in-law, a tall, plain, young woman whose plainness vanished as the face beneath its crown of brown braids, was lit by a glowing smile. She stepped forward now, to shake hands and greet the newcomers with an assurance lacking in her sister's demeanor. "I expect you'll find all of us a bit overwhelming in the beginning, but actually, we're pretty normal when you get to know us."

"You boys unhitch the horses," Sam told his two oldest children then shooed his guests ahead of him up the slope and through a low doorway, his booming voice telling them to, "Make yourselves ta home!"

It took a few moments for their eyes to adjust after stepping in from the sunlight to the darker interior. Will's hand on Hallie's elbow tightened as the inside of the dwelling became visible. Whether this, like his earlier handgrip, was a gesture of comfort or a warning to marshal her self-control, Hallie was not certain. Regardless, she was grateful for the support for just as she detected a strong, vaguely familiar odor, the heel on her right foot made contact with a small, slippery mass. She skidded wildly. Doing the splits and hanging desperately to Will's arm, she glanced downward. Now, clearly visible on the dirt floor was the remains of a daub of chicken manure.

Will gave a hoist, and Hallie gathered her bearings to find herself in what proved to the first of two rooms dug, side by side, into the hillside. The room they had entered was used as a barn, hence the manure, while the second provided shelter for the family. Sam proudly explained all this as they passed through into the living quarters...how much time and labor had been saved by this arrangement.

The second room had a small glass window on its outside wall instead of a door as did the first room. Hallie would learn, that this room was much larger than normally found in a "dugout" thus earning the "roomy" description Sam had used in his letter. A bulky, square table sat in the center encircled by wooden boxes of varying heights and three or four dilapidated chairs.

Obviously, the family had been eating when they had heard Sam's call. Plates of food, an overturned cup of milk, and a chair lying on its side testified to a hasty exit.

A kitchen range stood against the back wall, a stovepipe protruding upward through a hole in the sod roof. The side and back walls were solid banks of soil as the rooms had simply been dug out from the side of the hill. This, Hallie would also learn, was why the term "dugout" was used when speaking of these shelters so often relied upon in this nearly treeless country. The walls dividing the rooms and fronting the dugout were constructed of sod blocks. Such roofs as were found on these dugouts were often made with a frame of whatever material was available then covered with a layer of tarpaper and one of sod.

At one end of the room, bunk beds had been built, one above the other. Hallie counted six and wondered if the McNeils and the sister-in-law possibly shared these sleeping accommodations.

Piles of bedding, clothing, buckets and farm tools filled the corners. Flies buzzed busily over the forgotten food while a half-grown pup stood on a box licking from one of the plates.

The air from the open window had little effect on the odor of grease and stale smoke. Hallie's innards gave a lurch upward, threatening to embarrass her further. Will was giving her a worried look and Hallie realized her face must be turning white. She could feel beads of perspiration beginning to form on her upper lip.

"Are you all right?" Will whispered.

Hallie nodded, trying to ignore the floating flies in the water pail on a bench and the hen nesting in a box by the stove.

"Well, what do you think of her?" Sam demanded, making a sweeping motion with one arm, steadying the child on his shoulder with the other. "She's the biggest dugout in these here parts!"

"W-why, it's mighty fine, Sam. Nice and cool in here, too," Will replied.

Hallie couldn't utter a word. She pasted on a smile and sat down weakly in a chair the sister-in-law, Pearl, offered. She wished with every fiber of her being that she had never even heard of a place called Nebraska.

Pearl and Mattie were as different as sisters could be. Pearl had been blessed with enough energy and determination for both of them had she only been able to transfer a portion to Mattie. Pearl had been a teacher before coming with the McNeils to Nebraska to try her hand at homesteading. She had her own tiny sod house on an adjoining claim, built with a minimum of help. As they became acquainted Pearl would admit she had had several proposals of marriage since arriving in this woman-sparse county. She had refused them all. Perhaps, she feared to make the plunge, Hallie thought privately, having observed at close range Mattie's fiasco.

Hallie and Pearl enjoyed one another's company. Many afternoons when the dishes were done up from the noon meal, they would go to Pearl's soddy. They would take the older children giving Mattie and the little ones an opportunity for a quiet nap.

Pearl had brought schoolbooks with her when she made the move out from eastern Missouri. During these afternoons at the soddy, she spent the time tutoring Bert and Harry who were eleven and nine along with Nancy who was five.

The three children were instructed to wash their hands. Sam kept a barrel of water filled for Pearl from his well. When they were seated at the small table, school began. They were instructed in spelling and arithmetic as well as the rudiments of geography and history. Hallie was surprised to discover that their reading skills were beyond most children their age. She also noted that there were two sides to the McNeil children, one revealed in their own home and one at the home of their aunt.

The afternoons spent at Pearl's were a pleasant respite from the hubbub of the McNeil dugout. It was on one such afternoon when the children had completed a session of arithmetic and been given permission to run outside and stretch their legs, that Hallie complimented her new friend.

"You are very good with children, Pearl. You are a fine teacher."

"Thank you, but it isn't that difficult. Children love to learn. All they need is a little discipline and guidance."

Hallie agreed and thought to herself what a shame it was that Mattie and Sam did not seem to share this philosophy.

As though reading her thoughts, Pearl said. "Sam has always left the child rearing to Mattie." Pearl straightened a stack of books on the table then looked over at Hallie seated on the edge of the neatly made bunk bed. "Mattie used to try when she had things easier and fewer little ones. But...the management of a household has always been too much for her."

Pearl spread her hands in a futile gesture. "Mattie was so pretty when we were girls. She never wanted for a beaux, even if she couldn't boil water without burning it." Here Pearl laughed remembering. "Mother always said Mattie needed to marry a rich man...the fatherly type. Instead, she fell in love with Sam. And Sam has always thought the sun rises and sets on Mattie. It's just that...well, you've seen how things are."

Pearl sat down in one of the chairs by the table. "That's the main reason I came with them when they came out here. Mother was worried sick over them moving such a distance from home. What would happen if Mattie became ill…one of the children?" Pearl looked down at her hands and pushed at a cuticle with the tip of a thumbnail.

She raised her eyes to Hallie's. "I told mother I would go with them, help Mattie out, not that I get much accomplished in that direction. Mattie is an independent person even if she never makes much headway."

Pearl smiled resignedly. "Mother thinks they will give up and come back to Missouri, but she doesn't know Sam. He'll never go back as long as he has any chance of acquiring his own land out here."

The children burst in at this moment out of breath from racing. "Auntie Pearl, can we have storytime, now?" Nancy, hopping on one foot was spokesman.

"Calm down, now. You're in the house," Pearl reminded, and the three promptly settled themselves into their chairs with expectant grins lighting their faces.

"You're ready for a story, are you? What shall it be? Shall I read from Huckleberry Finn, or would you like to begin with something else today?"

"Read Little Daffy Down Dilly," Nancy pleaded, her pretty green eyes sparkling.

The boys groaned, but assured something would also be read of their choosing, they sat back in their chairs to listen as Pearl opened a small, worn book and began to read.

Such afternoons always held a storytime. Pearl read a variety of stories to the children though the boys favored those concerning history adventures and heroes; Lafayette, John Paul Jones, Washington, Lewis and Clark. These were their choices along with the tales of Indian battles. Hallie, stretched on Pearl's bunk, listening with closed eyes, could almost imagine herself a girl again in school back home, the voice of Miss Mayling reading after noon recess.

A pattern developed among the three women and the work involved with running the McNeil household. Pearl and Hallie watched the children between them and did the laundry. The washing of dirty clothing for so many was no small task. The diapers were difficult to get white after little Agnes and Sammy, had scooted about on the dirt floor with wet behinds.

The water for the laundry was heated in a boiler on the stove then carried to tubs in the yard. The tubs of water sat on benches. The women stood over the tubs where garments soaked, a washboard arranged with its legs in the tub water and leaning against the side. A wet garment was lifted onto the washboard where it was rubbed with a bar of lye soap then scrubbed until deemed clean. After the rinsing and being wrung out by hand, the wet wash was spread on the grass to dry in the sun. There was a clothesline of sorts, but the boys had swung on it until it nearly touched the ground. Besides, most of the clothespins had been lost.

Mattie was in charge of the cooking. Mattie's cooking was on par with her housekeeping. Hallie would not be able to recall one dish Mattie prepared during the two weeks they stayed with the McNeils that was not burnt or scorched.

The meat was always fried in a skillet sitting directly over an open stove hole so it would cook faster. The flames licked the black encrusted vessel until the pieces of rabbit or prairie chicken matched it in color. Often, Mattie forgot the salt. At other times, she was much too generous with it. Beans and potatoes were never boiled unless allowed to run low on water and end up with a scorched flavor.

One day, when Mattie wasn't feeling well, Pearl cooked the dinner. Sam couldn't figure out why the beans tasted so "flat". He added salt then chopped onion onto the pile of plump beans on his plate.

"Can't figure it!" He boomed. "They still taste flat, Pearl. You just ain't got the hand with cookin' that Matt has."

Will winked at Hallie. They knew what was missing. There was not a taste of scorch in the whole batch.

Pearl never said a word, but helped herself to another helping.

Sam was fond of his wife's bread, too. He always declared it would stick to a man's ribs and satisfy his hunger. "It's not like that feathery stuff some women make," he would state proudly.

It certainly wasn't! Mattie's loaves resembled brown and black bricks, the black prevailing. The crusts defied all but the sharpest knife while the center of a loaf was often gray and doughy.

Will manfully cleaned his plate at mealtime. Hallie on the other hand, would take small bites and sneak larger ones to the pup that quickly learned to lurk beneath her chair in anticipation.

The coffee at the McNeil's was yet another matter.

"It'll grow hair on your chest," Sam boasted as he smacked his lips over a cup of the thick, hot brew.

No hair sprouted upon her chest, but Hallie felt certain that when on occasion, she did take a sip of the bitter muck, her system shuddered and her toenails curled. It was little wonder, for a strict rule of the household was that the big, granite pot was never washed. Pearl confided she had emptied and scoured the grimy pot one time, only to have Sam swear the coffee unfit to drink for a week.

Each morning, fresh grounds were added to the pot, and when filled with water, boiled thoroughly. After breakfast, more water and a handful of coffee were added. The pot was set on the back of the stove where it simmered until the fire went out in the evening. Mattie and Sam drank endless cups of this solution. When the pot was about a third full of old grounds, they were dumped and the process started over.

Hallie was to learn that the McNeil coffee was much like life on the prairie...harsh fare for a novice.

Chapter 7

One evening when it was nearing suppertime, Will came riding in. He had been gone since sunup spending yet another day searching for just the right land to homestead. He had found several promising spots on some of his previous jaunts. None had quite satisfied him. Will took care of his horse then came into the dugout. Hallie could tell he was fairly bursting with excitement. But, it was hopeless to attempt a conversation during the supper hullabaloo.

Sam was the only one of the adults who could enjoy mealtime seemingly unaware of the confusion around him. One of the toddlers seated perilously on a stack of boxes, invariably fell off, upset his or her milk and ended up crying.

There was little if any system in serving the food if Pearl wasn't there. Pearl usually ate her evening meal at home. Mattie simply sat things on the table and everyone hove to. Between the rattle of cutlery, crying infants, and Sam's bellowed comments, normal conversation was out of the question.

When the meal ended the men and older children began to file outside, the men to enjoy their evening pipe of tobacco, the children to play hide and seek on the hillside. Will leaned close to Hallie as he passed and whispered, "Hurry up, and come out. I've got news!"

The two women cleared the table in record time as Mattie had caught Will's whispered words. "I expect he's picked a place, Hallie. I hope it's not clear off somewhere's."

"Oh, Will promised me we'd have neighbors so it can't be far." Hallie told Mattie who did not lose her skeptical expression.

At last the dishes were done and the babies bedded down for the night. Mattie and Hallie went out to join the men sitting on the hill above the dugout. These evenings were quite pleasant seated on the grass, the earth still warm from the sun, adding comfort to a person's backside.

Pearl walked over most evening to join them in the quiet dusk. They would sit contemplating the falling darkness with even Sam speaking with less volume, pipe smoke in the air, listening to the calls of the children playing on the far side of the hill and the chirp of the crickets hidden in the grass. Later, as the stars came out, coyotes on

46

some far hill would begin their nightly chorus sending the children scuttling in for home and bed. The women, tired from the day's labors often followed suit. The men would stay on, talking of the future, speculating on the settlers yet to come.

On this particular evening, however, as the women joined the men, Will took Hallie's hand and tugged her gently to sit beside him. He put an arm around her waist and gave a quick hug.

"I've found it, Hallie! I've found just the place! The sweetest valley you ever saw. Plenty of good level land for farming and grass galore! Hallie, wait until you've seen the grass!"

Grass! Good grief! Was Hallie's first reaction. What was so special about grass. That was all she had seen since they arrived. It was obvious, however, that it was important to Will. Hallie could barely see her husband's face in the settling darkness, but the strong play of emotions it displayed were evident. She could not recall seeing him so exhilarated, not even on that memorable night she had accepted his marriage proposal. Was it possible possessing land could mean more to Will than she did? Hallie shivered in the warm night as a little chill passed along her spine.

Will and Sam were gone a great deal during the following days. Will hired Sam to survey his choice of land. Sam strenuously insisted he would do it for free, but Will insisted. Sam had a family to support and land surveying had become the source of ready cash for the McNeils.

In Missouri, Sam's father had been a surveyor by profession. Sam had picked up some old equipment and the "know-how" from him. It was proving to be a mighty handy trade to have in this new country.

The two men made the long trip to Kearney so that Will could file on his claim at the land office located there. They also planned to bring back a load of supplies for both the McNeils and the McCains. They took Will's grays, pulling Sam's wagon as the McCain's wagon was still loaded with their belongings.

Will and Sam returned from the Kearney trip on the fifth day. Will announced that evening that he and Hallie would head for their claim the following day.

The next morning, Mattie's Dominicker rooster crowed reveille from its perch on the dugout roof just as the sun began to nudge the eastern hilltops. The men and boys began stirring from their blankets atop the haystack down by the corral, shaking the collection of itchy

47

hay stems from their shirttails. A little spiral of smoke began to rise daintily from the stovepipe ascertaining the breakfast fire had been started.

The chores were done while breakfast cooked, and then all gathered for what Hallie hoped would be the last meal with the McNeils for a good long while. She had grown fond of all of the family, even blustery Sam. But…their ways were not her ways and never would be. She could hardly wait to get out and away from all this…into her own home where cleanliness and order would rule. First, however, one more meal had to be endured beneath this sod roof.

Breakfast was already in progress when the men entered. The children were at the table attacking the piles of pancakes set before them. Pearl had come over to see the McCains off and was assisting with the breakfast process, cutting pancakes into bit size pieces for the little ones, etc.. Mattie, dingy flour sack pinned around her middle, stood over the smoking skillets, eyeing the frying puddles of batter, spatula in hand. Pancakes, under Mattie's jurisdiction, suffered the same affliction as did her bread. But, as with the bread, this deterred Sam and the children not at all. They devoured the steaming cakes by the dozen as Sam wiped at his whiskers calling for more, declaring as he did every morning, "You outdid yourself this mornin', Matt!" And as always, this oft used compliment never failed to bring a smile to his wife's tired face.

The men and older children, having finished eating, went out into the morning sunshine to ready the team and wagon. The women had their breakfast after the flurry of baking and serving the pancakes for the rest was over. Pearl had a technique she used in regards to much of her sister's cooking, especially the thick, heavy pancakes. Hallie had quickly caught the knack. This evasion was managed on this last morning as Mattie unsuspectingly ate away at her own stack of cakes. Pearl and Hallie busied themselves with picking up dirty dishes, sipping coffee and eating a bite or two they'd torn off a pancake they'd put in their plate, anything to avoid a direct confrontation with a stack of the doughy objects.

"Come on now, girls," Mattie would say. "You come and sit down. Eat before things get cold."

"In a minute," one would answer. "Just let me finish filling the teakettle," or "I've got to give these scraps to the pup." And Mattie never seemed to catch on to the evasion.

The stomp of horses' hooves and the rattle of trace chains out front proclaimed Will's readiness. Hallie grabbed her hat and tied the ribbons firmly under her chin. Her satchel was already loaded. Both Will and Hallie had expressed their appreciation and thanks to the McNeils and Pearl the previous evening. All that remained to be said were the "goodbyes" and "you-all come-to-see-us-soon".

The McNeil clan circled the heavily loaded wagon as Sam picked Hallie up and tossed her up to the seat next to Will.

"Now, you take care and don't let no coyotes get you while you're campin' out," he teased. "I'll be over in two or three days to help with the soddy buildin'."

Pearl handed up a bundle of food and a jug of water Mattie had insisted on preparing for them. She patted Hallie's hand as she passed the parcel over. "I'll ride over to see how you are doing, later on."

"I'll be looking forward to it," Hallie said, little knowing how much she would do so.

There was a last round of goodbyes. Will giddy-upped the team, and they were off.

It was going to be a beautiful day, and a relief to be free from the crowded dugout. Hallie tilted her hat back, letting the soft grass-scented breeze caress her face. She tucked her hand in the crook of Will's arm causing the already wide grin to broaden. Clucking to the team, Will began to whistle a tune they had danced to when they were courting.

Their route led them north through a series of undulating draws and hills covered with a blanket of beige fall grasses. Hallie decided the land did have a sort of regal serenity that some folks might describe as beautiful. She, however, preferred the lush foliage covered terrain of home, populated by friends and family. At the thought of home, and Missouri, a little lump rose in her throat. She gave herself a mental shake.

"None of that, my girl," she chided silently. "This new country is now your home. You've got to learn to like it." They crossed a sandy washout after a few miles where a thicket of wild plum bushes grew. Hallie was amazed to see the branches loaded with clusters of rosy red fruit.

"Look, Will! Fruit! Can you believe there's fruit out here?"

"Sure there is. I reckon most any kind will grow here if it was fenced off from cattle and taken care of," Will told her as he drew the team to a halt. He stepped down and began picking plums from one of the bushes, using his hat as a container. He handed one of the largest to Hallie. The outer surface of the plum was cloudy until rubbed. Like a mirror you had blown your breath on, Hallie thought. She bit through the smooth skin, exploring the escaping juice with her tongue. The tangy fluid was a delight. The flesh of the fruit was quite sweet while the skin was very tart…a most satisfying combination. Such fruit would make delicious jams and jellies. Will climbed back into the wagon and they went on, Hallie holding the filled hat in her lap. They munched the plums and talked as they traveled. They had not had a moment alone since they left Missouri. It was the first opportunity they had had to discuss their uncomfortable lodgings or their host and hostess.

They both agreed that the McNeils and Pearl were generous and kind, but they broke into laughter as they tried to find something positive to say about Mattie's cooking. Finally, they decided that "bountiful" was a fitting description…there was always more than you could eat. They began to laugh again.

Time passed swiftly, the miles filled with lively conversation and laughter. Hallie hardly noticed the distance they had come until suddenly the thought struck her.

"Will, haven't we come quite a ways? How far will it be between our place and the McNeils?"

Will shrugged. "Oh, not far. I reckon it to be about eight or ten miles."

Hallie's heart sank. That many miles to a neighbor! Surely not! No doubt other settlers lived up ahead. If not, there would be some coming before long. She was determined to let no gloomy thoughts spoil this day.

They drove on for another mile or so. Hallie found it difficult to judge distance in this undulating sameness. The horses drew the wagon up a steep range of hills, and Will pulled them to a stop. A broad valley was spread before them. Tall, swaying grass rose and fell across the expanse of floor like restless, tawny-colored waves fleeing before the wind.

The outlines of an old grassed-over creek bed could be plainly seen winding its course the length of the valley. Perhaps some long forgotten spring on a hillside had fed the little stream at one time. They would learn that occasionally, it still came to life when a heavy summer rain or melting snow sent trickles of water down the adjoining draws and gullies until they created streams. These streams would gush together at the valley's head, and for a few hours, roar madly down the old creek bed. It would flatten the stately grasses, causing them to writhe beneath the rush of water like millions of spindly water snakes struggling to reach the surface. But now, it lay sleeping peacefully, deceiving in its quiet slumber.

The sun stood overhead, its rays glimmering off the billowing grass to blind the eye with its golden onslaught. Far down the valley a hawk dived at a gray blur as a jackrabbit made for a hole in the creek bank. The hawk missed, gave an angry cry and rose again to his endless circling.

Hallie became aware that Will was watching her expectantly.

"This is it, Hallie! Isn't it something?"

Hallie hesitated, wanting to please her husband, but finding it difficult to phrase the proper words for this big, empty expanse of grassland. All she could manage were a couple of tired worn adjectives. "Nice," and "Big".

These seemed to satisfy her excited husband who slapped the lines to urge the team on down into the valley. At the foot of a low knoll, he stopped the team and draped the lines loosely over the edge of the wagon box, trusting the reliable grays to stand then stepped down. He offered a hand to Hallie so she might join him. Tucking the bundle of food beneath his arm, then taking the jug of water in one hand and one of Hallie's hands in the other, Will began to climb the knoll.

When they had reached the top, he pointed out over the sun-drenched valley. "Isn't it a sight and a half, Hallie? Why, you can see the whole valley right from this spot. I figure we could build a house on a hill like this, and you'd be able to see out over our whole place and across to the neighbors!"

Hallie attempted to match his enthusiasm, but a hint of her doubt must have shown for Will hastened to add.

"Why, before long this whole valley will be settled. There will be roads and a school, maybe even a church. Can't you just see it, Hallie?"

"Yes, Will. It could be a real little community." And she did her level best to visualize farms scattered across the valley floor with fence lines and fields, but it was difficult. Those empty miles of grass still lay before her. But…Will said others would come…. She must be more optimistic and share her husband's happiness.

No one could have doubted Will's happiness. All morning he'd worn a wide grin that pushed up the little laugh crinkles at the corners of his eyes. Those eyes that could so easily play havoc with Hallie's heart had been at their worst today. Each time their eyes had met her heart had given a little lurch, spilling out tiny bubbles of ecstasy right down through her middle.

They seated themselves in the warm grass, spreading the cloth in which the food was wrapped. They began to eat hungrily at the heavy slices of bread and the pieces of cold burnt prairie chicken. Between bites, Will spoke of his plans for their future. Hallie chewed valiantly at the tough meat, listening, eyes on the handsome, vibrant face across from her.

Their hunger appeased, they wandered hand in hand along the brow of the hill. They paused to gaze out over the grassy acres, seemingly alive beneath the agitating wind. Will turned to Hallie and drew her close. She lifted her face to his and their lips, warm in the noonday sun, met in a kiss that grew in urgency. Then with one accord, the two sank down into the tall, sheltering bluestem, wrapped in one another's arms.

Chapter 8

The team was unhitched from the wagon and bridles removed so the horses could rest and graze while the wagon was unloaded. Will had decided to leave that very afternoon for the distant canyons where cedars grew. Cedar poles could be used to reinforce the roof of the sod house they were going to build. As they had no source of water, Will would take some of their emptied wooden barrels to fill at a ranch along his route as he returned the following day.

Hallie was to stay at the camp to watch over their belongings and the milk cow.

"I'll just be gone overnight," he assured his doubtful wife. "Buttercup can manage without water until I get back. She filled up this morning good at Sams'. You'll have the water jug, but go easy with it. Better not try a bath," he teased.

And Hallie lifting up her arms to receive an armload of items Will was handing down from the wagon thought of the scrimping of water that lay ahead until they could have a well dug on their land. The lack of a stream or lake in the valley was a drawback, Will had admitted. The ranchers in the area by various methods, had already filed on such locations. Will had said he didn't blame them. He would have done the same if he'd had the opportunity.

Hattie had heard Sam say that some homesteaders had to haul water for years until they could afford a well. Some, like the Dikemans, had dug their own well, but Sam had warned against it. "Just plain foolhardy in this sandy soil. Dikeman had more luck than sense. Been more than one man killed trying it."

Remembering this, Hallie asked. "You're not thinking of digging a well yourself, are you? You know what Sam said about that."

"No, Hallie. Don't worry. I won't do that, but I will hire a regular well digger as soon as I can."

Will arranged the contents of the wagon to form three lumpy walls opening to the south. A shelter of sorts was thereby created when the wagon canvas was stretched and tied down to form a roof. The contents of the four barrels needed for hauling water were unpacked and placed in the shelter leaving Hallie just enough space to spread blankets for a bed.

"I reckon I'd better get gone," Will said. "Sooner I start, the sooner I'll get back."

While Will re-hitched the team, Hallie quickly wrapped the noon leftovers and a tin of crackers from the grub box for him to take. She was doing her best to appear nonchalant about being left alone. "After all, wasn't she a married woman sharing this adventure with her husband? Wasn't that how she'd put it when telling of their plans to wide-eyed friends back home?" Hallie prodded herself with this reminder as Will gave her a quick kiss then climbed up to the wagon seat.

"There's not a thing in the world to hurt you out here, Hallie. I'll be back before you've missed me."

Hallie doubted this as she stood with the afternoon sun hot on her back and watched the team and wagon climb the east ridge. Will turned to wave as the wagon topped the low hills then the rig and driver dropped from sight as they headed down the far side. Hallie turned with small fists clenched to face alone the valley in all its vast emptiness.

The sunlight glanced off the swaying blades of grass reflecting shimmering heat waves to blur her vision. The only signs of life were the hawk floating aimlessly in the cloudless sky and Buttercup grazing at the end of her picket line. The square of gray canvas stretched over their meager possessions scarcely marred the monotonous surface of the valley's floor.

"I can't stay here alone! How can Will expect such a thing of me?" Hallie whirled about taking a few running steps in the direction the wagon had taken. Her steps slowed then stopped as reasoning took control. She couldn't go running after Will like a forgotten child. Someone had to stay and watch after things. With a sigh, Hallie retraced her steps and began her lonely vigil.

Hallie spent the remainder of the afternoon on the east side of the shelter, resting in the shade of the low wall. A book of poetry had been among the items emptied from the barrels and supplied the distraction needed to help pass the hours.

She roused herself from her reading as the orbiting sun began to sink lower in the west. She pulled Buttercup's picket stake and moved her to a fresh supply of grass then restaked the pin. Buttercup began to munch contentedly and Hallie's thoughts turned to her own supper.

A battered plum thicket stood near their camp along what appeared to be a cattle trail zigzagging up the ridge. Many of the branches had been broken off or rubbed bare, perhaps by buffalo in the not so distant past, Hallie thought and more recently by the white man's cattle. She gathered an armload of twigs and branches to build a fire on the bare ground Will had spaded for this purpose.

Hallie put a handful of cornmeal from the cloth bag in the grub box into a mixing bowl, added a pinch of salt and a "glug" of water from the jug. This was mixed into stiff dough that she shaped into two small cakes ready to bake.

The fire was burning briskly and already forming a bed of hot coals beneath her iron skillet. A dab of lard was dropped into the skillet and when it began to sizzle, the cakes were put in. In a few minutes the under sides of the cakes were brown and could be flipped over with a long-handled fork to finish baking.

When the cakes were done, Hallie spread a bit of the butter on them. Mattie had thoughtfully sent a jar of butter with them. She sat on the wooden top of the grub box she had placed near the fire. It's really quite lovely here, Hallie thought as she munched hungrily at the crisp, steaming cakes from the plate on her lap. The sunset is positively beautiful. She gazed off at the western sky where bright reds and brilliant yellow were fading into flamingo pinks, lavenders and streaks of pale, spun silver.

A meadowlark called a last good night to his mate. Farther down the valley came the soft hoot of an owl as he began his nocturnal hunt.

The sun had long since slid behind the west ridge. Buttercup, only faintly discernible in the fast settling darkness, had eaten her fill and lain down for the night. Hallie scraped her plate and the mixing bowl then wiped them clean with a cloth before putting them away. There was no water to spare for dishwashing. She then followed Will's instructions by taking a spade and carefully covering the fire bed with a loose dirt. Her chores completed, Hallie snuggled down on a pile of quilts beneath her canvas roof to sleep.

She awoke with a start and lay listening in the quiet darkness. There was no sound. Even the night breeze had stilled. Something had disturbed her, but what? Then, a high penetrating howl rang out! She lay petrified as an answering call came from down the valley followed by a series of wild yappings. Were there wolves? Coyotes? Or both?

Will had told her about coyotes, and she had heard them over at the McNeils. Will had said that coyotes did not attack humans...that there was nothing here to hurt her...but did he know this for certain? Just then the amount of howls and yappings increased in number and in volume. Hallie, now completely terrified, visualized skulking gray forms creeping through the grass, closer and closer, to her open shelter. She prayed with chattering teeth and trembling limbs for her safety and poor defenseless Buttercup tethered like so much bait on her rope.

Hallie had been taught that praying was a must, but that God also helped those who helped themselves. She poked an arm out and felt among the pile of sticks she had gathered until she found one with some size to it. This would provide some protection, but as she continued to pray, she made a solemn vow to both God and herself. If by some miracle she should survive this night, she would learn to shoot the big rifle in its leather case among the house goods. Never again would she be this defenseless.

The hours crept by. The howls dwindled to an occasional yipping lament. At last, from sheer exhaustion, Hallie once again slept.

She awoke to bright sunlight and the soft, friendly chirping of sparrows in the old plum thicket. Hallie reached for her shoes, the only clothing she had removed the night before. The shoes were hastily tugged on, and Hallie went out to see if Buttercup had fared as well.

The cow was nowhere to be seen. Hallie dashed about distractedly, expecting to find remains strung about through the grass. Not one drop of bloody gore could she find. Finally, she calmed down enough to discover the picket rope and stake were gone. Undoubtedly, Buttercup had become frightened, jerking the pin free. Heaven only knew what had become of the poor thing!

Hallie laced up her shoes and grabbed up her hat to set out in search of either Buttercup or what the howling beasts had left of her. Despite her haste and anxiety, Hallie did have some of her wits about her. She noted the flattened grass where the cow had lain, the trampled area where she had apparently tugged repeatedly at the rope and then the faint trail of crushed grass blades leading west into the open valley.

This trail could be followed for nearly a mile before it disappeared altogether. Not a single hoof print could Hallie find among the closely matted grass stems. She tilted her hat brim down, shielding her eyes from the sun's bright glare as she looked far out across the valley. Nothing moved. Even the grass stood still during the absence of the pestering prairie wind.

Already, the heat was building, promising a scorcher of a day. Hallie bit her lip in perplexity, undecided which way to go. The tracks had been angling steadily northwest. It was a good bet the cow had continued on in that general direction.

By midmorning, Hallie had crossed the valley and had begun circling north along the west ridge, looking for tracks going out of the valley. She hoped that from a higher vantage point, she might be able to spot the cow. The sun beat down, the rays glittering as they were reflected from the wind-polished grass stems. Hot, tired, and thirsty, Hallie trudged on. Her heels sank with each step into the soft sand of the ridge. Sweat from the hot confines of her hat, trickled down her dusty cheeks, little salty beads gathering on her upper lip.

Hallie unhooked the top buttons of her dress, letting the tight, sweat-soaked collar hang open. Her whole body, beneath its layers of clothing, felt as though it were steaming. What she wouldn't have given right then for just one of the enormous shade trees from her old backyard, and a drink of icy, cold water from the pump in her mother's kitchen. And, running her tongue over sweat-salted lips, she realized for the first time what, "dry enough to spit cotton", truly meant.

A small gully washed from the side of the ridge appeared as though to prove to this complaining newcomer the grasslands could provide comforts for its inhabitants. A couple of plum bushes dotted with ripe plums grew along the upper edge, forming a small area of shade down in the gully as well as the tart fruit to quench a dry mouth.

Hallie filled a pocket with plums then slid down the bank to sit in the shade. She removed her hat a she ate a couple of the plums and rested her head against the crumbling dirt wall. She gazed up as she savored the tart juice. There above her, protruding from the soft soil, dangled a few hairy roots of the bushes above, exposed by the eroding winds and rains. A funny, gray spider about the size of a nickel was busily spinning an intricate web between two of the hanging roots. As Hallie admired the insect's handiwork, her eyes strayed on to a narrow ledge where one of the roots lay limply.

One end of the root moved! Beady eyes stared back at her from the other end. Hallie gasped and sat rigid. The snake coiled himself on the small shelf of dirt and waited warily. A slight movement by Hallie caused him to lift the rattle at the tip of his tail like a sassy thumb to send forth his message with clear intent.

Hallie sat there, her back pressed tightly against the dirt bank. The hat she had tossed aside rested not two feet from the snake's ledge. It was a good, sturdy, straw hat. She certainly couldn't leave it there. Perhaps she could locate a stick to reach it.

Hallie, keeping an eye on the snake and any possible companion it might have, climbed out of the gully. Farther north she sighted what appeared to be a cluster of willow-like bushes growing in a low spot at the base of the ridge. She clambered down and went to investigate. Surely, she could break off a limb there to use in the hat rescue.

She reached the willows and pulled several of the tall shoots aside searching for one she could break off. She found herself, face to face, with Buttercup who lay in the midst of the willows contentedly chewing her cud. Calmly, with only a twitch of an ear to discourage a fly, the cow stared back at her disheveled mistress. Hallie dropped to her knees, threw her arms around the cow's neck and hugged her as though she were a long lost sister. Fuss if you must, Buttercup's big brown eyes seemed to say as she batted their long, velvety lashes.

The hugging over, Hallie tied Buttercup's rope to a stout willow shoot insuring her staying put while she retrieved her hat. Actually, Hallie wouldn't have needed the stick for the snake was gone when she returned to the gully.

The sun was setting by the time Hallie, leading Buttercup, made the trek back to camp. Nothing had been disturbed in her absence. There was no sign of Will, the wagon, or the barrels of water. It had been a very long day without water. She wondered if Buttercup had scented moisture where the willows shoots had grown. Water probably stood there after a rain or when snow melted.

The water jug sat just inside the shelter's entrance where she had left it the night before. The water was tepid as she drank sparingly, barely quenching her thirst. She finished and shook the jug. Not a pint remained, she guessed. Buttercup was gaunt and sniffed at a bucket looking for water. Hallie wondered if she were to dig where the willow shoots grew if there might be enough seepage to water a cow. It was too far to go back tonight. Surely, Will would arrive shortly.

"Don't fret, girl," Hallie comforted, giving the cow a pat on her head. "You'll get a drink soon."

Hallie located a hammer in the tool chest and pounded the picket pin in until only its iron head could be seen above the ground. Buttercup was to do no more roaming.

Hallie hustled about ignoring her tiredness, determined to have some sort of meal ready when Will arrived. She lifted the lid of the grub box and studied the contents. There was not enough water to cook rice or beans, couldn't make coffee or tea. In fact, there really wasn't much choice with such a small amount of water to work with. It would take too long to bake some of the potatoes Will had bought in Kearney. She was much too tired and hungry to wait. It would just have to be corn cakes again, she concluded, reaching for the meal bag.

A fire was built, the cakes prepared and the skillet placed among the burning twigs to heat as Hallie listened for the sound of the approaching team and wagon.

A stomach cramp reminded her how hungry she was. Hallie rummaged in the grub box again, hunting for something to tide her over until Will came. There was a box of raisins stuck down in one corner under the salt sack. Her mouth watered at the prospect of nourishment. She sat down on the ground with her back resting against the wooden box, eating raisins and listened to the soft call of a nighthawk. Her head began to nod, tiredly her chin sank to rest against the dusty, damp folds of her collar, and Hallie was asleep.

Later, she had no way of knowing how much later, she awakened to find her neck had stiffened from its awkward position. As she straightened, she discovered a distinct crick in her back. Lightning flickered far to the west and the faint rumble of thunder could be heard. Hallie stumbled as she attempted to stand. One of her legs had fallen asleep. She braced herself on the side of the box rubbing her numb limb as she peered nervously into the darkness. The fire had gone out. Only a few coals glimmered dimly in their bed of ashes. It must be about midnight, Hallie decided. Still no Will. He should have been here hours ago.

"Oh, dear Lord! Where is he? Why doesn't he come?"

Something must have happened. An accident! He'd taken the shotgun. Guns misfire. He might have been crushed under a tree…the wagon. Her thoughts ran like so many scampering mice, as she began to pace back and forth in agitation. There was the sharp yelp of a coyote and she sucked in her breath taking a quick jerky step away from the sound. The back of her knees contacted the edge of the grub box with a resounding whack. Over she went.

This last indignity did it. Hallie began to cry and not very quietly. The coyote, all tuned up for his nightly serenade, hushed to listen to the unusual echo rising up to his perch on the ridge. Buttercup lowed sympathetically from the darkness.

The crying died down to an occasional hiccup. Grubby fingers rubbed away the tears. Scattered thoughts were marshaled into rational thinking. "You are nothing but a big baby," Hallie scolded. "Where is your faith? Will probably had to go farther than he expected. He'll be here in the morning."

The sensible thing to do, she decided, was to go to bed. But first, she would set out some tubs and buckets in case the fast approaching clouds brought rain. When this was done, Hallie knelt facing the on-coming storm and bowed her head. Her prayers reached out asking God for forgiveness for her doubts and asking Him to watch over Will...to bring him safely home. Then dusting off her skirt and massaging a skinned elbow, Hallie covered the fire ashes and found her way to bed.

Chapter 9

Morning found a bright, clean valley, washed by the passing rain. Hallie, bedraggled with wrinkled dress and dirty face, stepped out into this fresh, crisp world.

She had slept spasmodically during the night while the storm clouds growled overhead, spitting streaks of lightning and bursts of rain.

The bowl she had used to mix the corn cakes the night before had been knocked from the top of the grub box, probably when she had bumped against it. It had landed right side up and now sat rain-washed. It was filled to the brim with fresh rainwater. Hallie laughed aloud as she ran to retrieve the bowl with its precious contents. Carefully, she lifted it to her lips and drank deeply. Never had water tasted so good.

Her thoughts turned to Buttercup. The bucket and tub had caught several inches of water, but it would be wise to save that for cooking and washing. There were no doubt puddles in all the low places that would provide water for an animal. This decided, Hallie untied Buttercup and led her toward the old, grassy waterway whose path looped by not far from camp.

When she neared the creek bed a wondrous sound met her…the sound of running water. This was Hallie's first experience with the creek and its miraculous resurrections when for a few hours or even days water would gush down the normally dry bed. Always, when this occurred, she would be reminded of the creek in her father's orchard, and memories of her childhood home would come flooding back.

An anxious Will arrived that afternoon. He found a very peaceful, pleasant homecoming. A kettle of beans bubbled merrily over the fire while a skillet of corn cakes baked on the hot coals. The milk cow grazed contentedly on her firmly staked rope. A very tidy, very pretty wife stood serenely by the canvas shelter spreading freshly laundered garments out to dry on the smooth surface.

Hallie gave him a big smile and waved, calling out, "I thought you'd gone off to join the Indians."

Will grinned, his relief and surprise evident. I'll just bet he expected to find me all frazzled, Hallie guessed then admitted to herself how aptly that description would have fit at times during her husband's absence.

Will hopped down from the wagon and strode over to give Hallie a quick hug and brief kiss. "How did things go?" he asked. "Did you have any problems when it stormed?"

"Things went just fine. The rain was wonderful. It has the creek running."

She noted the poles poking out of the back of the wagon and dampness on the wooden sides of the water barrels denoting their filled contents. "I wondered about you. Did you have trouble?"

"Broke the handle on my ax first off. Had to waste time making a new one. It was a bigger job than I figured chopping those cedars. They are tough buggers. Then it took time chopping off the branches and dragging the poles out of the canyon."

"Well, you've got the job done, now. I've got supper cooking. You must be starved."

"No doubt of that. My belly button's been rubbing against my back bone all the way home." Will reached over the side of the wagon to lift a couple of fat grouse out by their legs. "I shot these a few miles back. Figured we could use some fresh meat."

Hallie took the birds and remarked on their having been shot cleanly through the head.

Will's grin widened. "Lucky shots, I reckon."

Hallie smiled as she watched her husband unload the barrels and poles then unhitch the team. She had returned to the shelter to lift the lid on the beans and check their tenderness with a spoon. She was practicing the advice her mother had drilled into her daughters. Hallie could recall her mother's words so clearly. "When a man comes homes he wants to be met with a smile and the smell of a good meal cooking not a litany of household problems." Mama had understood men, no doubt about that.

They ate supper by the dying embers of the fire. Hallie was seated on the box, Will on the ground, his feet stretched out, his back resting against the box and pressed companionably against Hallie's legs. It was then Hallie laughingly shared her hunt for the errant Buttercup and her meeting with the snake.

"I hated to leave you, like that, Hallie." Will tilted his head to look up into her face. "You handled things just fine, though. I knew you had the makin's for it. You've got grit."

Putting a hand out to smooth a stubborn sprig of hair on the back of her husband's red head, Hallie wished she was as certain of this as Will seemed to be. But then she had not told him of her tears or fright nor did she plan to. She let her hand slide slowly down the side of his face. She liked to feel the maleness of his bearded cheek. Will had let his whiskers grow since coming to Nebraska. What a comfort it was to have him here beside her. Tonight, she could ignore the encroaching darkness, the coyote howls. Tonight, Will was here.

Will was full of talk. He told her all about the people he had met at the ranch where he'd stopped for water. Their name was Hartwell. Friendly people who told him of the other settlers in the area, though Will had met some of them when he'd been out scouting for land.

"They're scattered out some," he admitted. "But, there's folks out here just like us. Good, regular folks wanting to get ahead."

"I'm surprised the Hartwells were so neighborly. I thought ranchers didn't like homesteaders coming in on open range land."

"I don't reckon any of them are too tickled over the situation. Some of them are being right down ornery about it, but it's like Mr. Hartwell said to me, 'Homesteaders have the law on their side. But, a lot of them won't stick it out. Them that don't can be bought out or their land preempted.' That's what he's figuring on. Getting back a good portion of his range in a few years. I reckon he will, too."

"Some that try homesteading don't know the first thing about land or crops. I can see for myself it would be better to run cattle or horses on this sandy soil, though the government insists you plow up part of it. I figure on getting in position some day, to do the same as Hartwells...get ahold of some of the claims others give up on. Meanwhile, I'm going to file on another 160 acres, what they call a tree claim. That'll give us a half section to begin on."

The talk went on to how well cattle wintered in the sandhills, how many acres Will hoped to cultivate the first year, how long before they could have a well.

Hallie listened patiently, waiting for an opportunity to bring up the subject of their house building. Sam was due to arrive anytime, now, to help with the project. They would need to draw up a plan showing the desired size of the rooms and how they should be arranged. She had accepted the fact it would be more economical to build with sod, but it could be well planned as to light and convenience, surely.

Will paused for breath and leaned forward to refill his cup from the smoke-blackened pot sitting on the cooling coals.

"Let's talk about the house," Hallie urged putting out a hand to squeeze his shoulder. "How big will it be? Don't you think it would be nice to have a kitchen window facing south like we had back home?"

Will took a sip from his cup then cleared his throat. "Well, it's like this, Hallie. I've been thinking, and..." he hesitated, clearing his throat again.

"You've been thinking. Why, I should hope so!" Hallie quipped. "We've got to get this all figured out so we'll be ready to start when Sam arrives."

The nearly full cup was placed on the ground and Will got to his feet. He stood with his back toward Hallie, his hands stuffed deeply into his trouser pockets staring down at the dying embers. Suddenly, he turned as though he'd reached a decision and squatted down in front of Hallie. He reached for her hands.

"Hallie, I had an offer today," he began. "A good one." Hallie stiffened. She had seen that look before, back in Missouri when Will had started all the talk about moving to Nebraska. What was coming this time?"

Will's rough, callused thumbs moved back and forth over the soft back of her hands as he began to explain.

"I told you the Hartwells are nice folks. Right off, we found out they'd come from Missouri, just like us. Why, they even came from Pettis County only they lived up in the north end. It makes them almost seem like kin, somehow. They come out here five years, ago. Course, he had money when he got here. Brought the beginnings of a herd when they made the move."

Will's eyes were on hers, his voice with that note of persuasion she knew so well, was telling how Mr. Hartwell was short-handed. One of his men had broken a leg when a horse fell on him. Another one had gotten homesick for Texas and headed south the day before Will stopped in.

"When he heard I knew horses, he asked would I like to work for him." Will paused and then hurried on. "I said I'd want to talk it over with you, and how I'd need a couple of days to get a place fixed for us to live. He said that was fine. I could start next Monday if I decided on it."

Hallie hadn't said anything, and Will urged, "Now, ain't that good news? Think of what we can do with some extra cash. Why, we can get our well dug in the spring, maybe even build fences for pastures besides putting up a house."

Hallie was trying to take this all in, grasping at the part about needing two days to build a place to live. What kind of a house could be put up in two days? She caught the phrase…"Dig right there to the left of the thicket."

"Dig what, Will? What are you talking about?"

"Ain't you listening? I said we could build a nice, little dugout right over there."

"A DUGOUT!" she gasped. "You want us to live in a DUGOUT?"

Will patted her hands and assured that it would only be for the winter. "It won't be half bad. The McNeils make out, don't they? Can't we manage, just for awhile?"

Hallie brushed a tear away that Will either didn't see or chose to ignore. She nodded when Will asked, "Now, don't you think it's for the best?"

Will was up at the crack of dawn. The fire was crackling before Hallie had time to lace her shoes. They ate a hurried breakfast standing, holding their plates. The coolness of the morning was a reminder fall was not far off. With the thought of fall came that of winter. This forced Hallie to face the knowledge she would be spending it living in a cellar…the like of which only the shiftless would have attempted to store their garden harvest in back home and then it would have probably gotten nipped by the cold.

When Will had strode off with purposeful stride, Hallie tried to think about the noon meal. Sam would no doubt have arrived by then and he was a big eater. They had the grouse and there were potatoes. Will had brought in an armful of dead branches from the thicket remarking there was not much more there to gather. He had added that they would have to burn cowchips as soon as they could get some gathered. Hallie gave an inward shudder thinking of it. What would her friends back home think if they knew she was going to be cooking with cow manure?

She buried three potatoes beneath the hot ashes and the dressed birds were put to cook in the heavy, cast iron skillet. The left over beans from the day before enhanced with molasses and dried onion were simmering in a pot at the edge of the fire. The corn bread could be mixed and baked nearer to noon.

The household tasks completed, Hallie went to help Will. He had hitched the team to the plow and was sliding it over nearer the area of the thicket letting it coast on its side, the shiny blade glinting in the sun. When the plow reached the stretch of grass that was to provide the sod blocks for the front of the dugout, it was righted. The harness lines were knotted together and pulled down over Will's shoulders so they tugged firmly across his back. This would leave his hands free to hold the plow handles.

"Giddy-up," he spoke to the horses. As they moved forward tightening the tugs, causing the plow to move forward its blade biting down into the sod. The first ground on the McCain homestead was broken.

The plow blade bit deep beneath the bluestem, turning back a thick strip of imprisoned soil…soil held tightly by the matted grass roots undisturbed until that day.

It was midmorning when Sam booted his horse down the ridge, his bellow of "Howdy, younguns," preceding him into camp.

Will dropped the spade he was using to cut blocks from the sod strips and hurried to greet him. Sam unsaddled and hobbled his horse to graze as Will explained the change in plans and the need to speed things along.

"Sounds fine to me," Sam said, spitting a wad of tobacco juice skillfully to one side. "You can always build a house later on, and there ain't nothing' snugger than a dugout for winter." He chucked Hallie under the chin and delivered a message from Mattie. "Matt says to tell you they sure miss your company. Her and Pearl are already badgerin' me to bring all of 'em over here for a visit."

To Hallie's amazement, she found herself replying in all sincerity, she hoped he would do so in the very near future. She had known she would miss Pearl…but Mattie and her untidy brood?

The men fortified themselves with a cold drink of water then set to work. The sod blocks Will had cut were laid to one side. Will stepped off the dimensions of the proposed dugout and the digging began.

Several hours of digging followed with only a short break at noon. A three-sided room was dug into the foot of the sandy hill, eight feet deep and nearly twelve feet long. The dirt walls were six feet high.

When the digging was finished, the men built wooden frames for the door and window from rough lumber Will had purchased in Kearney. The earlier plans for the sod house had included three ready-made glass windows, the rough lumber, a roll of tar paper and some nails. These items had cut deeply into their cash reserve.

"I passed on buying iron hinges for the door," he had told Hallie regretfully. "Leather makes pretty fair hinges, and we have to save where we can."

The following day the sod wall that fronted the dugout was built. The window and doorframe were set into place. A few of the cedar poles were laid across the top of the now enclosed room to support the flat roof. Wide strips of tarpaper were laid over the poles with heavy blocks of sod forming the third and final layer.

The last of the sod was in place shortly before dusk. Will declared they call it a day. The two men stood back, hands on hips, to admire their handiwork. Hallie couldn't see that there was much to admire. The outer wall of sod blended in with the hillside as any dirt bank would. All that was noticeable was the gaping doorway as yet doorless, and the one tiny window blinking in the rays of the setting sun like a solitary eye at the base of the hill.

Sam announced in his usual shout, "By golly, younguns, you've got you a fine little home there! You'll be snug as two bugs in a rug!"

Hallie heard this pronouncement from where she was preparing supper and had her own thoughts on the matter. But she smiled when the proud men joined her. She set out the plates on the grub box in readiness. Will had shot a rabbit that morning so there was meat to cook. Prepare and cook! Her father and brothers had always cleaned their own game before bringing it to the house. However, with Will in such a rush, she had been left to dress not only the grouse the day before but the rabbit today. It did have its reward, she admitted as she lifted the iron lid on the skillet and breathed the fragrant aroma of fresh, fried meat.

Supper over, they continued to sit by the fire. The men filled and lit their pipes while Hallie washed the dishes, using water sparingly. Finished, she sat down on the ever-present grub box to listen, watching the pipe smoke spirals drift off into the night air. She looked off into the darkness toward the newly prepared dugout. Her slender shoulders quivered with a shudder of revulsion. How would she bear it? She tilted her head back and gazed up at the dark velvet sky sprinkled so liberally with its millions of glittering stars.

How insignificant one feels out here, she thought. The ache of homesickness twisted in her breast as she visualized the emptiness surrounding them…the endless hills going on forever, a land so vast with a people so few.

"Yet, God is here," she reminded herself. With this comfort, Hallie closed her eyes to shut out the distracting stars and silently prayed, "Dear Lord, this is Hallie. How did I get way out here? How am I going to stand it? I've been pretending, going along with things for Will's sake, but Lord, you know I can't live in that hole all winter. You know I can't! I'll lose my mind. I know I will. Couldn't you please make Will change his mind and go home to Missouri? If you will, I'll never ask for another thing as long as I live! Please Lord! Amen."

The stars stared back at her when she opened her eyes with cold indifference. But from across the valley floor, a gentle wind, scented by the prairie grasses moved soundlessly over the campsite. The soft breeze caressed her face, ruffling and whispering through her dark curls. Faintly within her heart she heard, "It takes courage, Hallie. Courage and faith."

Hallie heard, but she whispered back…"What if I don't have enough?

Chapter 10

Life on the homestead officially began the day they moved into the dugout. At least that was how it seemed to Hallie. Until then she had felt transient...a guest...a mere camper in this prairie land. With a dwelling, such as it was, and Will working at the Hartwell Ranch, the truth had to be faced. She, along with the coyotes and the jackrabbits, had become a resident of the valley.

The McCains, not unlike the other valley inhabitants, were early risers. Long before daylight, they were up and about preparing for the day. Hallie would have her usual tussle with her miniature cook stove, poking and shaking its innards into action so breakfast might be cooked while Will was out saddling his horse. Will was using one of the workhorses to ride back and forth to the ranch.

They ate by lamplight, neither of them bent on conversation so early in the day.

It was a hurried meal with Will rarely taking time for the second cup of coffee, wanting to cover a good portion of the ride before sunup.

Will liked working at the ranch though the hours were long, and they were spent building another man's herd. "It's not just the money, though we sure enough need it," he told Hallie. "It's the learning that's going to come in handy. I figure somewhere down the road, when we build this place up into a real ranch, I'll want to know about raising livestock in this country." He'd given her a big grin. "We'll have us good cattle and blooded horses...something we can pass on to our younguns. We'll have enough land and stock that none of them will have to take off somewhere's on their own, unless they've a mind too.

And hearing this last part, Hallie had wondered if Will didn't miss home just a little himself.

Despite his determination, Hallie sensed Will did not find it as easy as he had thought to master the skills of a cowhand. Things were done differently out here in ranch country, she gathered.

"I reckon I can learn,' he told Hallie one evening as he eased his boot off a sprained ankle. "But, you end up playing the fool once in awhile." He chuckled ruefully as he related the incident that had produced the injured ankle. "Got myself tangled up in my own rope when I was trying to catch an old cow. We had her in the corral and I was on foot. I didn't have any trouble getting my loop on her. I'm getting half way good at that, but then she came charging past me and around the other side. Before I knew it, I was wound up like a kid's top. It gave the boys a good hee-haw by the time they got her slowed down and me unwrapped."

"You could have got yourself killed," Hallie fussed as she swabbed at a scrape on his cheek. "And those idiots thought it was funny!"

"It was funny. They're good old boys and don't mean anything by it. You get in a jamb, there's always somebody jumps in and pulls you out."

Will hobbled the two steps to the wash bench. As he washed in the water Hallie had left in the pan from her own washing, he remarked, "Joshing never has bothered me much. You know how it is growing up around a bunch of brothers. But, I got to admit it gets under my hide when somebody makes a wisecrack about the plowboy's riding horse."

"They have some nerve," Hallie declared indignantly. "They should have seen that horse you had in Missouri. I'm sure he was better than any they ride! I wish you hadn't had to sell him."

Will was wiping his face on the towel avoiding the scraped spot. "Don't go getting all het up about it. I showed them right off I could ride anything any of them could. Surprised them some, I could tell." Will hung the towel on its peg. "I'm just lucky Hartman furnishes his men good riding stock for the ranch work."

Will pulled his chair out and sat down at the little table where Hallie was dishing up their supper. "Can't you just see what I'd look like coming lumbering along behind the crew on old Pat?" Will chuckled again. "Him with those hooves each the size of a skillet."

Pat was the Percheron Will rode back and forth to work. He was a fine draft animal but certainly not suited for riding.

"You could use your first month's wages to buy a young, untrained horse from Mr. Hartman. Twenty-five dollars would be enough to get one, wouldn't it?" Hallie wanted to know.

"Probably would, honey. But, we can't waste money just to salve my pride. I'll get me a horse when the time's right. Might even catch me some of those mustangs that run wild around here, I get the time."

Will spooned beans into his plate. "I've seen some of them. Some are pretty fair horses. A man could get a good stud from back home and breed him to some mustang mares. He could build a decent herd that would turn out good using stock. Would be a way to get started till we could afford blooded stock."

Hallie agreed, but doubted the advisability of such a plan. Wild horses, indeed. She didn't think Will was truly serious about the matter. It was just something to talk about, and heaven knows, we need something new to talk about! She thought to herself. But, must it be horses? All Will ever talks about anymore are cows, horses, and the cowboys he works with! I'd give most anything to have a real good down home conversation with a female!

Hallie was lonely and bored. Will's days were filled with new experiences and people while her days consisted of empty, endless hours. There were limited household tasks with only Buttercup, and Mike, the other horse, for company.

Some mornings after Will had gone, the bed, still holding their body warmth, would tempt Hallie back beneath the covers, but not often. She had been raised in a family that considered it quite scandalous to lie abed after sunrise, unless of course, one was ill. Guilt would prick her conscience, and she would feel "shiftless" even if no one knew of her transgression other than herself.

So disciplined, Hallie would bustle about the dusky dugout doing her housework by the dim morning light furnished by the small window. The lamp would have been blown out to save coal oil or kerosene as some called it, right after breakfast.

Once the household chores were finished, Hallie would grab her shawl or an old coat of Will's, depending on the weather, and escape into the brightness of the out-of-doors. She stayed out for hours at a time. Only very persistent, very miserable weather could drive her back inside. Hallie tramped about the valley and throughout the neighboring hills and draws until they became as familiar as the fields and woodlot of her father's farm.

It was one such morning, after she had checked on the very expectant Buttercup that Hallie paused to talk to Mike and give the gray gelding his usual petting. Both the horse and the cow were tethered to picket ropes some distance from the dugout, grazing on the fall-cured grass. Mike lifted his head to acknowledge her presence.

71

Hallie rubbed his big, rubbery chin with its bristly whiskers and spoke companionably to him.

"Hello there, old boy. How are you doing? It's no fun being left behind every day, is it?"

The horse blew a gentle snort through his nostrils as though in agreement and lowered his head to get on with his grazing. Hallie studied the big horse and imagined herself up on his wide back. It was not the first time she had thought of this. After all, she knew how to ride. She'd ridden often as a child, but she had grown away from what had been a youthful obsession. At age fifteen when her father had asked Hallie which she would prefer, a sidesaddle for Christmas or a fur muff, she had hesitated for only a moment before naming the muff.

"I should have chosen the saddle," Hallie spoke aloud as she continued to contemplate the horse. The wind whipped the loosened ends of her hair across her face as she worried the idea about in her mind. One didn't have to have a saddle to ride. Her brothers often rode bareback for fun. The real problem was whether or not Mike would allow her on his back. Neither Pat nor Mike had been trained to ride. Will had had a time getting Pat to accept the concept of carrying a saddle and man on his back. The Percherons were gentle, and biddable animals, but because of their size and breeding, had been trained only for harness use.

Hallie knew all this, but the challenge stood before her peacefully munching grass and swishing his tail at a fly that had survived the frosts. She brushed the hair from her face and spoke coaxingly, "You'd let me ride, wouldn't you, boy? You'd not mind, would you?"

Having convinced herself, and hopefully the horse, Hallie proceeded. First, she needed a bridle. She would have to use one that went with the harnesses. These bridles were equipped with leather blinders that hindered a horse's side vision, but no matter. Mike was used to that indignity.

Carrying one of the bridles, Hallie returned to face Mike who now stood with head up far above her reach, staring off in the direction his companion had been ridden that morning. She looked up at the big head and considered. Mike liked having his chin scratched. Would he lower his head and stand still for the bit? This method failed. As soon as she stopped scratching to work with the bridle, up went his head.

This method abandoned, a wooden crate was dragged over to stand on. Mike took the bit like a gentleman, and Hallie buckled the bridle with a smug smile.

"So far, so good, boy. Now, let's see if I can get up there." Hallie contemplated the distance to the wide muscled back. The crate was not high enough...but the wagon was! Hallie led Mike over to the wagon and climbed the spokes of a wheel. Teetering on the rim, she jumped astride.

The big, gelding took no notice of the slight weight on his back. Hallie held her breath and nudged him gently with her heel. This signal meant nothing to the horse. She tried again. "Giddy-up," and slapped gently with the shorter checkreins she had substituted in place of the longer driving lines. This was more familiar. Mike took a step forward and turned his head, perhaps to see where Hallie had gone. The blinders obstructed part of this view, but he must have been able to see the hem of her skirt fluttering in the wind. This was no doubt disconcerting. Mike gave a few quick sidesteps with a nervous snort.

"Whoa, boy. Whoa." Hallie spoke calmly. Mike gave a snorty wheeze and with perked ears stepped forward as though willing to accept these peculiarities in exchange for his freedom from the picket rope.

Horse and rider left the dugout and Buttercup to move out on to the floor of the valley. Hallie was delighted. Not content to plug along, she gave Mike a kick in his fat ribs, urging, "Giddy-up!"

Mike obliged by breaking into a trot. To Hallie's dismay, she discovered riding bareback was quite different from riding with a sidesaddle. There was no stirrup to brace with, no horn to clasp with her knee. There was nothing to aid her but a hold on the horse's flapping mane. As Mike trotted, Hallie slid. She could not get a grip with her legs on his wide ribs. She slid first one side and then the other...then off!

She landed on her back, one hand still clutching the end of a rein. This brought Mike to a stop. He stood looking down at Hallie as she struggled to draw breath. She'd felt this way once before...the time she'd fallen from a high branch of an apple tree. She had been ten at the time. She recalled the sensation of feeling as though she would never draw breath again, but you did. In a few moments Hallie was able to suck in a shaky breath and sit up.

Hallie gained her feet and dusted herself off. How was she going to get on again? She didn't want to lead the horse all the way back to the wagon. Was the creek bank deep enough? It was and Mike cooperated nicely, standing quietly in the creek bed while Hallie mounted from the bank. "Good boy," she crooned. "Good boy."

Sedately, they continued on their way. "We'll have to take it slowly today, boy, but I'll learn. Just be patient with me." Hallie patted the big grays neck with grateful affection.

When Will arrived home that evening, he was informed of Hallie's exploit. "You could have broken your neck. You know that, don't you?" He scolded, but the twinkle in his eyes told Hallie that secretly he admired her courage and ingenuity. The rides continued. Hallie ventured farther out from the valley, day by day.

Will was putting in longer days at the ranch. It was often dark when he got home with the ever-shortening days and the fall workload. Many times the cowhands bedded down where they were rounding up cattle and sorting out those to be shipped to the eastern markets. Sometimes, days went by without Will getting back to the homestead.

It was during one of these stretches Hallie became particularly aggravated over her lack of fuel. She made do all fall with what she could locate, dry, twisted grass, twigs from the thickets, cowchips from along the trails. Will had the best of intentions, but he had never had the time to take the wagon to gather and haul a load of chips for her. He had told Hallie of a lake some miles distance where cattle congregated and the chips were plentiful. "We'll gather a load as soon as roundup season is over,' he'd promised his last time at home.

Meanwhile, it was a chilly morning. Hallie had used the last of the fuel she had managed to gather to cook her breakfast and to take the chill out of the dugout. "If only I had both horses to pull the wagon, I'd go haul those chips myself," she grumped.

Hallie was milking, her back huddled against the cold wind. She thought about the cowchips at the lake and her empty stove. She had poured some of the milk into the small bucket she used for feeding the calf his share when the idea came. Saddlebags! Great big ones! All she needed to do was make them.

After the milk was strained and the pail washed, Hallie began her project. She rummaged around under the tarp where they kept extra supplies and the tools. Folded at one end of the toolbox were several gunnysacks. She took two of the sacks and with a large darning needle, twine and a strip of torn canvas, she put together a pair of large, makeshift saddlebags.

That afternoon, Hallie rode westward, the empty burlap sacks dangling, one on either side of Mike's thick withers. She was not certain of the lake's location, but knew the trails winding through the hills would likely lead to water. If not, the lake, another water hole where chips would be easy to gather.

The trail she followed meandered through hills, some large, some whose peaks had disappeared, gnawed away by the hungry winds. Wind flung gritty sand from such denuded spots she would learn were called "blowouts", to sting Hallie's face, forcing her to close her eyes as she passed. The trail deepened, cut through countless years by the hooves of animals following the scent of water. The deep, rutted trail branched off suddenly at the brow of a hill into numerous, shallow fingers where thirsty critters had broken rank as they sighted water and hurried forward.

Hallie pulled Mike to a stop to look out across the little valley before her. It appeared to be about a half mile wide. Its natural shape and topography reminded her of a china dinner plate with its wide, flat outer edge inclining gradually downward into a shallow center. The gradual tilt of the valley floor sent runoffs from the rain and snow to form a lake in its middle. Its size probably varied with the seasons, Hallie surmised for the shoreline indicated that at times the water reached to the bunchgrass growing at the foot of the hills and again, during a dry summer, it might shrink to a mere mud puddle in the center. Two good rains in recent weeks had replenished it to a respectable size the October day Hallie first viewed what was known as Sand Lake.

Hallie, wrapped in Will's bulky chore coat, sat her horse and shivered in the wind. She retied her wool scarf, tucking the ends down in the loose-fitting collar in an attempt to block the wind's persistent whistling down her neck. She nudged Mike with her heel and rode down for a closer inspection. The big horse snorted, and pricked his ears at the unfamiliar scent of lake water and the sight of the strange, long-horned cows with their calves drinking on the far side.

It took a couple of thumps on his padded ribs before Mike took a few uneasy steps into the water. The tiny waves slapped teasingly at his shaggy fetlocks, causing him to snuff suspiciously as he lowered his head to drink. From her seat on the horse's broad back Hallie waited while he drank his fill. She wouldn't have to water him from the barrels tonight. How convenient it would have been to have land near water such as this.

Mike lifted his dripping muzzle and looked off in the direction the fleeing cattle had taken. He flared his nostrils filling his huge lungs with the crisp air then blew it out in gusty puffs. Hallie urged him back to shore where she dismounted and dropped reins. There was no danger of him deserting her. Mike had proven to be reliable.

Dry, manure chips dotted the shore in every direction. The hot winds of August and September had cured the summer cow patties and though the rains had dampened them they were again dry. The dry, gray-colored chips were about the size of her skillet lid. The sacks were stuffed full in no time. Hallie dragged the cumbersome sacks onto a sandbank where rubbing cattle had worn one side away. With this for a mounting block, the lumpy sacks were pushed aboard then Hallie jumped up behind.

If she was frugal, Hallie figured as she headed homeward, and heaven knew she had learned to be that, she would have fuel to last for the next few days.

Chapter 11

Hallie's trip to the lake was but the first of many. Sometimes, it would be with Will taking the team and wagon for a load of chips. Hallie's saddlebags couldn't begin to keep the little iron monster satisfied as it grew colder. Later, when Will found time, he often went to the lake to hunt wild ducks and geese. But, it was always one of Hallie's favorite destinations during those fall days when she and Mike roamed the countryside.

It was on one of these treks, Hallie discovered the deserted soddy. She had been riding south of the lake that particular day traveling up a narrow draw. Abruptly, it widened and setting back against the foot of a hill was a dilapidated soddy. Clumps of withered, brown grass hung over the edge of the sod roof like tufts of dry hair. Someone had salvaged the windows, frames and all. A wooden door hung whopper-jawed on rotting leather hinges.

What a sad, little structure it is, Hallie thought as she rode toward it. It would have a story to tell if it could only speak, she was sure of it. Someone had come to this lonely spot, built a shelter, and plowed the ground. The weedy plow ridges still marked where a small field and probably a garden had been planted at one time. Sand shifted dismally across the plow-scared patch. Someone had planned to build a home here just as she and Will were doing. What had gone wrong?

Did the soddy warrant investigation, Hallie wondered? Making up her mind, she slid down and went to tug at the broken door. The weathered hinges gave way, and the door hit the ground with a whomp. She jumped back guiltily. "Well, it wasn't doing a speck of good anyway," Hallie told the startled horse.

Hallie stuck her head through the doorway. A woman must have lived here. The walls had been plastered neatly with clay though at the corners it was beginning to crumble. A row of wooden pegs ran in a straight line across the wall at one end. At the other end of the room, near the stovepipe hole, it looked as though there had been shelves at one time. She stepped over a drift of sand on the sill into the tiny room, brushing aside the spider webs that crisscrossed the doorway.

The room was empty except for the ripples of sand on the dirt floor and a pile of refuse in one corner, nearly buried by sand. A child's leather shoe, cracked and worn through at the toe poked up from the sand. She shook the sand out of the little shoe trying to imagine the child who had worn it. Had it been a boy or girl? Plump or slight? Plump, she decided for the seams had been well stretched. She smiled as she set it back down picturing a sturdy little fellow in her mind.

She ran her fingers through the loose sand and discovered a shaving mug with the handle missing, its rim badly chipped. Hallie picked it up and let the sand trickle out. As the sand fell, a glint caught her eye. Poking her finger about in the fallen sand, she discovered a diminutive brooch the size of a nickel. It was in the shape of a miniature horseshoe with a wee wishbone tucked in its center carved from an orange stone of some sort.

Hallie held it cupped in her hand, admiring her find. Perhaps the woman who had lived here had kept this special brooch in the mug for safekeeping, way back on a shelf. When they moved away the damaged mug might have been tossed aside, and the brooch forgotten, tossed with it.

She wrapped the brooch tightly in her handkerchief and pushed it way down in one of the coat's deep pockets. It was far too pretty to be lost again.

There was little else among the discarded items; a tangle of knotted twine, a bent spoon, and an old, rolled up newspaper. Carefully, Hallie unrolled the ragged edges, checking for a name and date. There, in bold type, across the top of the first page was the title...Brandenville Gazette. In smaller type, just below, was the location and date...Brandenville, Illinois—July 17, 1878. Why, that was only two years ago, Hallie realized. People had lived here that recently! People from Illinois, if the paper was any indication. The paper was most likely from a small town sent out to the Nebraska prairie by relatives or friends left behind just as she and Will received their own newspaper from back home.

The second ragged page revealed a column proudly labeled "Society Items". Seated on the sand, wrapped in Will's old coat, Hallie began to read. She could fully sympathize with the ex-Brandenville matron, exiled here in her soddy, avidly reading these glowing accounts of the comings and goings of the citizenry of faraway Brandenville. It would have done little for the woman's morale to have read how the elegant Mrs. Ferguson appeared in her pale, green silk, hosting an afternoon lawn party. The reader, most likely, had been wearing a sweaty dress of gingham and hosting a swarm of flies while a trickle of dirt found its way down her collar from the sod ceiling above.

The newspaper was re-rolled and stuck into the pocket with the brooch. Reading material was too scarce to waste, even an outdated newspaper.

When Will got home that evening, Hallie told him about the soddy and her discoveries there.

"That's probably where the Petersons lived," Will answered and went on washing up for supper.

"Well, who were the Petersons, and what became of them?"

Hanging the towel on its peg, Will glanced over at her and then away. "It's not a story to lift a person's spirits. I didn't think it would do you any good to hear it so I never mentioned it."

"For goodness sakes! I'm not a child. Tell me about them!"

Will told her the story between hungry bites of cornbread and gravy.

"Mrs. Hartwell's the one told me about them. She knew the family as well as anyone out here did, I reckon. She said the Petersons came here in the spring of 77 not long after Mr. Hartwell got their big sod house built and she'd come up here to join him.

Will finished one piece of bread and took another spooning gravy onto it from the bowl Hallie moved over by his plate. "The Petersons put up their soddy and settled in. They had two little shaffers, one was about three and the other one was around four or five. The man plowed some ground and planted a crop. They must have raised enough to get by that next winter. They used water from the lake and came over to the ranch to get drinking water and their mail.

The wife was frail looking and didn't have much to say. Mrs. Hartwell said she figured the woman had an education from the way she talked when she did say something." Will had finished his bread and gravy and was now eating his dish of stewed dried apples with relish. "Hartwells didn't see anything of them during a stretch of bad weather. Then the man came riding in one day, said one of the boys was sick with chest congestion and did Mrs. Hartwell know what they could do in the way of doctoring. Both the Hartwells went back with him and helped take care of the little fellow. Mrs. Hartwell is good at that sort of thing, I understand. She said the house was spick and span even if there wasn't hardly enough space to swing a cat in."

"Did the child recover?" Hallie was thinking of the little shoe.

"He made it. They fixed some kind of a poultice Mrs. Hartwell had brought the makings for, and by the next morning, he was breathing easy. Mrs. Peterson was even more withdrawn after that sickness. She hardly came to the ranch anymore and come spring she never came again. Summer passed...must have been in 78, Peterson came over one day. He ordered winter supplies. You know how the Hartwells haul in supplies and folks can order from them...sort of run a store. Anyway, he had the little boys with him and they said their mama stayed home to clean house."

Will stopped here and having finished eating, began to work with his pipe, filling and tamping tobacco.

"You'd have thought she'd have wanted to come talk with another woman." And Hallie thought of how much she enjoyed her own visits with Mrs. Hartwell when she occasionally rode over to spend an afternoon and then rode home with Will.

"You'd have thought so, but like they said, she got strange like. And she did clean house while he was gone that day. They say she had washed the windows and dampened down the dirt floor. Brushed it smooth...done up everything. Then...." Will paused.

"What happened? How did Mrs. Hartwell know she cleaned her house like that?"

"Because, Peterson came back that day with his boys and asked them to send for the sheriff. He told them he needed help over at his place."

"You don't mean?"

"Afraid so. His wife had combed her hair all neat and pinned it up like she was going somewhere. Put on her best dress and took down her husband's pistol. Laid down on the bed and held that gun to her head...pulled the trigger. That's how him and those little fellows found her. Just about did him in, too, they say."

"Oh, how awful! Why, in the world would she have done such a thing?" But, Hallie could guess. It must have been the loneliness, the cramped soddy, the wind, the dirt...the emptiness.

"Hard to say," Will was looking at Hallie over the bowl of his pipe as he lit it from a bit of twig he had held over the lamp chimney until it flamed. "I reckon it's like Hartwell says, 'Life's hard on women out here if they don't have the backbone for it.'"

Hallie had stood up to stack the supper dishes. Will reached out to put his arm around her waist and pull her close.

"I reckon you get lonesome at times, Hallie. But, you're like Mrs. Hartwell, keeping yourself busy, riding and all. You and her are the kind that makes a go of it our here."

This was intended as a compliment, Hallie realized. Being compared to the highly respected ranch wife, but she found herself resenting it. Can't Will see how different our situations are? Mrs. Hartwell has a house…people stopping by every day. I keep house in a dugout…spend my days alone. And, Hallie asked herself how Will would feel if he had to trade places with her.

Hallie did not voice these rebellious thoughts. Instead, she turned to the stove and took up the pan of heating water. She turned back to set it on the folded towel placed at the end of the table to protect the oilcloth from the pan's hot bottom. Putting the stack of dirty dishes into the pan, she asked. "What became of Mr. Peterson and the boys?"

"Well, they had a sort of funeral and buried the wife at the ranch next to the grave of a cowboy that got killed riding a bronco. There isn't a regular cemetery closer than Dry Bend. Peterson sold his claim rights to Hartwell then he and his boys left…went back to Illinois."

"It's a pity he couldn't have gone a little sooner!" Hallie spoke with uncustomary sharpness as she rubbed at a streak of congealed gravy with her dishrag. She thought of the little brooch she had found that day. She would keep it…it was the least she could do for that poor woman…but she would never wear it.

Chapter 12

All was not gloom that October. Not only did Hallie have a birthday to look forward to, but, there was to be a "doings" at the ranch in early November. This function, hosted by Jacob and Ethel Hartwell, was an annual affair. Everyone for miles around was invited. The other cowhands had informed Will that nobody missed it unless they were so sick they couldn't crawl out of bed.

Best of all…the frosting on the cake…was that Ethel Hartwell had asked Hallie to work for her during the two weeks preceding the occasion. Hallie was delighted at the prospect of spending all those days in a real house and having another woman to talk to every day.

Hallie liked Ethel Hartwell though at first she had found her a bit intimidating with her forceful, no-nonsense demeanor.

Ethel Hartwell was a rather large woman, big-framed though not bulky. She walked with a graceful, straight carriage. She had a pleasant face and an abundance of blond hair just beginning to gray worn in an upsweep. Her voice, like her face, was pleasant and was seldom raised though it had a quality that brooked little room for argument. She was the type one expects and is calm under stress…a bulwark in a storm.

Childless, and in her early fifties, Ethel Hartwell directed her energies toward her husband's interests; cattle, land, and more recently…local politics. These political aspirations of Jacob Hartwell may have been at least a part of the motivation behind their hosting the fall affair. It certainly was a means of bringing far-flung inhabitants together.

Jacob Hartwell knew the names of every settler within a fifty-mile radius, or so folks said. The tall, gray, dignified rancher worked very hard at building a reputation for being both a friend of the homesteader and the cattleman. It was not an easy line to walk, but he did it well. Both factions appeared to trust him and depend upon his judgment when trouble between the two occurred…and it did at times…was bound to. However, there had been no blood shed in his area between the two groups. It was due, most said, to his influence.

The days Hallie spent helping at the ranch sped by. She was too excited to feel tiredness though she left the homestead before daybreak each morning accompanying Will on the ride to the ranch.

Ethel Hartwell greeted Hallie on the first morning with a matter of fact, "Good. You've come. We'll have a cup of coffee and then get started."

The ranch house and the other buildings sat in the middle of a stretch of flat grassland. The buildings were all of sod and single-storied though plans were being made to build a large, frame barn. The house was large and very comfortable despite its outer walls being made of sod. It had a kitchen and pantry, dining room, double parlors, four bedrooms and two wooden porches. The roof was shingled and every room had glass windows with deep sills created by the thick walls. The inside walls had all been coated with a mud mixture and plastered smoothly.

One of the first jobs Hallie was assigned was applying fresh, whitewash to the kitchen walls. As she brushed the solution on, she tried not to think of the ugly dirt ones in her own dwelling. She knew it would be even more difficult to cope with the dreary dugout after spending this time walking on wooden floors in rooms where there was actually space to move about.

Every portion of those days was enjoyable from polishing the furniture to waxing the wide-boarded floors in the parlors. Their rugs had been rolled up and put in the attic in preparation for dancing. The highlight of each day, however, was when Ethel Hartwell proclaimed it was "coffee time".

Ethel wasn't one for warmed over coffee. Nor did she stint on food. When the bread was toasted to a golden brown and the coffee had boiled, they would eat the buttered toast with wedges of cheese or thick slices of cured ham. There was always pie or cake in the pantry, and the cookie jar filled with molasses or oatmeal cookies.

The afternoon break differed from the noon meal in that it was a more leisurely affair with the main jobs of the day either completed or nearly so. The two women would sit, sipping and munching, visiting of family back in Missouri and the lives they themselves, had led there. Other times, the older woman would fill Hallie in on those who lived in their area of the prairie.

By the middle of the second week, these chats became more intimate in nature with both beginning to share information one will with a friend. Ethel Hartwell spoke quite simply of the row of little gravestones left behind in Missouri. It was the glitter of tears in the older woman's eyes that revealed the depth of sorrow those lost babies had left in her heart.

Hallie confided her own reluctance on leaving her family and her old life. Loyalty to Will prevented her mentioning how much she hated the dugout and dreaded the winter months that must be spent cooped up there. She did, however, express a concern she'd had these last few weeks. Ethel Hartwell listened, asked a few questions, and counting on her competent fingers, confirmed what Hallie suspected...she was in the family way. The first part of June would likely be the time an increase in the McCain family would occur.

"I'm not as happy as I thought I would be," Hallie admitted. "I'd be thrilled if we were back home, but..." She didn't finish, though Ethel Hartwell did.

"But, you're concerned how you'll manage out here. Lot's of women do, you know. It's a natural thing, having a child. You are young, and healthy. You should produce a fine, strong baby."

Perhaps she noted the doubt in her listener's expression for Ethel Hartwell hastily added, "Now, don't go thinking of the losses I had. Not many women have problems along those lines, thank the dear Lord!" She reached over to put a hand on Hallie's shoulder. "You'll do just fine. I'll be here if you want me. I've helped a good many into the world. It was just my own, I failed at." She pushed the cookie plate toward Hallie. "Now, have another cookie then we'll finish ironing those curtains."

The day of Hallie's eighteenth birthday fell on a Wednesday and passed without comment at the ranch. She had not mentioned it to Ethel Hartwell less she feel Hallie expected special attention be given the day. A letter had arrived a few days earlier from her family containing a practical money gift. Hallie put it aside to use for baby things. The letter had provided the usual news of home folks. Tears had blurred Hallie's eyes when she'd read those precious pages aloud to Will after supper on the day the letter came. Her mother had written Ida was feeling well and looking forward to the arrival of a little one in January.

Catherine had taken the same school again this fall and was being courted by a young farmer in that school district. Aunt Daphne was planning a Halloween party for the young people from the church.

Aunt Susie was put out because Uncle Tobias had purchased a new hearse for the mortuary instead of the new surrey his wife had been wanting. Hallie smiled as she imagined her mother's expression as she penned that bit of information.

Frank and Troy were back in school and growing like weeds. Amanda was helping at the dress shop in town, now she'd finished school. They'd seen Emily just last Sunday. She had sent birthday greetings and would be writing again soon.

Hallie's father had written a page in his cramped handwriting telling how the apples had produced and of the blight affecting one of the pear trees.

A lump had risen in Hallie's throat as she pictured her father strolling alone through his orchard. The letter should have eased her homesickness, but it didn't…it only made it worse.

Will didn't forget her birthday. He had just been very practical about it. "We'll borrow a catalog from Hartwells," he'd said earlier and duly carried it home in his saddlebags one evening. They had studied the pages, checking the prices carefully. In the end, three pairs of long, heavy stockings were ordered for Hallie as well as a flannel petticoat. Two pairs of long underwear were chosen for Will. "Those will be our birthday presents," Will had said. Will's birthday was just three weeks behind Hallie's. "Not fancy, but they'll feel mighty good this winter."

Finally, it was the night before the Hartwell's festivities. To make room in the cramped dugout they had devised a method of laying the table on the bed to make floor space for the bathtub. The tub was brought in after supper and tilted against the open oven door to warm its metal sides while the water finished heating in the teakettle and dishpan. Hallie did her best to trim Will's hair and beard. She had not yet mastered the technique of barbering, but she was improving.

To give one another a semblance of privacy, the lamp was blown out leaving only the light from the moon filtering through the small window. First, Hallie bathed and then Will. To conserve, they both used the same water. The tub of water was then set outside the door and used to soak Will's work clothes.

Refreshed and clean, they lay snug in their warm feather tick. Will was soon asleep, but Hallie lay awake, her mind awhirl with thoughts of the morrow. She would never fall asleep, she was certain of it. But, worn out from the long busy day, she too, soon slept.

Chapter 13

A covering of snow fell during the night though the morning dawned with a cloudless sky. The clear sky, Hallie felt, was in answer to her prayers and probably those of a good many other folk as well. No one wanted to have to stay home on this day because of bad weather.

Will did the chores while Hallie fixed breakfast though she was too excited to eat hers. She had pressed Will's suit that hadn't been out of the trunk since they'd left Missouri. Dressed in his suit and his beard and hair neatly trimmed, Will was as handsome as ever, Hallie was pleased to discover. Her own outfit was a wool suit she had made for herself the previous winter. It had a close-fitted jacket of red and gray plaid trimmed in red piping with a flared gray skirt. And when she had pinned in place the smaller of the two hats kept in their boxes beneath the bed, Hallie hoped she made a presentable appearance.

There was no point in asking Will how she looked, Hallie knew from experience, for he would say she looked fine if she'd had her hat on backwards. The only mirror they had was the little one Will had used for shaving until he'd abandoned the practice. She bent her head sideways attempting to see in the tiny shaving mirror if her hat was on straight.

"It's fine!" Will assured as predicted, when Hallie did ask about her hat. "Come on, lady. Let's get started. The horses are champing at the bit."

No more than I, Hallie thought as she followed her husband through the dugout door. She turned and yanked at the stubborn door whose leather hinges had not proved that successful. She felt a sense of release as the door closed on her little dungeon and she turned her face to the brightness of sunshine on snow. A whole pleasurable day spread before them.

By mid-morning folks could be spotted headed toward the Hartwell Ranch from any direction. Winding through the snow-clad hills came wagons, buggies, horsebackers, and a few just using the two feet God had given them.

Everyone was dressed in their best whether it was clean, mended work clothes or cherished garments kept stashed away protected by camphor balls. However, there were a couple of rough old bachelors who Hallie would meet who did there "duding up" by simply scraping the top layer of grease and grime from their britches with the blade of a hunting knife and wiping a portion of tobacco juice and other debris from their bushy beards.

At the ranch, the McCains parked their wagon along side another arrival. This wagon was driven by a ruddy featured young man of about thirty. He was accompanied by an attractive woman with bright eyes and a charming smile. She was attempting to control an excited toddler on her lap while vainly reaching for the coattails of two rambunctious little boys bent on crawling over the side of the wagon. The husband came to her aid with a firm warning to his older offspring. The pair, one now balancing on the rim of a wheel and the other astraddle the tailgate, was obviously twins.

"Howdy, Will. Looks like we're going to have a pretty fair day."

"Howdy, Geoffrey. Fine looking boys you've got there."

The occupants of both wagons climbed down, and the twins began to wrestle like puppies in the snow. The toddler tugged hopefully at his mother's hand wanting to join his brothers.

Hallie thought she had never seen such handsome children. All three had golden curls and big, blue eyes that fairly sparkled with fun and intents of mischief. Their plump cheeks and lips were tinted with a rosy glow enhanced by their recent ride through the November chill. Would she and Will be blessed with children such as these?

It was obvious the two men had met before, but introductions were now made to and of the wives.

"This is my wife, Catherine," Geoffrey Mitchel offered proudly, and Hallie was pleased to hear the same note of pride in her own husband's voice as she was introduced.

The Mitchells lived several miles east of the McCain homestead. Will had mentioned meeting Geoffrey at the ranch a time or two. He'd told Hallie he was sure they'd make good neighbors. He had also promised to take her over to visit them some Sunday, but for lack of time, it had always been postponed like so many other things.

The twins were hauled up from the snow to be brushed off and introduced. They were five year olds, named Theodore and Terrance. The toddler who had made his escape to plop his fat well-clad bottom down on the snow, was Jonathan. These dignified names didn't seem to fit such little "rounders". Hallie was not surprised to discover they were nicknamed, Teddy, Terry, and Jonny.

Hallie and Catherine, chatting companionably, walked up to the house, the boys romping ahead of them. Hallie carried a cake she'd baked the day before, wrapped in a clean, white dishtowel. She'd gotten eggs from Ethel Hartwell to make the heavy, spice cake and had frosted it liberally though it had lowered the level of her sugar bucket drastically. The pungent smell of warm molasses and beans suggested the covered kettle Catherine carried was most certainly, baked beans.

As was the prairie custom, every household would contribute to the feast whether it was dried apple pie or only fried prairie chicken.

Hallie knew Ethel Hartwell had been cooking for days for she had helped with a good deal of it. And the crew cook had had his ovens at the cookhouse filled with immense roasts and huge hams for the big day. There would be no lack of food.

Ethel Hartwell met them at the door. "Come right in, ladies. Oh! What's this you've brought? You know you shouldn't have, but take it to the kitchen. I'm sure it will be enjoyed."

Similar greetings were given each guest who arrived. As soon as they had unburdened themselves in the kitchen they were directed to a bedroom to remove their wraps. Once rid of coats and hats, the women found something they could do to help. The kitchen and dining room were hives of activity. None of this curtailed the conversation. There was a constant hum of female voices above the clatter of crockery, pot lids, and the giggle and squeals of the smaller children who had been kept inside under the watchful eyes of their mothers.

Hallie was stacking plates at the end of the dining room table when she heard, "Hallie! There you are!" It was Pearl, her youngest niece in her arms, her face alight with gladness at seeing Hallie.

The two women hugged and exclaimed over how long it had been since they had seen one another.

"We've spoken of coming over a dozen times," Pearl declared, "but Mattie hasn't felt well lately. I've been there helping with the children most of the time."

"I'm sorry to hear that about Mattie. Was she able to come today?"

"She's here," Pearl indicated with a nod, the doorway leading to the next room. She's there visiting up a storm with Bessie Dikeman. You remember the Dikemans are the folks where you stopped on the way to our place. Bessie is as good as any tonic to pep a person up."

Pearl and Catherine exchanged greetings and a few friendly comments. They had met on previous occasions. Hallie excused herself with a promise she would be, "Right back," and went to get another stack of plates.

Children scampered through the house and out into the yard. They were delighted to have playmates. Through the windows you could see games of hide and seek beginning and a circle being stamped in the snow for a game of fox and geese.

All forenoon, people kept arriving. By the time the big dinner bell by the yard gate was rung at noon, a crowd of over a hundred was assembled. The meal was served in shifts. Long tables made by laying boards across sawhorses, had been set up in the dining room so forty-five to fifty people could be seated at one time.

Women and older girls took turns washing dishes so a clean supply was kept ready. By two o'clock, the last straggler had been "stuffed to his gills", as Bessie Dikeman put it. The pace in the kitchen and dining room slowed considerably. All the women had eaten and could now take a "breather". They sat in small groups visiting. Some of the mothers who were nursing infants, retired to a bedroom where they could visit and feed their young ones in peace. A few toddlers gave up the chase and fell asleep among the piles of coats in the back room or on their mother's lap.

The men and older children were out-of-doors. The sun shone just enough to cause icicles to form on the south edges of the shingled roofs. The bigger children held up smaller ones to grab the frozen pendants then all stood about licking the wintertime lollipops.

One of the groups of women that gathered during the afternoon to visit was made up of Mattie, Pearl, Catherine, and Hallie, though such groups fluctuated in size as women moved about to chat with others.

Mattie slumped tiredly against the back of her chair looking pale and drawn. Hallie's heart went out to her. Mattie was such a kindhearted person, just not up to the demands of her large family. And now...poor soul...she was expecting another child in a few months by the looks of things.

Ethel Hartwell moved about the house stopping with first one and then another to visit for a few minutes. Hallie noticed how she reached out to tousle the hair of a little tyke running by in hot pursuit of another vanishing beneath a table. Why were some women blessed with more children than they knew what to do with, while some like Ethel, were denied any?

And Pearl. Hallie looked over at her friend…so personable and, yes… attractive. Why was she letting the years slip by? Helping her sister was commendable, but what of her own life? Why, she'd acted as though she didn't even notice the glances cast her way as she had deftly refilled coffee cups and bread plates at dinner. Pearl could have her pick of the unattached males around here if Hallie was any judge.

Perhaps Pearl really hadn't noticed those glances. Hallie decided to remedy this oversight with a bit of teasing. "Catherine," she began. "Did you happen to notice the attention a certain young lady was receiving as she waited on tables today?" Hallie looked over at Pearl with raised eyebrows then back at Catherine.

There were answering smiles all around. "I most certainly did," Catherine picked up on Hallie's intent. "Why, that nice looking Peter Bergstrom was waving his cup for a refill every five minutes."

The others in the group chuckled and winked or nodded. But, Pearl only smiled and changed the subject.

"I've heard there's been a few cases of measles," she said. "Have any of you heard of any?"

"No, I haven't," there was concern in Catherine's voice. "My boys haven't had them. I dread going through a round of sickness."

Mattie told them with tired acceptance that her older ones had had the measles, but the two little ones had not."

"Well, we won't worry about it." Pearl reached over and patted her sister's arm. "The older ones didn't have any complications, and Agnes and Sammy probably won't either when they do get them. One good thing, you had both varieties when you were a child. They say it is dangerous for a woman to contact the measles, especially the German measles, if she is in the family way."

A discourse on the treatment of measles followed. Hallie, grateful that she too, had had both types as a child, went over to visit with Bessie Dikeman. Bessie was as cheerful and talkative as ever. Hallie recalled wryly how crude she had thought Bessie's soddy the night they had stayed there. How comfortable she would find it now.

Hallie was introduced to numerous new faces during the afternoon. She knew she was not keeping all the names straight much less where the women all lived. She did manage to keep a good number of them sorted out. The Whipple women, a mother and two daughters, were large, hearty individuals. The mother who must have weighed two hundred pounds, instructed Hallie when introduced, "Call me Angel, everybody does. My husband, bless him, started calling me Angel back when we got married and it stuck."

Ebee, the husband, who Hallie met later that evening, was an undersized fellow whose head came only slightly higher than his wife's shoulder when they danced. Ebee Whipple, assisted by a strapping-sized son, dug the water wells in the area.

Another lady, a Mrs. Huebanks, ran a mercantile store with her husband in Dry Bend. Dry Bend was a little town off to the east though neither Will nor Hallie had been there. Will purchased what items they had needed so far, from the stock the Hartwells kept on hand for that purpose. The Huebanks had three daughters, all grown and living in the Omaha area where the Huebanks had originally lived. The daughters were married, and there was a raft of grandchildren Mrs. Huebanks missed a great deal. "We go back on the train two or three times a year. Visit the girls and their families. I don't suppose we'd get back that often except we do the ordering for the store while we're there." She had smiled wanly. "It's not easy, living out here, as I'm sure you have discovered, but men, at least some of them, seem bound to try new places."

The McNeil's had new neighbors. Their name was Loomis and they had made the move from Kansas by team and wagon, according to Pearl. They had arrived only a day or two before their first child was born...delivered by the husband in the back of the wagon.

Rachel Loomis was slender and taller than most women, discounting the Whipples of course. She had a great mass of red hair she wore twisted and bound with a leather thong. Her dress was dark and covered with a heavy, loose fitting apron. It was as though she dressed to hide the contours of her body. Hallie guessed her to be in her early twenties though her face had a hardened look as though she had seen a great deal of the world and found it wanting. The husband was older, perhaps twenty or thirty years older.

"They are strange ones," Pearl confided as she and Hallie moved on after they had been introduced. "They're friendly enough yet they don't seem to want to neighbor. I wouldn't have been surprised if they'd stayed home today."

Hallie would remember faces of those she met that afternoon and evening, but many of the names would become confused. For instance, there were Mary and Agnes Daws or Dawson, Hallie couldn't remember which, two pretty sisters from the eastern part of the state whose parents had died the year before. They had arrived recently to make their home with an uncle and aunt on a ranch, miles to the north. The girls confided they thought they would die of loneliness if they didn't have each other. Mary and Agnes were drawing scads of attention from the cowboys, and Hallie doubted they would lack for company in future. Out here, unmarried females were a rare commodity.

The afternoon sped by and as darkness began to fall, the fiddlers tuned up. The sound of music quickly lured the men and children to the house...music and the food spread on tables placed against the south wall of the dining room.

The children trooped in, shedding damp wraps, standing about the coal heaters to soak in a bit of heat before turning their attention to the stacks of sandwiches and rows of tempting desserts lining the tables. There were potato salads, baked beans, cookies, cakes, and pies. When a bowl or platter was emptied, it was quickly replaced with a freshly filled one from the kitchen. At the end of one table was a punch bowl kept filled with Ethel Hartwell's special recipe of cranberry and apple punch. Whole cloves and bright, red cranberries floated on the top of this refreshing drink. The contents of the punch bowl sank rapidly only to be refilled from what seemed an endless supply. The Hartwells always ordered a barrel of cranberries to be brought out with the winter supplies from Kearney each fall.

The furniture in the parlors was carried out to the porches and the waxed floors sprinkled with cornmeal to enhance their slickness. The fiddlers, two men from Dry Bend, were in full swing by then accompanied by one of the Hartwell cowboys who played a guitar.

Feeny Huebanks, the storekeeper whose wife Hallie had met earlier, stepped forward, clapped his hands together and gave a stomp or two with one of his well-polished boots. In a loud, singsong voice, he began to call a familiar square dance. In no time, four circles were formed, two in each parlor, and the dance was on!

Will came to claim Hallie. When the square dancing circles dispersed, a lively two-step began. Will swung her out onto the floor. "Having fun?" He asked, holding her close.

"Oh, yes! I hope it never ends!"

Will laughed. "It'll end, but not for hours. Sometimes, they say, it goes on till morning. I reckon by the time you've danced with most of these characters, you'll be all tuckered out." Will motioned with a nod of his head to the collection of single men congregated just inside the door.

Hallie did dance with an endless parade of eager cowboys and other men folk of various ages and sizes. Everyone danced, young and old. The women took turns helping out with the supper tables so no one was left out of the dancing. Even Mattie was coaxed in to a slow waltz with Sam. Watching them, Hallie was touched by the tender way Sam guided Mattie along the edge of the floor, shielding her from the boisterous crowd with his body.

As she attempted to follow the erratic steps of a queer, little man who said he taught school in Dry Bend, Hallie observed Pearl being partnered by Peter Bergstrom, the bachelor with the oft-empty cup at noon. He wore a smile stretching from ear to ear, but Pearl didn't seem all that pleased with his obvious enthusiasm.

Hallie's partner just before the musicians had a supper break, nearly upset her stomach. His name was Grover Ditmore, an elderly man wearing greasy overalls, and smelling to high heaven. It was doubtful he'd had a bath in years. Throughout the evening, he went about asking first one woman and then another, to dance. Few refused. Most were good sports and must have, as Hallie did…drew breath as few times as possible while dancing with him. It was like that at these prairie dances…to refuse an invitation to dance was considered poor manners. Will had forewarned Hallie before they came.

Aunt Daphne would be pleased, Hallie thought looking around the crowded rooms. There were no prairie wallflowers. Few women sat out dances unless they were in Mattie's condition, or crippled up like Granny Tickmess, a tart little woman who lived with her son and his family several miles south of the Hartwells. Even the youngsters joined in the dancing. If they didn't know the steps, and few did, they improvised. Hallie observed little two and three year olds, standing on the sidelines jiggling in time to the music.

The dancing and eating kept up a steady pace as the night advanced. At last, dawn began to break and the strains of "Good Night Ladies" drifted out across the prairie hills. The exodus from the ranch began.

Before many of the guests had reached their distant homesteads, ranches, or houses in Dry Bend, big, soft flakes of snow began to fall. The temperature dropped no lower than the high thirties. The wind remained calm, allowing the travelers to pass along through a snowy wonderland. A fitting ending to a wonderful, wonderful time, Hallie thought as she cuddled close to Will and watched the snowflakes fall.

Chapter 14

The snow fell all day increasing in intensity with a rising wind. By evening a blizzard was in progress. All night it raged, drifts growing ever higher, and then...spent...the storm slunk away leaving a frozen wasteland in its wake.

Will pulled open the door the next morning to find a shoulder high drift blocking it. "Hand me the dishpan, Hallie. I'll dig with it. Remind me to bring the shovel inside the next time a storm threatens."

The fire in the stove had long since gone out. Cowchips did not hold a fire like wood or coal. The room, however, wasn't terribly cold as Hallie dressed. The dugout was insulated by its earthen walls.

Will had made his way to the pile of cowchips stacked by the dugout wall and returned with his arms full. "I was afraid the chips would be soaked." Will said dropping his load into the bushel basket by the stove. "But, they were all right once I dug under the top layer." He began building a fire in the stove. "Good thing I went ahead and took those days off to get a supply of chips hauled in." And he struck a match to the handful of kindling twigs then began adding small chunks of crumbled chips until the fire burned briskly.

Will had hesitated at asking for time off, but Mr. Hartwell had been agreeable on the matter. "Signs all point to a rough winter," he'd said. "You'd better get set for it."

The promised trip to Sand Lake with the team and wagon had been made. In fact, three trips had been made and the pile of chips next to the dugout stood high. The pile of dried cow dung was not an attractive addition to their home site, but it was a comforting one.

Shelter had also been provided for their four head of livestock. Will had gone to the canyons once again for cedar poles. These poles were placed across a washout whose proportions had been increased by a good bit of digging on Will's part. He piled some old hay he had hauled from the ranch over the poles to form the roof of their temporary barn.

Will had purchased a few loads of newly cut hay from the ranch. This was stacked in front of the washout creating a wall of sorts. Only enough space was left to lead an animal in or out of the shelter.

These preparations proved to be timely, for with the storm following the Hartwell affair, winter set in with a vengeance…one that would long be remembered in those parts. Two more heavy snowfalls came in December along with several light ones. Will managed to make his daily trips to and from the ranch and to haul their water, but it became more difficult each day. The horses walked knee deep on the level, and deep drifts that buried low spots had to be circled. The ranch was attempting to get hay to some of the cattle. Normally, the cattle could subsist on the dried winter grass covering the hills and low lands, but now it lay buried beneath the snow.

During December, there were still a few open patches of grass on some of the side hills where the wind had left only a light covering of snow. In such places, the hungry animals were managing to subsist on the meager forage. But, Jacob Hartwell and the other ranchers in the region were getting concerned. If the snow kept coming…what then?

All through the month Hallie remained in good spirits, despite having to spend so much time inside due to the inclement weather. There was Christmas to look forward to, and an invitation to spend the holiday with the McNeils.

"The weather has to improve by then…it just has to," she would tell herself as she kept busy making small gifts for all the McNeils using scraps of material from her sewing box. There were potholders for Mattie and Pearl, hair bows for the little girls, and marble bags for the boys.

"Shall I make Sam a handkerchief with his initials?" Hallie asked Will one evening as she searched about in her sewing box for another spool of thread.

The wind gave a low, moaning howl outside their door. Will got up from the table where he'd been reading from an out-dated agriculture magazine he'd brought home from the ranch. He went to peer out of the frost-streaked window as he replied, "I maybe should pick up a couple plugs of tobacco at the ranch store for old Sam."

Hallie giggled. "I expect you're right. That would suit Sam better than a hanky." Hallie had located the color of thread she needed and was unrolling a length for her needle. "It's handy to be able to get things like that at the ranch, especially with all this bad weather."

As was their custom, the Hartwells permitted their hired men, to buy what they needed; tobacco, socks, and such like from the several wagonloads of supplies brought up from Kearney each fall. The cook was in charge of keeping the record book. At the end of the month or whenever they drew their salary, the cost of these items were deducted.

Will checked the door latch that had a habit of jiggling loose when the wind blew. He came back to take his chair at the table jarring the lamp as he did so. It was difficult for Will to move about in the confines of the dugout though he never mentioned the fact.

"My getting work at the ranch was a stroke of luck, in more ways then one," Will stated as he picked up the paper to resume reading.

Hallie had to agree with this, though it had been difficult having Will away and if he hadn't worked at the ranch they would have gotten a house built. But...Will was right. His working at the ranch benefited them in many ways. She shouldn't complain even if she did so in silence.

Mail had been reaching the ranch intermittently, between storms. In mid-December, one of the homesteaders who lived south of the ranch a few miles managed to make the trip to Dry Bend with his team and wagon. He dropped off what mail had accumulated at the post office for the ranch folks and neighboring homesteaders at the Hartwells. This would be the last mail to get in for the next two months.

Will had taken his own team and wagon that day so he could haul water home. He had replaced the wheels on his wagon with crude sled runner made with a couple of slender cedar poles. This made it much easier to get about in the deepening snow. Hallie was milking Buttercup just outside the barn shelter when Will came driving up all smiles. "Brought you something, Hallie. Come clear from Missouri!"

Hallie nearly dropped the pail as she rushed to the wagon to see the big, wooden crate sitting beside the water barrels.

"Oh, Will! It must be Christmas things! I can't wait to see what they've sent!"

There was no question of waiting until the holiday to open the box. Neither Will nor Hallie could have stood the suspense though he was not as quick to admit it. As soon as Will shoved the heavy crate inside and shut the door, he asked, "Should I open it for you, Hallie, or do you want to have supper first?"

Hallie's answer was to hold out the hammer.

Will pried off the lid. The venison roast simmering on the back of the stove, sending out its tantalizing aroma, was doomed to be ignored for nearly an hour.

Hallie ran her hands over some of the bundles, caressing them. "Oh, Will! Just think. These were home not long ago. Can't you just see everyone wrapping them, putting them in here for us? They were probably talking about us. Wondering how we are." The wistfulness in her voice was unmistakable.

"I reckon they were." There was a husky note in Will's though he quickly covered it with a cheery, "Here, Hallie. What do you reckon this is?"

There was the rustle of paper and the pop of breaking string as bundles and bags revealed their contents. "Look! Black walnuts!" Hallie exclaimed gleefully. "Oh, won't they make good Christmas goodies?"

More delighted comments were made as two-dozen bars of Mrs. McCain's homemade soap were discovered, sacks of dried apples from the Melrose family, bags of pecans, and jars of pickles and jams from both kitchens. There were little bags of a variety of flower and vegetable seeds, spools of thread, cotton flannel…a whole bolt of it, and several skeins of yarn.

Hallie looked over at Will as her hand felt the cuddly softness of the yarn. They smiled at one another both perhaps visualizing the tiny sweater and booties the yarn would provide. One or both of the grandmothers had had the foresight to send the yarn and flannel.

There was a length of pretty, blue wool for Hallie and a piece of heavy shirt material for Will. There were also some small packages marked "Do not open until Christmas". These were placed on the shelf above the bed.

In the middle of the crate were a dozen huge, Jonathan apples carefully wrapped and tucked in among the sacks and bundles that had protected them from the cold, chilled to the core, but not frozen.

Tears sprang to Hallie's eyes as she unwrapped one of the scarlet globes and lifted it to her cheek. She rubbed the hard, waxed surface against her skin. With eyes closed, the fragrant smell took her back among the trees in the orchard…to the creek…her father walking there. With a sigh, she opened her eyes to admire the apple itself. How would she ever bring herself to eat one…destroy one? Of course, she did. Who could resist fresh fruit when they hadn't had any since the wild plums and chokecherries back in September?

Those glorious, juicy apples were kept along with the few potatoes they had, in a sack at the foot of the bed between the feather tick and the comforters to insure any chance of freezing when the fire went out at night. They would choose an evening for "apple eating" and after supper they would cut one in half then each would enjoy their portion. They ate slowly, seated before the stove, savoring each crunchy bite to its fullest.

The apples lasted until the middle of January.

Chapter 15

The day before Christmas was cloudy, but the wind was quiet. The last snowfall that had fallen two days earlier lay undisturbed, fresh and pristine, on the crusted, older snows.

Hallie, busily cracking black walnuts was singing a Christmas carol while Will, sitting on the floor by the stove, worked with some leather straps.

It had been decided it would be easier to ride the horses than having them drag the cumbersome wagon sled the ten miles to the McNeils.

"You sure, Hallie, you'll be all right riding that far?"

Will was fretting over this decision as he assembled what was to be a sort of side-saddle for Hallie to use on the trip.

"If I strap a heavy blanket on Mike and attach this here thing with stirrup loops and a hand hold, it might make you more comfortable...safer, too, I reckon."

He shook his head as he worked with a buckle he finally tossed aside. "I still think the best thing is for you to just use my saddle. Are you sure you can't?"

"We've been over that, Will. I'd better not ride astride with a baby coming. You know I told you how Mama always thought that was why Mavis Bevins lost her baby."

She gave a whack with the hammer and a shell flew. "Don't worry. I'll be fine with that rig you're fixing. Now, just go ahead and finish it up. It's soon dinner time."

Will didn't look reassured as he retrieved the buckle. He doesn't really think we should go, Hallie realized. He's doing it because he knows I've got my heart set on it. She positioned another stubborn walnut on the upturned flatiron. The nutmeats were intended for a batch of fudge Hallie was planning to make and take to the McNeil children.

"It will turn out all right," she assured herself. "And it just wouldn't be Christmas if we don't go."

That evening, Will and Hallie were like excited children as they hurried through supper and the dishes so they could begin the Christmas Eve they had planned. Hallie hung the damp dishcloth to dry on a peg above the stove. The teakettle was refilled from the water bucket to heat for their sponge baths. It was much too cold to uncover the tub and drag it in through the snow for a real bath. Will added chips to the fire then took down the Bible from it shelf while Hallie put the Christmas packages on the table.

Solemnly, they sat down at the oilcloth-covered table. The Bible was opened to the passages in Luke that so beautifully tell the story of the birth of the Christ Child. Will began to read.

"And it came to pass in those days, that there went out a decree," and Will went on reading the familiar verses as Hallie listened, her chin resting in her hand, her elbow propped on the table, her eyes half closed, envisioning those unfolding scenes.

The fire crackled. The lamplight glowed softly, illuminating the strong, young faces against the dark walls of the dugout. A guest, had there been one, observing his host and hostess, might have wondered if that other couple of long ago awaiting that all important birth, had not been people much like these; a youthful pair, far from home, but blessed with faith and hope.

Will finished reading and unaware of any such similarities, closed the Bible to smile over at his wife. "Next year there will be three of us sitting here like this. It'll be real nice, won't it?"

Hallie reached out and put her hand on Will's where it lay on the Bible. "I'm glad you're happy about the baby. Some men aren't they say."

"Well, I'm not one of them," Will stated firmly. "I reckon a family is a mighty fine thing for any man to have. Life wouldn't amount to much without one."

"Have I mentioned lately that I'm glad I married you?" Hallie spoke softly.

Will leaned across the table to place a kiss upon her lips. "You're not just saying that? You're not sorry?"

"No, Will. I'm not." And Hallie meant what she said. It was only the move to Nebraska, she regretted, and Will was wise enough not to ask about that."

What he did ask after another kiss was if it wasn't time to open the presents.

They opened the gifts they had for each other first. Hallie had made up Will's shirt material sent in the crate from Missouri keeping her sewing project out of sight when Will was in the dugout. Will's gift to Hallie was a new writing tablet and a box of hard candy from the ranch supplies.

"I'd have gotten you something nicer if I'd gotten into town," he apologized.

"You know I love candy," Hallie assured him, "and there's only a few pages left in my old tablet. You couldn't have made better choices."

So the evening proceeded, warm and homey in the little dugout as they opened the packages from the family; knitted scarves and knitted mittens, embroidered handkerchiefs, a beaded necklace, tobacco pouch, items chosen and sent with love from both the Melrose and McCain households.

Of all the gifts, those that would be cherished for years to come, were the books. There were two thin volumes of poetry for Hallie. Will as head of a household, received a voluminous book listing the various ailments of both man and beast with specified treatments. This large, cumbersome book would be handled with care and studied many a time.

The gifts having been thoroughly admired, inspected, tried on and read, were put away for the night. All was in readiness for the next day. Hallie had won her skirmish with the walnuts. The fudge was made and packaged tightly so as to withstand the rigors of the ride. The fudge, along with the little gifts was stowed in a gunnysack that could be tied to Will's saddle. Their warm clothing was all laid out. Will and Hallie, after quick baths, lay asleep.

Shortly after midnight, the wind began to blow, timidly at first, moaning softly as though it suffered. The mournful sound roused Hallie. She lay listening. "Oh, dear Lord. If it be thy will, please calm the wind. Let the snow lie in peace," she prayed.

The wind kept on. The crescendo rose an octave higher, and as Will moved beside her, she realized he also was awake and listening.

Neither spoke, no doubt visualizing what was happening outside. The last, fluffy snowfall lying loosely on the frozen surface of the old snows, like a downy covering of goose feathers, was all the wind needed to create a ground blizzard.

Hallie couldn't help it. With a sob, she turned to cry against her husband's shoulder. "Oh, Will. Why did it have to blow tonight? It's going to ruin our going!"

Will had no answer. All he could do was hold her close and murmur, "I know, honey. I know."

And Christmas Day was spent at home in the dugout. More snow had fallen toward morning supplying even more for the howling wind to swirl and heap into drifts across the defenseless prairie hills. Hallie spent much of the day sitting on the bed wrapped in a quilt, knitting and reading...trying to keep warm. Even the dugout felt the effect of the icy wind.

She did her best not to think of how their families would be celebrating this day back home; the special church service, the wonderful food, the gifts beneath the tree, loved ones, friends, warmth and gaiety. No, those were not thoughts to dwell upon.

The fire Will managed to keep burning in the stove was small competition against the blizzard winds pushing in with snow at fine as flour though the cracks around the rattling door and window frames, threatening with each thrust to tear them from their moorings. Once, when Will went to check the animals and get more fuel, the wooden latch on the door must have failed to catch. He'd been gone a few minutes when an extra strong gust hit. The door flew inward, pulling madly at its leather hinges, filling the tiny room with snowy, frigid blasts.

Hallie sprang from her quilt cocoon and grabbed the door, pushing with all her strength to close it. She won the struggle and gasping, forced the latch into place.

The room was in shambles. The wind had caught the oilcloth flipping it over the lamp still setting on the table from the night before. Fortunately, it was not lit. The lamp and the oilcloth lay on the floor in a tangled heap, the coal oil fumes from the broken lamp base permeated the room. The dishpan had sailed from its peg and lay on the floor among the books and papers kept on the shelf.

The new doctor book Will had been reading before going out, lay on the floor slammed shut, its cover splattered with coal oil. A page torn in the mishap, protruded from between the closed pages fluttering in the draft coming from beneath the now closed door.

Hallie began to clean up the mess. She wiped the cover of the book with a cloth, straightening the damaged page. The oilcloth could be salvaged with hot, soapy water. The lamp and its chimney were beyond repair. Heaven only knew when they'd get another.

The Christmas blizzard made any type of travel almost impossible. The water situation became critical. Snow could be melted on the stove for their use, but the amount needed to water the animals would have made too great an inroad into the pile of cowchips.

"Probably be spring before we can gather more," was Will's prediction. "I'll just have to try and circle around through the drifts with the team and wagon and get the barrels filled at the ranch."

The trip to the ranch and back took all day, but at least Will was able to pick a trail through the hills the team could negotiate pulling the wagon perched on its pole runners.

Keeping the water in the barrels from freezing solid, once Will got them home was a problem for which he found a solution. One barrel, for house use, was kept in the corner of the dugout. This took up valuable space, but there was little choice. The other barrels were placed in the back corners of the livestock shelter. The body warmth of the closely confined animals kept these from forming more than a thin layer of ice on the top of the water.

The days of the old year drew to a close.

Chapter 16

On one of the first Sundays of the new year, 1881, the sun peeked out as though to prove to the besieged land it was still there. Will came in carrying the milk pail.

"Looks like a good day to go visiting," he announced cheerily.

Hallie was on her knees, posed on the edge of the bed attempting to smooth the far side of the feather tick. She frowned. "I don't think that's humorous, Will."

"Wasn't supposed to be. But, if you don't want to go over to visit the Mitchells, I won't fuss at you."

"You are serious! We can really go?" Hallie was off the bed with a bound and throwing her arms around Will's neck.

Will laughed at her happiness and removing her hugging arms, directed. "Stop your lollygagging, woman. Get yourself ready while I hitch up the team. It looks as though it's going to be a pretty fair day. We'll go over, do some visiting, and see if Geoffery still has any ear corn he wants to sell. A little corn would stretch our hay feed."

The day was cold but almost painfully beautiful. The rolling hills, wearing their heavy white coats, glittered beneath the pale winter sun. Every inch of surface was jeweled with effervescent ice flecks as though Jack Frost had flung fistfuls of crushed diamonds, far and wide. A few sturdy branches of plum or chokecherry thickets rose out of the snow like black ink etchings against the pure whiteness. The only animation visible in all that stiffly frozen world was their team pulling the wagon sled. No hawk in the sky, no prankish rabbit to dart ahead of the grays.

"It's like driving across a winter painting, isn't it? Hallie remarked. "As though we're all that's living."

Will nodded. "The deep snows have driven most things, including a lot of the cattle, south toward the Platte River."

Then as they rounded a hill, they sighted a small band of antelope huddled on the leeward side, hoping most likely, to absorb a little warmth from the indifferent sun.

"The poor things." Hallie exclaimed softly so as not to frighten them. "They're all skin and bones."

And indeed they were. The ribs and hipbones of the animals stabbed sharply against their unkept coats. Doleful eyes watched the humans pass by. The older ones seemed to sense there was no danger from these humans.

"These have stuck around until the snow has gotten too deep," Will said. "There is not many places where they can paw down to reach the dead grass. They're tough little buggers, though. Most of them will make it."

The Mitchells came rushing out of their soddy when their visitors arrived, as eager for company as the McCains. Catherine informed them she had a pot of beans simmering on the stove and a deer haunch roasting in the oven. "Come on in, Hallie, while the men put up the horses. All I need to do is put a couple of extra plates on the table and we'll have dinner.

The twins were beside themselves at the joy of having visitors. They took Hallie's wraps, chattering like a pair of frisky chipmunks, filling her in on all their news...of the puppy they had acquired...how smart he was. Each attempted to out do his brother with important information.

"We had the measles!" Terry told her with a strut to his walk.

"I got them first," Teddy bragged.

"Yes, but I had them the worst! Mom said so," persisted Terry.

Hallie glanced over at Catherine who confirmed this with a nod. "Yes. They came down with them just a day apart about two weeks after playing with all those children at the Hartwells' back in November. Neither had any ill effects, and little Jonny had a mild case. We were fortunate."

While the measles were being discussed, Catherine had whipped up a batch of biscuits and popped them into the oven. She, too, burned cowchips, Hallie noted, though Catherine had the luxury of a full size cook stove.

The Mitchell soddy consisted of one large room with a partial loft for storage. There was a bed at either corner next to the back wall with the edge of a trundle bed visible beneath one of them. Wires, hung with gingham curtains, crisscrossed the room in such a way that when drawn, the room was divided for privacy.

The room was crowded, but well kept. Keeping house in one room with three youngsters would be a challenge for the best of housekeepers, Hallie knew with a certainty. There was a small window in each of the four walls with a ruffled valance of the same gingham pattern as those used as room dividers. The floor was dirt, but braided, rag rugs lay in the areas not covered by the furnishings consisting of beds, stove, a round table and six chairs, two rocking chairs and a cupboard. It was apparent the cupboard had been crafted by someone who was not a carpenter. Nevertheless, it was sturdy and large enough to hold kitchen supplies. It even had narrow work counter across its front. Hallie wondered if Will could construct one for her when they had their own soddy.

By the time the men came in and had washed up, the biscuits were browned nicely. Everyone sat down to a meal of simple but savory food.

The afternoon was all too short, but thoroughly enjoyed. Hallie vowed it had made a new woman of her, getting out for the day and to come calling. Catherine laughingly, gave her a hug. "It's given me a new lease on life, as well," she assured Hallie. "Being shut up all these weeks with three children and the measles hasn't been a picnic."

Will stuck his head in the door to inform Hallie that the corn was loaded. He had purchased several bushels from Geoffery. "I reckon we'd better get started if we're going to make it home before dark."

It was obvious the women were reluctant to say goodbye, but Geoffrey cheered them by promising, "I'm going to take our wagon and make a sled like Will's done then I'll bring the family over to see you folks."

Hallie, who was carrying Jonny on her way to the wagon, spoke teasingly. "I'd love to take you home with me." She gave him a squeeze and a kiss on one plump cheek before handing him to his mother.

The twins, overhearing this remark, promptly informed her they would go home with her. Geoffrey chuckled and told them Hallie did not need double trouble at her house.

The visit ended in laughter and with plans for getting together at the McCains soon.

More long, winter days passed accompanied by more snows and unusually low temperatures. Will spent much of his time seeing to the needs of their livestock and hunting. Game of course was scarce, but grouse and prairie chickens could be found in the canyons where the cedar trees and thickets provided them food and shelter. He did not hesitate to shoot more than they could eat at the time for any extra game could be cleaned and kept frozen in the wooden crate he'd set outside the dugout door.

Will had not worked at the ranch for several weeks. Work there was at a standstill except for feeding what livestock was kept in small pastures and pens near the ranch buildings. The main cattle herds that normally wintered in the hills, had drifted south along with the other cattle in the region. How many had survived, and would be found, no one knew.

Every few days, Will made the trip for water. If the weather was not too severe, Hallie rode along, but often she was forced to remain home because of the cold. It was one such day she ventured out just to get a bit of fresh air. Will was due back shortly and she paced back and forth along the path he had made from the dugout to the animals' shelter, listening for the sound of his returning.

She paused to look out across the stark whiteness of the valley. It appeared hazy in the west and a snowflake floated down to land on her cheek followed by another. Hallie sighed…snow again. Would it never stop? She moved on then paused for she thought she detected the jingle of harness traces. There was Will's voice.

"Giddy up, there!"

The team, their warm hides steaming in the cold, appeared on the ridge, tugging the sled behind them. Instead of stopping on the top as he usually did to give the horses a breather, Will urged them straight down, water sloshing as they came. That was not like Will, Hallie knew. Something was wrong!

"Bad news, Hallie," Will announced somberly as he pulled up beside her. "Sam came to get Mrs. Hartwell to help with Mattie early this morning. Things were going bad for her. The baby got here all right, but come backwards or some such. Mattie had a real hard time of it, I reckon."

Suddenly, the cold seemed to penetrate her clothing, and Hallie clenched her teeth to keep them from chattering. "Oh, the poor soul! She wasn't strong to begin with. I wish there was something we could do. I wish we knew how she is doing!"

"There's more, Hallie."

"More! What else? Tell me!"

The expression on her husband's face frightened her even more than his words.

"Geoffrey rode in to the ranch while I was there. He was needing Mrs. Hartwell to tell him what to do for Catherine and Jonny. They're both down sick. He thinks Catherine has pneumonia."

Hallie gasped. Pneumonia was a dangerous illness even when you had a doctor to care for the patient.

Will continued, "I told him we'd come and do what we could until Mrs. Hartwell gets through over at Sam's. Do you think you're up to it?"

"Yes, of course. I'll get things ready to go right now!" Hallie rushed toward the dugout, her shoes crunching the packed snow of the path as she went.

She moved automatically as she hurriedly packed items into a gunnysack, her heart seemingly frozen within her breast. Two friends so very ill, both needing a doctor and none to be had. She would be a poor substitute, but at least she could provide nursing for Catherine and Jonny. She placed a packet of dry mustard seed in the sack along with what other medicine she had on hand; camphor oil, castor oil, goose grease, turpentine, and ginger root. Hopefully the Mitchells would have some onions. Onion made a good poultice for congestion, her mother always said, but their last onion had been used months ago.

The heavy doctor book was taken down from the shelf to be wrapped in a pillowcase then added to the sack contents. Will was at the door by then with the barrel of water for the dugout and asking if she was ready to leave.

"Put on those felt boots of mine over you shoes," he instructed. "We'd better take some bedding along, too. You can use it to keep warm in the sled, and when you need to rest at the Mitchell's, we can fix you a place." While Will was explaining this, he was rolling up their bed covers, feather tick and all. Quickly, they loaded everything into the sled, and with the dugout door firmly closed, they were off.

They made the trip to the Mitchell's, covering the cold, snow-drifted miles behind the tired team. The gallant grays seemed to get their second wind for this added journey through the settling dusk.

The twins' pup from his bed in the hay pile, barked a nervous welcome as he heard the team approaching. Geoffrey, his face haggard, came out to meet them.

"Am I glad you've come!" He exclaimed as he helped Hallie down from the wagon. "It's good of you to come out in the cold, like this," he told her as he took the bedding Will handed him.

"Put your horses in with mine," he instructed Will, motioning to the three-sided sod structure that served as his barn.

Hallie, carrying the gunnysack, followed Geoffrey up the dark path to the soddy door.

Catherine and Jonny lay in the same bed. Jonny was sleeping fitfully his face flushed with fever. Catherine was awake, but her eyes were glassy. Her face was as flushed as her son's and her fever had dried and cracked her lips. She tried to speak as Hallie came up to the bed, but the effort brought on a fit of harsh coughing.

"Don't try to talk," Hallie soothed as she tossed her wraps aside and went to wash her hands at the bench. "We'll get you fixed up in no time. You and Jonny, both."

"There is no time to pamper fear nor doubt," was Hallie's silent admonishment to herself as she quickly set about working with the withered onions Geoffrey found in a sack under the cupboard. As she cooked and mashed, Geoffrey talked in a low voice, his worry and exhaustion evident.

"Catherine caught a cold. Nothing much, we thought. She was doing fine then Jonny came down with one…had a bad earache with it. Catherine was up and down nights with him. I tried getting up with him, but he'd end up crying, wanting his mommy.

Well, Catherine's cold settled in her chest. I could tell it was tightening up on her, and she was running a fever. I finally got her to give in and stay in bed. She agreed if I'd put Jonny there beside her."

Geoffrey looked over at the bed where the patients lay then back at Hallie. Anguish choked his voice. "I've done all I know how to do. Jonny seems to be resting better at times, but Catherine. She's worse. You heard that cough. Sounds to me like her lungs are plumb full. I figure it is pneumonia?"

Hallie agreed. "From what I've read in the doctor book," she had studied it quite a bit since Christmas, "I think you are right about the pneumonia." She gave a stir to the onions, cooling them slightly. "I wish Ethel was here to help, but an onion poultice is a good one, according to the book. I know my mother used to make them when any of us had the croup or a bad chest cold."

Within minutes, Hallie had prepared two poultices. She held the first one in readiness as Geoffrey opened his wife's gown then she pressed it to Catherine's chest. Catherine was then turned enough that one could be applied to her back.

Hallie rubbed warmed goose grease mixed with camphor oil to Jonny's small chest covering it with a warmed towel beneath his undershirt. He roused fretfully and rubbed at his left ear, then drowsed off again. Hallie warmed a few drops of castor oil in a spoon over the lamp chimney. She tested it with her finger then carefully let the oil drip into the offending ear.

All through that prayer-filled night, the Lord was near. Hallie never doubted that, yet her patients did not improve. At times, Catherine appeared to breath easier, yet each breath continued to have that harsh, shallow quality, and her temperature would not go down.

While Geoffrey had sponged his wife's hands and face with cool water, Hallie did the same for Jonny, again and again. Jonny grew more restless, rubbing his little ear and whimpering. He must have an ear gathering, Hallie concluded. This was a complication often associated with the aftermath of measles or from cold congestion. Hopefully, the warm oil drops would ease it. She didn't know what else to do.

The snow had stopped falling by morning, and Will went out to do Geoffrey's chores. He had watered Buttercup before they had left home and turned, Daisy, the calf in with her mother so she could nurse. Buttercup would not need milking until their return. With the extra hay he had given them, the pair could make do at least for today.

Hallie came out to join him at the barn for a few moments, a shawl clutched about her head and shoulders. "What do you think we should do, Will? She implored. "Do you think you should see if Ethel is back? I'm frightened. I don't know what else to do for Catherine, and she's worse, not better!"

"I know, honey." Will put his arms around her and held her close. "When Mrs. Hartwell can leave Mattie, she will. We left word. I've been watching toward the ranch. I reckon they'll be coming directily." He lifted her chin with a mittened hand. "You're doing just fine. Nobody could be doing much more, I don't reckon." He released her and gave her a gentle push toward the soddy. "Now, you scat back in where it's warm. I'll be back in soon as I finish up here."

The day dragged on. Hallie lost all track of the hours, only measuring time by the changed poultices and the sponge baths. As she tended her patients, Hallie prayed, numb to the fatigue gripping her body, fearful of what lay ahead. Catherine's temperature was higher, she was sure of it, and Jonny was more fretful than ever.

Hallie heated warm cloths by the stove, and Geoffrey held them to his small son's ear, talking softly to him as he held him in his arms in one of the rocking chairs.

The twins had been good as gold all day. Will had read to them and played quiet games to keep them distracted and occupied. But, every now and then, one of them would come to the side of the bed and pat his mother's hand. They would offer words of comfort. "You'll feel better soon, Mommy.", or "We been real good, Mommy."

Hallie could hardly hold back the tears at these times, or when the little boys would carry a toy to Jonny, trying to coax a smile from the baby. As evening drew near, the two sat on their chairs, chewing dutifully at the slices of bread and butter Will had fixed for them, their faces solemn and filled with worry.

Just at darkness, the pup barked, and the Hartwells rode into the yard. Will went out to meet them, but no one came in for several minutes. Waiting anxiously, Hallie wondered what was keeping Ethel. When she did come in, Hallie could tell at once the older woman was near exhaustion. Her face was white and strained. The straight shoulders sagged.

Geoffrey helped Ethel Hartwell remove her wraps and offered her a chair by the fire to warm herself. This she did, but only long enough to take the chill from her hands, then went to check the patients. She questioned Hallie about the treatments she had used then assured her that she had done everything one could do with what they had to work with. This was some comfort, and yet, Hallie had hoped Ethel would bring some special potion...something that could accomplish what her own methods had failed to do Will and Mr. Hartwell came in and took off their wraps. Jacob Hartwell found a seat out of the way of the busy women. Will set about brewing fresh coffee and setting out cold venison with slices of bread and butter.

Will brought a cup of coffee to Geoffrey who still sat holding Jonny. He took the coffee, but refused Will's offer of a sandwich.

Teddy and Terry, along with Mr. Hartwell came to the table, and in a few minutes, the two women came to sink wearily into chairs.

"How was Mattie when you left?" Hallie inquired, having waited until a quiet moment to ask.

Ethel Hartwell glanced up at Will as he handed her a cup of coffee. She set the cup down carefully before looking over at Hallie. "She's gone, dear. We did all we could, but we couldn't save her. She passed away at about 1:00 this afternoon.

Hallie's mind went blank...the tired, concerned face of Ethel Hartwell swam before her. The cup she held slopped hot coffee onto her hand, but she didn't notice.

She started to sway. Will stepped forward to grasp her shoulders.

"Hallie! Get a hold of yourself. There's no time for grieving. Not now. You have to be strong. Help with Catherine and the baby"

And somehow...she did.

Chapter 17

Ethel Hartwell and Hallie nursed the sick mother and child throughout the night. Another day dawned, cloudy and cold. The threat of yet another storm hung in the air. Will said he thought he'd better go see to Buttercup and her calf. Mr. Hartwell felt he should check on things at the ranch. After doing the Mitchell chores and seeing the soddy was well supplied with fuel and water, the two men left. They would return by evening.

The battle inside the soddy continued. Hallie, listening to Catherine's labored breathing, realized she was weakening. They were losing the fight. Ethel knows it, too, she thought observing the tense lines on the woman's face across the bed from her. Hallie lifted one of Catherine's hands, the skin so hot and dry, to hold and will strength from her own healthy body to pass into the failing one on the bed. "Dear God," she prayed. "Please don't let this forsaken prairie claim the life of another mother. Please, not another one!"

Jonny began to cry. Hallie laid the hand of her friend gently beneath the covers. She had better heat another cloth for that ear. Jonny was crying steadily now, pushing away the cloth she brought. Geoffrey lifted the pad, attempting to quiet the child and exclaimed, "What's this?" He held up the cloth pad now smeared with blood and pus where it had rested against the troubled ear.

Ethel Hartwell came over and assured, "It is all right, Geoffrey. The gathering in his ear has broken and it is draining. As the pressure goes down, the pain will go away. He'll get better now."

Catherine, however, grew more feverish and restless. At times she seemed to know those about her, and then again, she lapsed into periods of hallucination, caused by the high temperature, Ethel Hartwell said. Once, toward evening of the second day, she began to struggle and gave a weak scream. She gasped out that there was a snake beneath her bed. They assured her it was gone. She quieted for a time, only to imagine she was back home with her parents. She called Ethel Hartwell, "Mama", and Ethel couldn't hold back the tears. She patted Catherine's hand, murmuring, "Yes, dear. Yes, dear. I'm here."

It was the middle of the second night. Hallie was rocking the baby who had awakened and drank some warm broth. Ethel Hartwell and Geoffrey were sitting on either side of Catherine's bed, keeping watch. The twins had long since gone to sleep in the other bed. Will and Jacob Hartwell were dozing in chairs by the stove. Perhaps Ethel had fallen asleep for she started up when Geoffrey suddenly jumped to his feet, calling his wife's name. Hallie rushed to the bed with the child in her arms. The rasping breathing from the bed had stilled. As the three watched, helplessly, Catherine looked up at them with imploring eyes, struggled for one last impossible breath and died.

The next few days were a nightmare from which Hallie thought one must surely awake. But…the agony of sorrow and loss went on. The bodies of the young mothers were taken to the ranch. Will and one of the cowboys built coffins from rough lumber the ranch had on hand. Ethel Hartwell lined the crude boxes with white sheeting and made pillows edged in lace.

The coffins were set on benches, side by side, in one of the parlors to await burial. The husbands, sunk in sorrow, sat nearby their now motherless children clustered about them. Pearl and Hallie would attempt to distract the children by taking them into another room to read to them or offer something to eat. But, before long, they would wander back, one by one, to sit in the parlor. They would be left with only the babies to watch over.

It took nearly a day to prepare the graves. The snow had to be scooped away near the graves of Mrs. Peterson and the unfortunate cowboy. Armed with crowbar and ax, the men fought the frozen earth until they had reached a respectable depth.

The funeral service was a simple one, held at the graveside. There were only those from the ranch, Will and the bereaved families huddled in the cold wind beside the open graves. Jacob Hartwell read the Twenty-third Psalms. Will would tell Hallie this later for she had stayed at the house to watch over Jonny and the newest McNeil infant. The group had then attempted to sing, In the Sweet By and By, but most choked up and dropped out. Only Ethel Hartwell had carried on, singing the words bravely above the sound of muffled sobs. Fell Walters, one of the cowboys, had joined her then singing in a high, sweet tenor on the last verse and then even Ethel Hartwell's voice had failed. Fell Walters had finished the hymn alone.

Hallie stood by the window holding the tiny baby in her arms, watching the coffins being carried up the hill followed by the mourners. "If I live to be a hundred," she told herself, "I will never see a sadder day."

The new baby having difficulty adjusting to cow's milk, fussed in her arms, its tiny, wrinkled face reminding Hallie of an old woman's, long disenchanted with life. Jonny clung to her knees, fretfully asking over and over, "Where's Mommy? Where's Mommy?"

"She's gone, my sweet. She's gone," Hallie murmured.

All these motherless children, Hallie thought. What is to become of the poor things? Geoffrey can't manage his three alone. They are too young to be left with fires and lamps when he had to be outdoors. Hallie knew the Mitchells had few relatives back east, and none they felt close to from what Catherine had confided. The McNeil children would be all right for the present for Pearl would of course help Sam with them, but what of the future? Pearl would want a husband and children of her own. Sam had a lot of relatives back home, however. Perhaps, a widowed aunt or some such would come out to be his housekeeper. But, would anyone agree to live in that dugout as Mattie had?

From the window, Hallie could see the others starting down the hill to the house. Will had an arm around Sam, guiding him along and carrying one of the smaller children in his other arm. Pearl was just behind, shepherding the rest of the weeping McNeil brood ahead of her. Ethel Hartwell was leading the twins while her husband walked beside Geoffrey. The cowboys were waiting respectfully at the open graves until the families should enter the house. Not until then would the thump and rattle of frozen dirt clods upon the coffin lids be heard.

The baby had quieted and Hallie laid her down and begin putting out the food the crew cook had prepared earlier. Roast beef and scalloped potatoes, bread and butter with a pan of applesauce cake. She sat out a pitcher of milk for the children and checked to see if the coffee was done. Jonny heard footsteps on the porch and ran to the door. "Mommy come," he called out. But of course his mother was not one of the chilled group filing into the house.

Wraps were removed. Ethel Hartwell coaxed everyone with a solicitous, "Now, you try just a few bites of something. A body has to keep their strength up in the cold like this."

Dutifully, most accepted what was put before them, but few could bring themselves to eat no more than a mouthful or two. Geoffrey sat hunched in his chair by the table, a cup of coffee forgotten in his hand. Jonny and the youngest McNeil boy, Sammy, were having milk and cake at the end of the table, distracted for the moment.

The twins sat on either side of their father, pressing against him as though fearful of losing him, too. Hadn't they just left one parent on the frozen hillside? They were guarding the remaining one well.

Sam refused to sit down. He stood silently by the heating stove, his coat and cap still on. Mrs. Hartwell carried him a cup of coffee, but he declined in a voice that broke. "Sorry, ma'am...but...I just can't swaller nothin' just now."

She squeezed his arm gently. "That's all right, Sam. I understand."

Pearl managed to get most of the McNeil children to eat a few bites by allowing them to have coffee like the "big folks". Then she busied the older ones, getting the younger ones bundled up for the ride home. The baby had been fed her warmed cow's milk with a teaspoon while the others had eaten. Now, Pearl put on her own wraps and bound the baby in a heavy wool quilt, insulating her against the cold. Pearl thanked everyone for their many kindnesses then moved her charges to the door.

Sam, in a daze, was unaware of these preparations and still stood by the stove, his eyes on the floor. One of the cowboys had gone to fetch the McNeil team and sled to the door. Pearl called out softly to Sam, "It's time to go, Sam. We must take the children home."

He glanced up then startled to see his family in readiness by the door, he followed them out mumbling broken thanks as he went.

Hallie watched the sled out of sight, Pearl sitting ramrod straight in the hay filling the sled bottom, the bundled baby in her arms, her sister's children surrounding her. A foreboding filled Hallie...a sense of something she could not name.

The question of how the Mitchell household would manage was yet to be solved. Will and Hallie said they would be glad to keep the children for a while, but it had to be admitted they lacked the space in their tiny dugout.

Fortunately, the Hartwells suggested the children stay with them. Geoffry could come visit as often as possible. When warmer weather came, Terry and Teddy at least, would be able to return to the homestead. "Why, you'll be able to go back home and help your daddy come spring," they were promised.

Though this arrangement was a far cry from the close family unit the Mitchells had previously enjoyed, there was little choice. Gratefully, Geoffry expressed his appreciation of this generous offer.

The McCains would swing by the Mitchell place on their way home that evening to do chores. Geoffrey would then be able to spend this first night with his little sons at the ranch. Tomorrow would be soon enough for him to face his empty soddy on the lonely homestead.

Chapter 18

Winter closed in. It had honored an age-old custom of battle. The opponents had been allowed to bury their dead, but the truce was over. One blizzard followed another. Will managed a trip to the ranch between storms where he heard many of the homesteaders were suffering from lack of fuel and nourishment, even dry shelter.

The McCains had plenty of frozen meat on hand and though the chip pile was shrinking, with careful use they hoped to get by. There were times when it was impossible to travel, when the water barrels would become empty. It was then they struggled to melt enough water for the livestock. To conserve the fuel, and yet melt snow, Hallie would heat a teakettle of snow water to a boil. This hot water could then be poured over the buckets of snow Will brought to the dugout door. This created a sort of slush in the buckets and when stirred would melt down into needed water.

It was during one of these spells Hallie ran out of flour. They were low on coffee and had been rationing themselves to one weak cup at breakfast. Their potatoes had been gone for some time. They still had a supply of dry beans and there was their larder of wild game. Hallie stretched the bag of dried apples, cooking only small amounts as a special treat. And there was Buttercup, precious Buttercup, to supply them with milk, butter, and cottage cheese. They were fortunate indeed, compared to many that hard, hard winter.

Despite having enough to eat, the sameness of their diet left room for cravings, especially if you were a young female in the family way. One day, when they had neither flour nor cornmeal, Hallie, standing at the window peering through the frost, found herself longing for a slice of corn bread...a warm, steamy slice with butter melting on its top. It was then Will came into view carrying a few ears of corn clasped against his chest on his way to the barn shelter. Could she grind some of that corn into meal? It would be worth a try.

Will obliged when Hallie asked about the possibility. He brought a few ears into the dugout warning her they were as dry as a bone and not the best quality.

When the shelled kernels were ground in the coffee grinder, they produced a meal that made a much coarser corn bread than they were accustomed, but it did satisfy Hallie's longing. She also discovered, that when soaked and then simmered in salted water, the meal made an edible mush. Garnished with a spoonful of their precious molasses and some of Buttercup's cream, it could provide a tasty supper.

Laundry, always a problem with their limited use of water, was even more difficult with all the snow and cold temperatures. To make room for the tub and wash bench, the table had to be placed on the bed. When Hallie did managed to wash and rinse a few garments, there was the drying. If a rope was stretched across the little dugout and clothing hung on it to dry, there was no space left to move about.

It was on one of these washdays when Hallie, having finished the washing, was standing at the window. She spent a great deal of time at that tiny window looking out through an area scraped free of frost. Behind her she could hear the persistent drip from a pair of Will's trousers she had been unable to wring out properly after rinsing out the soap.

"I wouldn't mind all this so much if I could just get outside more...have some sunshine for a change," she told herself. "Since Catherine died, Will doesn't want me to stick my head out the door except to go to the outhouse for fear I'll catch a cold and get pneumonia! And he is so grim and cranky. Like yesterday when he finally made it over to the ranch for water. He came home and plunked that sack of flour on the table, hadn't brought any coffee or sugar. Said, 'You'll have to make do, Hallie.' As if I don't! Saying he didn't want our bill at the ranch to get any bigger, now that he's not working. That Hartwell's probably won't hire him back in the spring if the ranch has lost as many cattle as Mr. Hartwell fears. Why, Will was talking as if I'm some sort of a spendthrift!"

Hallie left the window, sidestepped the dripping trousers, and went to stand by the stove. She held her hands out to the warmth. She understood that Will was worried about money matters. How they were going to meet all the expenses ahead? They needed to have a well dug. There was barbed wire to buy in order to fence a pasture for the livestock and to keep roaming cattle out of the crops Will hoped to plant. Will had not drawn his salary, simply leaving it on the books until spring. The price of what they had purchased so far would be deducted, but hopefully what remained would pay for the well and the wire with perhaps some left for supplies. It was a concern...no doubt of that...but must he take it out on her?

And Will was always fretting about her health. She knew it was because of Mattie and Catherine. He complained that Hallie was pale. "You'd better drink more milk," he'd say or ask. "Do you feel all right? You look peaked," he'd accuse as though it were her fault, or at least so it sounded to Hallie.

"What I need is sunshine," she wanted to snap back, but held her tongue. She'd seen her face in the shaving mirror and she was as pale as a ghost after spending so many days cooped up in the dugout. "And someone to talk to!" she would have added for the more Will worried, whether it was about Hallie, money, fuel, or water, the less he talked.

At times, he sat staring at the glowing cracks in the stove door, completely absorbed in his thoughts. Hallie's attempts at conversation were apt to receive only a grunt or two in response. Will was not listening.

How could two people in such a small space be so far apart, she would wonder? Will never smiled or teased as he had in the past. Didn't he have any idea how difficult it was to be shut up in this dugout, carrying a child, no one to talk to and very little to occupy her time. Hallie had read what few books they possessed over and over. She had made up the flannel from the Christmas box into diapers and baby garments, knitted a sweater with a cap and booties from the yarn. This must be how it feels to be in prison, she thought, but then of course, those poor souls have no hope of spring.

Desperate for something to fill the hours, Hallie took an old petticoat and cut it up to make bibs and little shirts. She made diminutive stitches, working slowly, adding dainty embroidery designs so that the project would last for days.

Whenever Will was away after water or hunting, Hallie would bundle up and go outside despite Will's concern. She would visit Buttercup and Daisy, talking to the cow as though she understood. Buttercup would chew her cud, twitching an ear as though listening sympathetically. Sometimes, the cow would low softly in response as though to say, "I know how it is dear. I'm tired of being shut up, too, you know."

Hallie would walk back and forth on the packed path. Once, when it was above freezing, she walked to the top of the ridge back of the dugout following the tracks made by the sled. It was exhilarating at the top. She filled her lungs with the clean, cold air. She could see for miles in every direction.

To the east lay the Mitchell homestead. For just an instant she pictured Catherine busy in her little sod house, and then in the next second, she remembered. Catherine wasn't there. Geoffrey was there, baching, alone.

She turned to face the hills stretching between her and the McNeil's. How were they faring? Was the new baby thriving? They had had no word of the family since the funeral.

Hallie always felt better after these visits with Buttercup, the fresh air and exercise. If Will ever noticed the smaller footprints in the snow, he never mentioned them. He might have seen an unusual glow to his wife's cheeks after he had been away, but he must have been too absorbed in his problems for he never mentioned that either. And Hallie continued these occasional, brief outings.

February finally passed, and March came in like the proverbial lion, with yet another storm. Hallie had to speak sternly to herself. "Yes, you can stand another month of winter. Remember, Mama always says the Lord doesn't give us more then we can bear." And Hallie peering out at the falling snow through her peephole in the frosted window thought grimly…maybe not…but almost!

But, to Hallie's great joy and no doubt that of every other living creature in the sandhills during the spring of 1881, winter did call an unexpected retreat. The sun began to shine, timidly at first as though it were out of practice, but becoming more assertive each day until the snow and ice began to melt. This made slippery conditions for both man and beast. Hallie, however, made the most of the sunny weather and accompanied Will on his next trip after water.

She had such a good visit with Ethel Hartwell, and it was reassuring to see the Mitchell boys. They seemed adjusted to their situation. One of the Hartwell cowhands had made the trip into Dry Bend and brought out the mail. There were letters from Missouri for the McCains and an accumulation of newspapers. The mail had brought word to the Hartwells that a Reverend Sorenson who had traveled through the area the summer before holding meetings, was planning another such circuit. If possible he would hold a meeting at the Hartwell Ranch the last Sunday of March, weather permitting. If this arrangement was acceptable, he wrote, he would be obliged if the word of his coming was passed around.

"Of course, we will tell him to come," Ethel Hartwell said. "We can all use a good sermon after the winter we've had! Do us all good to get together, besides."

That evening when the chores were done and supper over, the letters were carefully opened to be savored as they were read by the light of the kerosene lantern Will had borrowed from the ranch.

While Will read the news from his family, Hallie scanned the pages of her mother's letter then went over it again slowly picturing each one mentioned. Ida and Tom had had their baby on January tenth...a girl...christened Louisa Marie. The boys were growing and becoming more help to Papa. Amanda had been to Zella Middleton's birthday dance party. Catherine had had a bout with the flu. She had missed a week of teaching. Cousin Emily was clerking at the drugstore. George Brodee, the proprietor's middle son, had taken Emily home from church two Sundays in a row. Papa said to tell Hallie and Will he would be sending apple seedlings before long.

The letter from Will's brother, Rueben, was full of questions concerning land in Nebraska.

"He'll be coming out to homestead, one of these days," Will prophesied with satisfaction. "You mark my word. He'll be coming." Will grinned over at Hallie. "Who knows, those younger brothers of yours, get a little older, they just might get the idea to settle out this way, too."

Word had been passed throughout the community so when the designated Sunday for Reverend Sorenson's arrival came, quite a crowd gathered at the Hartwell Ranch. Most folks, unless they were close neighbors, had not seen one another since the November doings at the Hartwells. Will had seen Geoffrey a couple of times at the ranch since the funeral, but they had not seen nor heard a word of the McNeils.

Hallie watched people file in as she sat on a bench near the back of the opened parlors. She wondered what changes the past winter had wrought in each of their lives. She looked down at her lap where her gloved hands rested. I've changed...and Will. He is so gloomy...doesn't notice when I struggle to make a decent meal...never notices how I look except to say how pale I am. But...then anyone would be hard pressed to come up with a complement about her appearance. My hands are hopeless, all red and rough. My hair is dull and my figure is gone! Hallie drew her shawl

123

more closely thankful it hid the growing bulge of her front then went back to watching those coming in.

There were the Mitchell twins their eyes bright with mischief and high spirits. Thank goodness, little children forgot their sorrows easily. Geoffrey walked just behind the twins and was carrying Jonny. Geoffrey appeared tired and thin, poor fellow.

Oh, there came the McNeils! Hallie turned eagerly and started to stand up. But Pearl, carrying the baby and the other children in tow, just nodded and smiled as she moved on to find seats up front on the far side of the room. There was no sign of Sam, but when Hallie looked back toward the door she spotted him talking to Will. The two of them then went to speak with the minister.

"Well," Hallie said to herself, "Sam looks almost presentable. He has his beard trimmed and I can't see a trace of tobacco juice on it. A clean shirt and pressed trousers. I do declare. The children were all as neat as pins, too. Pearl has brought some changes."

Planks had been laid across chairs to increase the seating capacity. When everyone had found a seat, the minister came forward. Reverend Sorenson was a small, unassuming man in appearance. The only thing striking about him was a pair of piercing blue eyes and a deep base voice startling in one his size. He smiled out over his impromptu congregation, and said, "Let us pray." The service had begun. Hallie couldn't recall when she had hung on every word of a sermon. She had not realized how much she had missed church...how hungry she was to hear the preaching of God's word. The others, including Will at her side, must have felt the same way for the roughened, wind-burned faces were intent, seemingly absorbed in each word. Even the children sat quietly as though aware of the importance the grown-ups were giving to this man's words though a few were beginning to tug at a parent and whisper an urgent request.

As the final words of the closing hymn dwindled away, the minister raised his hand to gain attention. "I would like you all to remain seated, please. I have a special announcement."

The children, ready to wriggle toward the aisle, paused and looked up at parents inquiringly.

"I've been asked to perform a wedding at this time, and you are all invited to stay and witness the ceremony."

This was greeted with a pleased murmur of anticipation, and with everyone looking about, speculating as to whom the prospective bride and groom might be. One of the cowboys has probably found him a wife among the homestead families, Hallie was thinking. But, all the girls sat primly in their seats just as curious as the rest.

It was then Hallie saw Pearl rise, hand the baby to the oldest of the McNeil boys, and walk forward with Sam. Will was getting to his feet beside Hallie. She felt his hand on her elbow urging her to do likewise.

"Come on, Hallie," he whispered. "They want us to stand up with them."

Hallie was being escorted forward, her mind in a turmoil. What in the world was Pearl thinking of? She can't do this thing! Such was her agitation, Hallie did not even think to be embarrassed at being put on display in her "condition". She attempted to catch Pearl's eye when she had reached her side. She wanted to say, "Don't do this! There's got to be another way!" But, Pearl kept her gaze fixed on the picture hanging on Ethel Hartwell's wall above Reverend Sorenson's head.

The vows were spoken while Hallie stood by helplessly. It was all wrong. Pearl should be marrying a young man, one she loved, one with whom she could start a fresh life. "Where does duty to others and duty to oneself begin?" Hallie asked silently. All she knew was that a wedding should be a happy occasion, and this one made her feel ill!

The minister pronounced the couple standing before him, man and wife. Pearl was now Mrs. Samuel McNeil, stepmother of six children.

The McNeil wedding was the climax as far as Hallie was concerned to the winter...a killer of a winter that had cast favors upon no one. The homesteaders had endured somehow, but Mattie and Catherine had not been the only deaths that occurred. A man some miles north had gotten lost in a storm and froze to death. A baby had died and several instances of frozen hands and feet were reported. The ranchers had also suffered though their losses had primarily been financial.

The blizzards coming, one after another, from the north had driven the cattle from the hills south toward the river bottoms. Whole herds had vanished from their customary grazing lands, drifting before the winds.

With the coming of warmer weather and as the drifts began to recede, cowboys were sent in search of the lost stock. Only a small percentage was found alive. Vast fortunes dissipated in stinking heaps along the rivers and gullies where starving and freezing cattle by the thousands had died. The English and eastern money withdrew from the sandhills. Only those who were to make ranching a way of life, intended their roots to grow deep and strong in the sandy soil, stayed on. They would swallow their losses and try again.

Across storm beaten hills, the homesteader climbed from soddy and dugout to face the spring. "At least there's moisture from all that snow," they told themselves. "It should make a good crop," they said to their neighbors. "Maybe next winter won't be such a hard one," they said to their wives.

And the true settlers faced the future with what resources they could muster...with hope the most abundant.

Chapter 19

The high-pitched call of a coyote drifted in through the open window. Hallie slowly opened her eyes and pushed the bed covers aside. She sat up carefully, putting her legs over the edge of the bed then stood up. With her hands cupped beneath her child-heavy stomach, helping her body adjust to the upright position, she moved to the window. She rested her arms on the sill, and let her gaze travel out across the sleeping valley. The orange ball of the moon had begun its drop behind the distant hills. The first feeble light of another day could be seen from the east.

The moon dipped its colors then slid from sight as he watched. Pale streaks of sunlight shot bravely through the chill of the April morning. She wrapped her arms about her flannel-clad shoulders, lifting one bare foot from the dirt floor and placing it on the warm instep of the other. Behind her from the bed, Will sighed and rolled over on to his back still sleeping.

Hallie moved over to the bed and began dressing. She tugged on her heavy stockings and flannel petticoat before removing the warmth of her gown.

Will was waking. He gave a half-hearted, "Good morning' as he climbed over to the edge of the bed, slid his feet down to the floor to begin his dressing. He cast a critical eye at the sunlight creeping timidly in through the window while his trousers were but halfway on. Not satisfied, he stepped to the door and flung it wide. He stepped into the other leg of his trousers surveying the sunlit valley. Here and there, small crusty patches of old snow clung stubbornly to sheltered spots, but they were growing fewer each day.

Hallie came to stand beside her husband, and together they let the morning sun wash over them, elated at the prospect of spring...the end of winter.

"It's going to be wonderful to have a garden with fresh vegetables," Hallie spoke. "And the apple seedlings Papa is sending should arrive soon"

Will put his arm about his wife and hugged her to his side. "It was a long winter, but we made it. There are a million things we're going to do now!"

Spring, despite sending enough warmth to melt the snow and fill the creek bed with icy, torrents, was not speedy enough for men such as Will. The locked earth must soften and release the imprisoned frost. It had to gather warmth in its dormant soul to trigger growth. Will fretted, testing the soil with his spade each day, longing to begin breaking the sod he would need for spring planting.

At last, the day did arrive when he declared the ground fit for plowing. He went to drag the plow from its dry spot beneath the canvas. He readied the implement, polishing the blades with an old sack until it shone…running his thumb along the lower edge to test for sharpness.

The plow, pulled by the grays, skidded on its side to the wide level ground Will had chosen for planting. While Hallie watched, he sat the plow upright and went to adjust hame strap on the harness. The bright-bladed plow stood posed, the shining steel mirroring the dry grass from the past season. The old grass was matted above, protecting the tender greenness tinting the sod below its brittle stems.

It is as though it were waiting stoically for the first thrust of the plowshare, Hallie thought. Waiting to have its roots torn from the sandy loam it has claimed even before the buffalo and the Indian. But like the buffalo and Indian, its fate is sealed. And she watched the plow bite deep.

The battle fought with the sod was not an easy one. It was grueling work, wearing at the muscle of man and beast. The grays bore the brunt of the work, their massive shoulders straining against their leather collars as they moved steadily forward, dragging the plow in their wake. Will came behind, holding the plow steady and on course, faring little better than his team. By evening, his back and legs were one solid ache. But come the night and the chance of rest, his exhausted muscles rebelled by writhing and knotting painfully, waking him from a sound sleep.

Pat and Mike, out on their picket lines, suffered none of this. They grazed then dozed, standing upright, with big heads hanging low, chins brushing the crushed heads of the old bluestem, the hooting owls and lonely coyote's howl lulling their slumber.

Will would rise from the bed almost with relief, it seemed to Hallie when the light of a new day crept down the hills and over the dugout roof. He would go out to do chores, and she might lie there for a few tardy moments, organizing the day in her mind. What to fix for breakfast? Was there enough cream saved for churning or would it be better to wait one more day? She'd have to bake bread. She'd sliced bread for supper last night from their last loaf.

Such moments were not prolonged for Will would be in shortly for breakfast. Hallie slid her feet over the edge of the bed, and pushed herself into a sitting position. She tugged her nightgown over her head and shivered. A trickle of air was seeping in through the crack in the door Will had failed to latch. She leaned forward reaching for her petticoat on the chair. Beneath her breast the baby gave a vigorous kick. She put her hand over the place on her stomach, feeling where the tiny foot pushed. "So, you're awake, too, little one. Well, just behave and let me get dressed. I've got to cook your daddy's breakfast," Hallie admonished as she pulled on the petticoat.

After Will had eaten and left for the field, Hallie cleared the table. She stacked the dirty dishes in the pan of water heating on the stove then took down the big, crock bowl to start her bread making. The covered jar of starter was taken from its warm spot beneath the stove and just the right amount poured into the bowl. A trip was made outdoors to fill a pitcher with milk from the covered, stone crock kept in the shaded coolness of the freight box.

Having filled her pitcher, Hallie paused to look out at Will plowing. She gasped and the pitcher hit the ground splashing up milk to drench the front of her skirt. Hallie was unaware of this for riding out of the creek bed not thirty yards from Will, came Indians on horseback. The sun glinted on knife and gun. She screamed a warning, and Will glanced up. Instead of making a run for it as Hallie expected, he simply pulled the team up and waited for the Indians to approach.

Hallie stood frozen, expecting to see her husband slaughtered before her very eyes. Nothing was happening. They were taking their time about it. She'd heard Indians liked to prolong such things. By the looks of it Will was communicating with them, talking and gesturing.

As Hallie watched too frightened to breath, Will wrapped the lines around one of the plow handles and leaving the team, began to walk toward the dugout. The Indians followed on their mounts. They are going to kill us together, Hallie concluded. Her arms made a sheltering movement as though to protect the unborn child. "Oh, dear Lord! Please let us live to raise our child!"

Will was close enough by then to see the fright on her face. He motioned for her to go inside. Somehow, Hallie turned amazed her legs would carry her, and with jerky steps obeyed. Will followed her in a few moments, the Indians left clustered out front.

"They only want something to eat, Hallie. It's just a hunting party strayed down from the reservation. If we feed them I think they'll just head on out of the valley."

In a few quick motions, Will took the dishes from the dishpan and piled them back on the table. The water was steaming in the big, flat pan. "Get me that sack of corn meal, and we'll cook up some mush."

She handed him the sack with shaky hands. Will dumped half of the contents into the hot water, stirring with the big spoon Hallie had laid out to mix her bread.

"Poor in some salt. It will give it flavor,' Will instructed. Hallie did so while glancing out the window where their guests could be observed lounging by their shaggy ponies. When the mush was thick, Will carried it out to the waiting Indians and set the steaming pan on the ground. The sight of the food brought garbled jargon from them as they quickly moved to crowd around Will who was stirring the mush in an attempt to cool it.

It had cooled only slightly before the hungry men squatted down and began dipping into it with their hands, blowing noisily to cool their burning fingers as they carried the hot food to their mouths.

The mush didn't last long. One Indian who appeared to be the leader of the group, belched and grunted out the word, "Bread," and gestured toward the dugout.

Will came back inside where Hallie was watching and listening by the window.

"How much bread do you have?"

"There is just the rest of that loaf we had at supper last night."

"It won't give them more than a taste, I reckon, but I'll take it out to them. I'll try to get them to understand it is all we have."

The Indians seemed satisfied and smacked their lips over the portion each of them received. The big Indian thumped his belly and announced, "Good!" He then squinted toward the dugout and spoke again. Hallie could not hear what he said. There was some gesturing and she saw Will shake his head from side to side several times.

The Indians grunted a few words among themselves then mounted their ponies and rode off down the valley without a backward glance.

Hallie came out to stand by Will and watch the ragged, little band out of sight. She gave a relieved sigh, and went to gather up her dishpan that she took over by the water barrel for a good scrubbing.

Will chuckled and asked, "Don't you want to know what that Indian asked before he took off?" Will didn't wait for her reply, but launched into his story with what Hallie would later suspect to contain some exaggerated details.

"Didn't you hear him ask about the squaw that made the bread?"

Hallie admitted she had missed that part.

"He said he had a couple of good wives at home, but he figured he could use another if she could make bread like that."

Hallie looked up, shocked, from where she knelt scrubbing away at the pan.

Straight-faced, Will continued, his eyes on the toe of the boot he was using to scrape a line in the soft dirt, acting as though he had not noticed Hallie's puffing up like an indignant pouter pigeon. He ended his little narrative. "That sure was one fine looking horse, he was offering to trade."

With a wicked chuckle, he dodged the mush-flecked water that came flying his way and headed back to the field.

Chapter 20

The spring weather did much to lift Hallie's spirits. She found plenty to do and the bouts of homesickness and loneliness that had plagued her during the winter were kept at bay by sunshine and busy hands.

The hills and valley were tinted in pale greens while the clumps of plum and chokecherry thickets, so bare and ugly in winter, had pushed forth little knobs of tight, green leaf buds. The yellow-breasted meadowlarks sang clear, crisp notes perching on a dried sunflower or waddled importantly about through the grass searching for just the right place for a nest. Above the dugout in the plum thicket, a bobwhite seemingly the sole survivor of the covey that had lived there last fall, called his name over and over, as he searched for his lost mate.

The heavy snows had killed most of the quail in the area, and only a few would be seen that summer. Down by the creek bed, however, the drumming of a grouse received an answering challenge from farther down the valley, both birds drumming a series of hollow booming sounds like competing musicians.

Hallie hanging clothes on the line Will had put up for her, smiled as she listened. The child moved within her body, as though protesting its confinement. "Have patience, little one. You'll be with us soon."

As May approached the ribbon of turned sod had widened to a respectable field of perhaps twenty-five acres. "I think I'll call it good for this spring," Will spoke of his plowing when he came in at noon. "The horses are getting worn down. By rights, a man should switch teams at noon when he's doing heavy work such as plowing. But, there just wasn't any help for it this year."

"You've done the best you could," Hallie consoled her husband. "You've given them a good rest each noon, and you've not used them on Sundays like some would."

"I reckon," Will agreed. He reached over to put his hand on Hallie's shoulder. "I know it's been hard staying home on Sundays and not neighboring so the horses could rest. But, you do get to go along when I go for water."

Hallie did enjoy those trips for water and Will did his best to avoid the rough places so she wouldn't get jolted badly by the wagon.

A post office was now officially established at the ranch. The McCain's mailing address was now Hartwell, Nebraska instead of Dry Bend. Ethel Hartwell kept a pot of coffee on the stove for any that stopped in for their mail. It was a good place to catch up on the news of the community.

Will could have had his job back at the ranch for a good number of Hartwell stock had been located down in the river country plus Jacob Hartwell was having some more trailed up from Texas to replenish his herd. Will declined the offer despite their need for extra money. The homestead simply had too many demands this time of year.

Those short visits at the ranch were a great comfort to Hallie. She always returned to the homestead with her confidence bolstered after a few of Ethel Hartwell's straightforward comments concerning the expected baby. Sometimes though, when she lay awake at night, she was prone to think of Mattie and how she had died. A tingle of fear would run up her spine. It would soon be time for her child to be born. What if there were complications? "Stop worrying," she would scold herself. "Women have babies every day." But a nagging little voice would persist, "Some of them do have problems."

They had not seen Sam or Pearl since their marriage. Sam did come to the Hartwells for their mail and had left word that he'd be bringing the family over some Sunday in the near future. This promise was kept a week later when the McNeils came driving up in their wagon.

"Decided to come and take you folks and the younguns on a picnic," Sam boomed as he pulled the team to a stop in front of the dugout. There was hugging and joking as the visitors climbed down. The baby, four months old, must be admired. The plowed field commented on. Buttercup's calf inspected.

Pearl helped Hallie pack what she wanted to contribute to the picnic though Pearl said she was sure she'd fixed plenty for all of them. Hallie tied a dishtowel around the crock of cottage cheese she had made on Saturday. "I find when it's seasoned with cream and diced wild onion it makes a good change," she told Pearl who said she would have to try it.

The rabbit meat that had been simmering on the stove when the McNeils arrived was put in a bowl with a lid and Hallie wrapped up two loaves of fresh bread and a jar of butter.

They all climbed into the McNeil wagon where piled hay made the bumpy ride less jolting. Everyone was full of bits and pieces of news which they shared as they rode along.

"I lost a tooth," Nancy volunteered, and grinned to display the gap it had left.

"I shot a skunk last week," Harry told them. "He was getting into the new chicken coop."

This surprised Hallie...not the part about the skunk...the part about a new coop. Pearl must have convinced Sam to move the chickens out of the dugout.

There was laughter as Will told of the Indians offering to trade for Hallie. "By golly, that Injun knew a good thing when he saw it." Sam grinned over his shoulder at Hallie where she sat on the hay with Pearl and the children.

"I'd trade Nancy for a Indian pony, did I get the offer," Bert teased, dodging a blow from his sister. "She can't bake bread, but she could fetch and carry."

The much-teased little sister was ready to aim another blow when Pearl interceded and smoothed her ruffled feathers. "Don't pay any attention, Nancy. Any trading gets done, it just might be a certain boy that could fetch and carry."

The distance to the lake passed swiftly with all the bantering and chatter. They found the lake had filled with snow water far beyond its natural boundaries. As the wagon approached, flocks of ducks and geese swirled into the air to land on the far side. There was no scarcity of migrating birds for they had been south during the winter. They had not suffered as had their fellow creatures left behind.

The children were delighted with all this and set off almost immediately to search for nests. "You can look for'em but don't bother'em." Sam warned his brood. "Wild things will desert their eggs if humans go handle'em."

Pearl and Hallie spread quilts on the sand and laid the baby on one. She was so sweet, all coos and gurgles and toothless smiles.

The men had unhitched and were down by the water, letting the horses drink. The men stood talking in the sun, free to take their time instead of being pressed by work as the week days demanded.

Hallie sat down beside Pearl and the baby, holding out a finger for one of the tiny waving hands to clutch. The women were silent, looking down at the baby between them unspoken questions hanging in the air above the gurgling infant.

Pearl's hand came to rest upon one of Hallie's. "You think I did the wrong thing, don't you?"

Hallie didn't know how to answer. After all, it was not her business. "Not wrong, exactly. I just felt you had a right to a life of your own."

"This is a life. It may not be the one I envisioned, but I feel it is going to be a good life. The children need me, and I love them."

"But, marriage? Maybe you love the children, but you don't love Sam."

"No, not yet. Perhaps that will come, too, someday. Sam understands. He doesn't expect me to be a wife in every sense."

"I hope it all works out," Hallie told Pearl, their hands clasped now. "I just want you all to be happy."

"I know. And we are…happy as most people are."

They visited for a while then began setting the food out on a sheet they had spread over one of the quilts. The children were far down the shore, but it looked as if they were coming back toward the wagon, no doubt guided by empty stomachs.

Will and Sam were sitting by the wagon resting their backs against a wheel, deep in conversation.

"My, that potato salad looks delicious," Hallie remarked as Pearl uncovered a large bowl, slices of hard-boiled eggs decorating its top. "I miss having my own eggs."

"I'll lend you a couple of setting hens and give you eggs to hatch out," Pearl generously promised. "You'll have a flock started by fall."

"That would be wonderful! It's so difficult to cook without eggs though Will buys a few from the Hartwells, at times. Thank goodness, we've got milk and cream. I don't know what we would do without it."

"Dinner's ready," Pearl called and Sam gave a whoop that brought the children running.

Bert dashed up a few lengths ahead of the others. He plunked down at the edge of the food-laden sheet and looked as though he might be tempted to grab a sample. Pearl, however, gave him a stern look. "Wait for the others, Bert, and until we have said grace.

The other youngsters came panting, the little ones bringing up the rear. When everyone was seated the older children bowed their heads and the younger ones quickly followed suit. With a nod from Pearl, Sam lowered his head and mumbled a few words of blessing.

Would wonders never cease? Hallie marveled. Will must have shared her thoughts for he raised his eyes and gave a little grin.

When the meal was over, the adults sat visiting while the children scampered about, pursuing the elusive sandpipers or tossing clods of dirt into the lake to hear the delightful little "plops" as they hit the water. Little Sammy gave up the chase to come lay his head in Pearl's lap and was soon asleep.

Thunder, off to the west, called a halt to the outing. Deep blue clouds were building on the horizon. A rainstorm was coming. The food was packed up and everyone bundled into the wagon while the team was hitched to the wagon. They started homeward. Sam urged the horses into a brisk trot over the level stretches, slowing them where it was rough in respect to Hallie's condition. The storm was moving rapidly their way.

During the time it took to cover the distance to the McCain homestead, the storm clouds had caught up and were boiling overhead. The wind had risen and was whipping the loose dirt across the newly plowed field. Will and Hallie pressed the others to wait out the storm with them and they willingly agreed.

"It look's like it could be a bad one," was Sam's prophesy.

Chapter 21

Thunder crashed. Lightning flashed and cracked on the other side of the valley. The women took the children into the dugout along with the picnic things and watched the roiling clouds from the doorway. The men had unhitched the team to put in the shelter. The McCains team with the cow and calf had been tethered to graze that morning far out in the valley. There was not time to bring them in closer.

The wind was growing fearsome, forcing the women to retreat and close the door. From the window they watched as the wagon canvas covering the tools and supplies was lifted and sent sailing high in the air. The sky had grown so dark Hallie took down the lamp they had ordered from Dry Bend and lit it. The lamplight was comforting in the storm-induced darkness of the dugout.

Sammy whimpered, "What's the matter, Mama Pearl? How come it got so dark?"

"It's just a rain storm, honey," Pearl soothed as the smaller children huddled against her with even the baby seemingly sensing danger.

Suddenly, there was an ominous silence with the only sound the hurrying tread of the approaching men who burst inside without preamble, shoving the door shut and then pushing their weight against it.

"A twisters a coming!" Will shouted.

The wind resumed with a deafening roar. Something crashed against the door causing little Agnes and Sammy to scream in fright. Almost instantaneously, the roof over their heads was lifted like the lid of a kettle, allowing wind and rain to sweep in. The cold deluge extinguished the lamp flame shattering the hot chimney and drenching everyone to the skin. The roof came back down with a heavy crunch, showering them with crumbling dirt, filling their ears with the wrenching screech of bending stovepipe.

They crouched tightly together in the wet darkness, fearful of what the next onslaught might bring. The children clung to the adults, anticipating they knew not what. The baby cried, outraged by the cold bath she had received.

As quickly as it had come, the storm passed on, and the sky lightened. The result of the tornado became evident. The roof sat cater-cornered on the dugout, gaping daylight. The interior and its occupants were coated with a layer of wet dirt. The bent stovepipe had fallen on the bed, adding soot to the overall mess.

When the door was opened, they discovered the McNeil wagon on its side with one wheel missing. The pile of items Will kept stored beneath the canvas, was strung far and wide. The roof on the animal shelter had been ripped from its moorings, its poles and sod blocks dumped in a heap. The McNeil team stood tied to the manger. They snorted and rolled their eyes nervously as the men approached, expressing their distrust of those who had placed them in such a frightening situation.

The grays and Daisy, the heifer calf, had disappeared along with their picket lines and stakes. Buttercup was still tied to her stake where she had been left that morning. Now, she lay stretched out, kicking feebly, on the soft, freshly washed grass. A pitchfork that had stood by the entrance of the barn shelter before the storm, now protruded from her side, its long tines buried full length. Frothy, pink bubbles rimmed her muzzle. The big, black, kindly eyes glazed then closed.

It was Harry, the McNeil's oldest, who ran to the dugout to impart the particulars of this additional loss. Pearl and Hallie were searching for something dry to wrap the baby. Hallie was down on her knees in front of the wooden chest when she received this last report. She bit her lip and swallowed hard on the lump that pushed up in her throat. She would not cry! There were no tears to spare in this country. One could not use up tears on a cow.

Hallie handed Pearl a flannel shirt of Will's and rose heavily to her feet. She held her lips in a tight line to prevent them trembling, her mind a turmoil. Everything they owned was either wet, dirty or strung heaven knew where. The dugout was ruined...dear Buttercup dead. What were they to do with the baby's arrival so near? And pushing to the forefront of her troubled thoughts was one of home. Surely now, Will would give up and move back to Missouri.

The children, except for the baby, had followed the men outside to inspect the damage. Pearl removed the wet, filthy top quilt from the bed. "Hallie, why don't you lie down and rest a few minutes? You should, you know."

138

Hallie shook her head, and insisted she help straighten up the dugout. Bert came to the door and asked for the dishpan. The men were going to butcher the cow and salvage the meat, he said. Hallie gave him the pan with shaky hands. She knew it was the sensible thing to do, this butchering. But, she shuddered inwardly at the very idea of eating a bite of dear, faithful Buttercup.

Clouds were building in the west again, threatening more rain, and it would soon be dark. The two older boys were sent off in search of the missing stock while the men worked at the butchering. "Keep an eye out for that canvas, boys," Sam called after them as they started off on foot.

The canvas was located just over the ridge caught in a plum thicket. The grays and the calf were dragging their picket ropes and grazing in a draw about a mile north of the valley. The animals showed no sign of injury. Evidently, the tornado had just frightened them so badly they had pulled free and ran for safety.

Thunder was again rumbling as the boys and the stock returned. The boys, with instructions from the men, stretched the canvas over the dugout roof and weighted it down with some of the sod blocks from the damaged barn shelter.

The women had done what they could to the interior. The stovepipe had been straightened to some extent and its end poked up through its hole. A fire was started in the stove and the filled teakettle put on to heat. The baby had eaten and then fallen asleep on the bed. Hallie was wiping off the covers of their few precious books.

Bert came in with the dishpan now containing the heart and liver from the carcass. "Will said some of this meat would sure taste good for supper," Bert relayed this message as he set the pan down on the table.

With an air of determination, Hallie dipped water from the barrel outside the door. The meat would have to be washed and cooled before it could be sliced. She took a firm grip on the warm, slick, reddish-brown liver with one hand and washed at the blood with the other. She would not think of Buttercup...she would not! But, the cows face with those big, soft eyes rose up between her and the dishpan. Hallie gagged and dropped the offensive thing with a splash, slopping water onto the table Pearl had just wiped clean.

Pearl spoke with a no-nonsense pronouncement. "You've had quite enough for one day, Hallie." She handed Hallie a towel. "Dry

139

your hands and lie down…get off your feet. If you won't think of yourself, think of the baby!"

Pearl settled Hallie beside the baby and took over the chore of preparing supper. By the time the men had finished and laid the carcass to cool in the McCain's wagon box, there was a platter of crisp, fried meat to serve along with the leftovers from the picnic.

The dugout could not provide room for everyone to eat comfortably, instead, plates were filled and the men and children went outside to eat. The fresh meat was a treat to the others, but Hallie could not bring herself to put a piece on her plate.

Little splats of rain began to fall just as the last bites were disappearing from the plates. There were growls of thunder overhead followed by a sudden downpour. Everyone crowded into the dugout out of the rain. The clouds were watched closely from the open door in case any of them should start dipping ugly tails of destruction earthward again. None appeared, however, and the rain passed on as suddenly as it had arrived.

It had grown dark. The McNeil wagon still lay on its side where the tornado had dropped it. Bert and Harry took a couple of blankets, damp but useable, and went to curl up in the shelter of the overturned wagon. Will and Sam said after they'd had a few peaceful puffs on their pipes they would join the boys. Hallie and Pearl fixed pallets on the floor of the dugout for the three younger children then the two women, the baby between them, stretched crosswise on the bed, tired feet dangling over the side. Shoes were all anyone removed that night.

The men had settled down on the ground leaning backs against the side of the dugout as they smoked. Takes more than a tornado to disrupt a man's smoking ritual, Hallie thought as she lay working her foot up and down, attempting to ward off the "Charlie horse" threatening an exhausted muscle in her right leg. The smell of tobacco smoke was pleasant and it along with the men's voices, lowered in deference to those sleeping within, was carried by the night breeze into the room.

Even breathing came from where Pearl lay, indicating she was asleep as were the children. Hallie knew she should say her prayers and try to sleep, also. But, her body gave no indication it could relax and do so. She sighed and moved restlessly taking care not to disturb the baby next to her, trying to keep her mind from dwelling on their problems or she knew she'd never fall asleep.

Sam, attempting to keep his voice lowered, spoke up. "It's been quite a day, ain't it?"

"You could say that," Will responded. "Started out fine and dandy, but it sure went to the bottom of the heap."

There was silence for a bit then Will said, "I shouldn't of brought Hallie out here, Sam. She'd a been better off if I'd kept grubbing on that worthless farm back in Missouri."

Hallie listened with mixed emotions. On the one hand, she was hoping against hope, Will had decided they should leave the homestead. On the other hand, she was distressed at the pain in her husband's voice. He had wanted so badly to attain land of his own.

"The dugout was bad enough," Will continued. "What with the baby coming and all. Now, we don't even have that. Can't you just hear what her folks would say if they could see how I'm taking care of her?"

"Ain't you being a little hard on yourself, Will? This, what happened today, wasn't nobody's fault. We'll figure out a way around it, see if we don't."

It was quiet outside then Sam spoke again, "I reckon we'd best set to and get your soddy put up now stead of waitin'."

"There's not time, Sam. You got your crops to get in and so do I."

"Don't reckon a few days one way or the other, is goin' to matter that much. Pearl can take the younguns home tomorrow after we get the wagon wheel fixed. Then you and me can get a nice little, old sod house put up in no time a tall.

Chapter 22

The morning following the storm, Pearl and the children readied themselves to start home. The missing wheel had been found and put back on their wagon. A hearty breakfast of friend steak and pancakes had been served. Half of the butchered beef was loaded into the McNeil wagon. Fresh meat could not be kept in warm weather unless preserved in some way. Pearl had explained to Hallie the method she planned to use to dry her portion of the beef. Lean meat could be kept for some time if dried.

"I hate to leave you in this muddle," Pearl said once again as she loaded the last child into the wagon. "Someone has to see to the chickens and the milk cows at home, though."

"I know you have to get back. I'm just sorry your visit had such a dramatic ending." Hallie gave a tired smile to the children looking down at her from the wagon. "We did have a fine picnic, though, didn't we? We'll have to have another one soon."

They all agreed this was a very good idea, but Sammy piped up with one emphatic suggestion. "Don't want no 'tornader' next time!" He placed his chubby hands over his tousled head as though to ward off any such windy threat. There was laughter as the wagon pulled away.

When the wagon and its load of waving children disappeared from view, Hallie walked back to the dugout to face the task of working up the meat. It had to be cut up and salted thoroughly then dried beneath sheeting in the sun. Fortunately, they did have a good supply of salt. The salt sack had been stored under the bed with the flour and sugar so had stayed dry. Hallie began the tedious job of working salt into the strips and chunks of beef.

The men came to contemplate the dugout. "I reckon on taking out the window and leaving the wood frame," Will said. I'd leave the door and its frame if I had enough lumber left from what I bought in Kearney back in the fall." Will rubbed his whiskered chin. If we did that this dugout could make a chicken coop or some such."

"There's that old soddy of the Petersons," Hallie remembered. "Others have taken the windows and the shelves, but there were still the roof supports and the door."

"By, golly! Hallie. That's an idea. Me and Sam will go get what we can from there. Grounds too wet to start plowing sod yet." The men went to hitch the team to the wagon and presently drove off bound for the abandoned soddy.

"Should be back by noon," Will called out to Hallie at the table that had been moved outside where she could work on the meat more easily. "We'll be ready for some of those steaks, again."

"Yes, I expect you will," Hallie mumbled under her breath watching them drive off. She would have preferred a drive through the greening hills to working with this mound of raw meat! Papa and the boys had always done the meat cutting at home. Oh, her mother had seen to the making of headcheese and the frying down of the sausage when a hog was butchered, but she had never been called on to slice up a pet milk cow! And the tears Hallie had held back until now, overflowed making clear droplets on the reddening surface of the breadboard she was using to protect the tabletop.

The men were back by one o'clock, and after devouring the steaks Hallie had fried, set about making frames for the door and windows that would be used in the sod house. Grim determination saw Hallie through the rest of the meat slicing and salting. The drying process would take a good number of sunny days.

With the remainder of the day, the men took the wagon box off and replaced it with cedar poles to make a flat bed. This created a vehicle easier for loading and unloading the heavy sod blocks to be transported to the building site.

The following morning the first load of sod had been cut and taken to the knoll where the house was to be built when the grays perked their ears and Pat gave a welcoming nicker. A minute later, horsebackers appeared on the ridge top. It was Geoffry on his bay gelding and the twins riding double on one of the Mitchell's work horses.

Sam let out a whoop. "Here comes another strong back just made for sod packin'!"

Sam went to meet the horsebackers and stretched up a dirt-smudged hand for a hearty handshake. "Howdy, Geoff. How are you and these boys of yours?"

"Fine. Just fine. We ran into Pearl over at the Hartwells getting her mail yesterday. She told us you'd had a right smart breeze over this way. So me and the boys thought we'd ride over and see if you could use any help."

"Can't say help's not welcome." Will slapped Geoffrey on the back as his neighbor stepped down from his mount.

With three men to work on the house, the walls rose rapidly.

Hallie was kept busy baking bread and roasting and frying beef from the fresh portion she was trying to keep cool in lidded pails in the water barrel. The twins were good help and full of news. Mrs. Hartwell had filled them up not only on her good cookies the day before, but on all the comings and goings of her mail patrons. They vied with one another, filling Hallie in on local gossip.

"You know all them critters that died last winter? Well, there's folks skinning them so's they can sell the hides," Teddy informed her. "Sure would be a stinky job, I figure."

"A fella lived way off by himself, broke his leg," Mrs. Hartwell said." This information was from Terry. "He just pushed the bones together and tied it tight to a board to keep it straight tell it healed. Must a hurt something awful, don't you figure?

Hallie agreed that it must have.

Teddy then had to tell Hallie that their little brother was talking real good. "He calls Mrs. Hartwell, 'Mommy', now." Blue eyes looked up at Hallie. "I don't think Daddy likes for him to."

And Hallie wondered where all this would lead. Ethel Hartwell had hungered for a child for so long, but Geoffrey was not the type to give up a child.

Geoffrey and the twins rode back and forth to help each day. They took their meals with the McCains except for breakfast. The house was completed in five days. It measured 24X24 feet inside and had two rooms. The doorway faced south away from the cold north winds that blew in winter. The three small windows had been placed strategically, with one in the south wall and one in the east of the larger room so they might catch the maximum of sunlight. The remaining window was built into the west wall of the bedroom so it could catch the very last ray of light at the end of the day.

The partition between the rooms was only as high as the top of Will's head and opened at one end to provide a doorway between the rooms. There was no ceiling other than the rough roofing boards that slanted down to the outer walls from the low ridgepole overhead.

These boards were covered with strips of tarpaper that in turn were held in place by a layer of sod.

Clay, found in a low spot in the creek bank, had been used to plaster the dirt walls so they were smooth and clean. The floors were dirt, but Hallie sprinkled them with water. The Mitchell boys had tramped them down. The process was repeated several times until the floor surface was firm enough to be swept with a broom

The Mitchells, loaded with thanks and pockets filled with cookies, had promised to come back for Sunday dinner and to bring their mending. Geoffrey had confessed he was not very handy with a needle.

Will took Sam home on the afternoon the soddy was finished taking their heartfelt thanks with him. Will would stop at the ranch to fill water barrels on his way home.

Will arrived back at the homestead late that night after Hallie had given up and gone to bed. He'd stopped for the water and the mail. There was a letter from Emily and the newspaper. He brought two hens Pearl said were starting to act "broody" and enough eggs, carefully packed, for two "settings".

They spent their last night in the dugout.

Chapter 23

The move to the soddy was a simple matter. In fact it was finished by breakfast time. The stove was moved in the wagon and set up first. While Hallie built a fire and prepared their first meal in the new house, Will made a second trip for the remainder of their belongings.

After they had eaten, Will helped set up the bed then went off, anxious to get at his farm work. Hallie walked about the new rooms with their clean, plastered walls, marveling at the feeling of spaciousness they gave her. She could actually circle the table without barking a shin on a chair, grub box or bench. And, what a luxurious feeling it was to have the bed in a proper bedroom instead of smack dab along side the table and stove!

She stood for a few moments in the opening between the rooms and surveyed first one and then the other with a proprietary eye. The pieces of furniture were so few the rooms, despite their meager dimensions, looked a bit bare. A touch of color, here and there, would help brighten things up. Curtains…geraniums blooming in those deep window sills. A braided rug or two would be nice when she could accumulate enough rags to make them. It would take time, but eventually, she could make this soddy quite homey.

A shouted greeting and the sounds of an arriving team and wagon broke her reverie. The south window revealed two men climbing down from a dusty, canvas-covered wagon. Will was coming toward them on the run. The taller of the pair turned and Hallie caught her breath. Why, it was Rueben! Will's brother had come to Nebraska just as Will had predicted.

The other young man looked vaguely familiar. During the excited greetings, they would discover that he was the oldest son of the Swedish family they had met on the train trip to Nebraska.

"Family is all fine," he assured Hallie. "Ve got vork like ve planned, but ve don't none like the city." And later, Danjel would tell his story in halting English.

The Andreasons had owned a tiny farm in Sweden. The soil was worn out from centuries of use and barely fed the ever-growing family. Like so many, they heard of the wonderful opportunities in America. They sold their farm and used the money to buy passage to

146

the land of opportunity. They had reached Omaha and the relatives there. Jobs for the father and Danjel were secured, but still they listened to the talk of free land farther west with longing. Chafing at the constrictions of his job in the train yards, Danjel had urged his father to let him go inspect this land they spoke of. If it was truly there and free for the taking, why shouldn't the Andreason's claim their share?

By chance, Rueben and Danjel had taken the same train out of Omaha. They'd struck up a conversation and discovered they were planning to leave the train at the Prairie Rose depot. When Rueben disclosed he had a brother in that area named Willard McCain, Danel could not believe his good fortune.

"Vin it vas decided I should come look for land, ve thought of you good peoples. You vould give advice to greenhorn like me. But, I never thought I should find you for sure like this." He grinned happily at the friendly faces around the table where he and Rueben were hungrily eating the pancakes and fried meat Hallie had fixed for them.

"I told him he just as well come along with me when I found out he'd met you folks and was wanting to settle out here like me," Rueben put in. "Figured there was plenty of room from what Will had written."

"You couldn't be more right," Will was quick to reply. "We need good neighbors and I hope you'll find what you want right here in the valley."

And that is how it worked out. Three more homesteads were to be established before the spring had progressed much further. Rueben staked out the quarter of land south of his brother's. Danjel staked out two quarters across the valley, one for his father and one for himself. Before the week was out, Danjel had caught a ride as far as Kearney with a freight wagon and was on his way to Omaha. He was anxious to get his family moved out to their homestead. They would need to make haste if they were to get a crop and garden planted that spring.

Rueben would stay with Will and Hallie until he was able to build himself a soddy. He would get the material he needed when he went to file on his claim. The most pressing task, as it was for all new settlers, was to get a crop in the ground. The plow had been unloaded from Rueben's wagon and he, like Will, was soon at work.

The spring days sped by. There was so much to do and only so many hours of daylight to do it. Will fretted when he thought of the list of things that needed doing. There was corn to plant, oats and potatoes. A garden. Fences. Fire guards to plow and the Whipples coming anytime now, to dig the well.

The ground in the fields was plowed and harrowed in readiness. The sowing of the oats was done by hand with Will carrying a supply of seed oats in a shallow bucket and casting handfuls in wide even motions as he walked up and down the field.

The corn was planted in "hills" with three or four kernels in each, evenly spaced along the newly turned furrows. When this was done his thoughts turned to the proposed potato patch. They had skimped on potatoes all winter and then ran out. Will vowed they would raise enough this summer to see them through the coming year. He had purchased seed potatoes in Dry Bend and these they cut into chunks, leaving an "eye" on each piece. When one of these pieces was planted in the ground a sprout would grow from the eye to become a plant.

Hallie helped Will plant the potatoes. He walked ahead down each plowed row, pushing the blade of the spade into the turned sod at two-foot intervals. He would shove the embedded blade forward so there was space behind it for Hallie to drop one of the potato pieces. The spade was then lifted out leaving the seed piece buried. Will stepped firmly on the spot pressing the dirt snugly around each one then moved on to the next, Hallie following with her pail of potato pieces.

The potato planting seemed to take forever. Will appeared unaware of how difficult it was for Hallie to stoop and bend. He hurried up and down the rows under the warm morning sun, eager to finish this task and begin another. Hallie trudged along trying to keep pace. Her back began to hurt. Sweat was trickling down her face. She kept on, determined to stick it out, but by the time the patch was three-fourth finished, she began to feel lightheaded and sick to her stomach.

"I've got to quit, Will," she told him as she stopped to wipe her face with the hem of her apron.

"All right, all right! Hand me the bucket and go on to the house." And he had proceeded down the row awkwardly manipulating both the spade and the bucket as he went.

Hallie felt too ill by this time to care if Will did sound "put out". She went across the rough plowed furrows wanting nothing but to reach the coolness of the soddy and her bed.

She lay on the bed praying the backache would ease and not turn into labor pains. It was possible, but the first of June was still two weeks away. The pain lessened after a while. The nausea passed and knowing the men would be coming in soon, hungry and expecting dinner, she struggled to her feet and went to heat up the leftover rabbit stew from the night before.

The men found a hot meal on the table, but the cook greeted them with a wan smile. Hallie's heart sank when Will announced that the potatoes were planted and there was plenty of plowed ground left for the garden planting. She was not up to any more such chores today.

Will must have come to this realization also, for he gave her an apologetic grin. "I can plant the garden truck, Hallie, if you'll just tell how you want it done."

Hallie unpacked the precious seeds, those they had brought and those sent at Christmas time. Will planted them with care; turnips, beets, carrots, onions, cucumbers, peas, squash, pumpkins, beans, and some of her father's jet black, watermelon seed.

Her mouth fairly watered as Hallie recalled the taste of those giant melons, their juicy, red flesh chilled by the icy water of the spring. She could not resist planting a hill herself. As she patted the dirt firmly over the freshly planted seed, she offered a little prayer. "Please, dear Lord, help them grow. I could eat a whole one right now...rind and all!"

Truly, they were starved for fresh fruits and vegetables. Their diet of meat, bread, and beans with only occasional relief of dried apples or raisins was not only unappetizing but far from healthy. Hallie had watched gratefully, as the first green rosettes of dandelion greens thrust through the ground along the creek bank. There would be greens to cook within a week. This common plant was valued highly by the prairie housewife as the first fresh vegetable of the season. Other wild, spring fare were the tender lambs quarter used in its early stages of growth and the frail, wild onion that could add a touch of flavor to everyday dishes.

In her advanced state of pregnancy, Hallie craved the missing milk and cheese Buttercup had provided. One night she dreamed she was lifting a glass filled to the brim with cold tangy buttermilk to her lips. Just as it touched her mouth, her hand began to tremble, and the glass fell spilling its contents. Hallie awakened, hand pressed to her mouth, and felt tears of disappointment trickling down her cheeks, so vivid was her dream and so strong her craving.

She lay there thinking of Buttercup and how she had milked the little cow…how the streams of milk had cut briskly down through the rising foam in the bucket…the warm fragrant smell. Milking had never seemed like work for Hallie had enjoyed the whole procedure. First the milk had been strained through a clean cloth and set aside in a cool place until the cream had come to the top. The cream, thick and golden, was then skimmed off with a ladle to be used on desserts, morning mush, seasoning vegetables. Milk not used for the table was set back until it "clabbered" and could be made into cheese. The extra cream was saved until there was enough in the churn to make butter. It had been restful to sit and lift the dasher up and down until bulgy, yellow chunks of butter materialized to float in the gold-flecked buttermilk.

Hallie had heaved a sigh of regret and turned over to find a more comfortable position. "No use crying over spilt buttermilk," she'd told herself and grinned wryly in the dark at her silent witticism before, once again, falling asleep.

Chapter 24

The trips to the ranch for water were becoming an ever-demanding job. Since Rueben's arrival there were four horses to water as well as the heifer and the house needs. The brothers took turns going for water, but those hours kept one or the other from fieldwork. Hallie rationed the house use severely so she need not be the one to report an empty barrel.

The tiny flower sprouts had come up from the seeds she had planted along the south side of the soddy. They were struggling valiantly to grow despite being watered with soapy laundry or dishwater. Hallie was doing her best to pretty up her yard, planting the seeds, transplanting wild rose bushes and goldenrod along the base of the drab sod walls. Without a well these plants would not survive the summer heat when it came. The apple seedlings had arrived and been set out. They could not live without regular watering.

Therefore, it was little wonder, Ebee Whipple and his son, Nute, received a hearty welcome the day they finally drove in to begin digging the long awaited well. Ebee was a little bit of a fellow not more than five feet tall and with his bony frame and jumpy motions, reminded Hallie of an agitated grasshopper. His smallness was deceptive for Ebee's stringy muscles had unusual strength, and in his scrawny rib cage, the heart of a stalwart soul. Ebee, standing in a loop of rope, could drop down into the shaft of a dark well too narrow for his brawny son, to set about digging without a qualm. No one knew his age, not even his treasured wife, Angel, or so it was rumored.

The McCains would learn during the course of the well digging, that the Whipple family had arrived in Dry Bend when the town consisted of one squat sod building housing a store and post office. Ebee and Nute had filed on claims near the proposed townsite, built soddies and a blacksmith shop. They let it be known they were skilled in well digging and blacksmithing...anything from shoeing horses to crafting branding irons or mending wagon wheels.

Angel, with her strapping daughters, did the farm work and cared for their growing herd of livestock. They were not the type to let any grass grow under their feet, folks were apt to say when speaking of the Whipples.

A site had to be picked for the McCain well. Ebee who had the "touch" for water witching, would pick the site. Will had designated an area beside the house knoll as the most convenient. Ebee began his search there. First he cut a forked branch from a green plum bush, skinned the bark off and cut it down to a Y shape some foot and a half in length. With the branch clasped in both hands and his arms stretched out before him, he began pacing back and forth in the proposed area. Suddenly, the branch quivered ever so slightly as though an unknown force pulled from below. The tail of the fork was tugged downward until it pointed straight to the grass at Ebee's feet.

"This here's the spot!" Ebee pronounced with certainty, and the digging began.

Ebee and Nute took turns digging in the progressing shaft that was to be of a size large enough to accommodate Nute's girth. A windlass was erected as it deepened to lower and hoist buckets of dirt the digger filled at the bottom of the three to four foot wide shaft.

It was difficult, exacting work. Even the wooden curbing installed to hold back the crumbling sand walls as the shaft deepened did not eliminate all danger of a "cave in".

It seemed to Hallie that with four men now to feed, she cooked and washed dishes from morning until night. The men ate ravenously after their labors. Preparing the huge meals called on all her ingenuity. Not only did she lack eggs and milk, the only meat she had was the salted dried beef. She soaked the beef to get as much salt out as she could, but it still retained enough to make it overly salted when cooked.

She knew a steady diet with dried beef served at every meal would become tiresome to the men. She was determined, despite her long list of "have-nots" that Ebee and Nute should have no tales of culinary deficiencies to carry away from her kitchen. Will was just as sensitive as to what might be said about the table they provided. It was not the season to hunt. The wild birds and animals were raising their young. But, Will said he would see she had some fresh meat to cook.

"I'll see to it, Hallie. Stop fretting," he assured her as he tucked her grocery list into his shirt pocket. Water had to be hauled ever day, now with the Whipples team added to the list of animals needing water. On this day, Will was the one making the trip. He planned to drop the barrels off at the ranch, go in to Dry Bend for supplies and then bring the water home on his way back.

"I figure I might just as well draw my wages and settle up. See where we stand," he explained to Hallie.

When Will got home just before dark, the men went out to unload the barrels and Will came to the house, laden with groceries. "Got you an extra bucket of sugar and a couple more pounds of raisins than you had on the list." He slid a sack of flour off his shoulder to the floor. "I got more stuff in the wagon…a good chunk of beef I bought from the Hartwells. They had just butchered a steer. They wanted to give it to us, but I paid. I figured we're not so hard up we can't pay for what we eat."

The ranch butchered often in order to feed their crew of men. As their meat would not keep any better than anyone else's, they often gave portions away or to those who could, sold it quite cheaply. Hallie was grateful they were among those who could pay. She felt positively rich as she set about fixing supper with items from her new supplies. Why, she had a whole case of canned milk…and what was this? Three-dozen eggs packed carefully in a box of salt!

Thus supplied, Hallie was able to turn out meals that would not only stick to a man's ribs, but appeal to his palate as well. Roast beef with bread dressing, boiled beef and dumplings, thick stews on corn bread, baked hash, biscuits and gravy, boiled greens or dried beans boiled with some of the dried beef. Her desserts were not fancy, but seemed to satisfy with such items as spice cake, bread puddings or raisin pie. Hallie was stretching the eggs as far as she could keeping them cool at the far end of the soddy away from the kitchen and the constantly heated cook stove.

Rueben was free with his compliments, and Will assured Hallie her meals were fine enough for anybody, but still she was concerned. The Whipples always ate their fill, said "Thank you kindly, ma'am," then went outside for a smoke. If Hallie had but know, Ebee Whipple would go about for years proclaiming the best biscuits he ever ett was turned out be a purdy gal over in McCain Valley. Hallie, worn to a frazzle baking, cooking and washing, gardening and caring for the two batches of newly hatched chickens, could have used such praise to boost her lagging energy, had it been given when so sorely needed.

It took most of the week to dig the well to water level and to install the wooden curbing. During that time, they all became better acquainted. This did not take place during the busy days. It was in the evenings spent outside as the men sat around the door in the soft, summer darkness smoking and talking. Hallie would hurry with the dishwashing, Rueben doing the drying, so they might join the others and listen to some of Ebee's endless supply of stories.

Ebee was an accomplished storyteller, and though he might be prone to exaggerate, just a little, Hallie thought, it only enhanced his story. One story he told she never forgot. It was about a man who fell into an old well on an abandoned claim. Hallie had gotten chills as she sat on the stoop in the warm darkness picturing the man, down a hundred feet in the ground, enclosed in a narrow shaft, water to his waist. His only tool had been a small, pocketknife. Cutting and probing with the inadequate tool, he had cut hand and toe holds in the rotted curbing. He had managed to climb to a height of perhaps fifty-five feet the first day. Exhausted, he had then made a sort of shelf with some of the curbing boards so he could rest for a few hours.

Again, he had moved upward. Twice he nearly fell when a handhold gave way. At last, so weary he could barely hold on, he reached the top. He had pulled himself over the edge by grasping the long blades of bluestem that had hidden the well opening. "He said, he just laid there stretched out praisin' the Lord," Ebee concluded as he took another pull on the stem of his pipe and then blew the smoke out in little puffs. "That was old Rollie Lindberg that happened to. You remember him, don't you, Nute?"

Nute said he did. "I remember him telling how he had dreams about being in that well for years afterwards, said it still bothered him to look down a well." Nute lapsed into silence again for he was not the talker his father was. He would sit chewing at the end of a stem of grass while the other men puffed on their pipes just listening.

"My boy don't smoke," Ebee was fond of saying. "He's afraid it'll stunt his growth." He always laughed heartily at his little joke.

Ebee discovered that Will especially enjoyed his tales of the wild horses that roamed the region. He would wind up his evening repertoire with a narration on this theme. The men would sit, perhaps leaning their backs against the sod wall of the house. Hallie would be in her usual place on the stoop. Pipe bowls would glow in the dark, the bright moon overhead. The evening would draw to a close in a discussion filled with speculation and conjecture on the many aspects of horse hunting.

"I'd give a heap to catch me a good horse!" This was from Will at the close of the first such session.

There was the sound of a slap to a shoulder as Rueben told his brother, "You just never know, Will. You and me, we might just get some gathered one of these days."

"Not without a couple of good riding horses, Rube. It takes a good horse, I reckon, to catch a good horse."

"Now, don't be too sure about that, son," Ebee spoke up. "There's more than one way to skin a cat if'n you set your mind to it."

There was a soft chuckle from Will's direction. "You're right on that score, Ebee. Maybe if we was to do a little figuring we could get the job done with what we got."

Chapter 25

It was evening on the day the Whipples put the finishing touches to the curbing they'd built around the top of the newly dug well. The curbing was a good three and a half feet above ground level creating a safety barrier around the mouth of the well. It was a good well, and though for the present, the water would have to be lifted by bucket and rope from its dark depth, some day a pump and even a windmill would be installed.

It was an unusually hot day for the beginning of June. A heat haze hung over the valley, and a line of blue-black clouds edged the skyline in the west. A weather breeder, the men all predicted.

Hallie, despite her elation over having all the water she needed, was feeling more than a little "wrung out" as she prepared supper. The stove seemed to radiate enough heat for three stoves its size.

"Where was all your heat last winter when it was needed?" she grumbled when a blast of heat hit her in the face as she opened the oven door to check the baking biscuits.

When she straightened a pain caught at her back. She put her potholder down and rubbed at the offending spot. Mercy, but it was hot. She tugged at the front of her smock where perspiration held the material of her undergarments to her skin like glue. She unbuttoned the top buttons of her smock and blew down inside her collar cooling a patch of skin. How good that felt. And she thought of bedtime when she would take a cool bath in the tub...a real bath with no concern about how much water she used.

There was not time for further indulgence, however. Hallie buttoned her collar and began setting the table. The men would be coming in for supper shortly. The tableware was laid out, and Hallie had taken the biscuits out of the oven when she heard the first, faint rumble of thunder. Rain was coming.

It will cool things off, she thought gratefully as she stacked the last biscuit on the platter. The men were at the wash bench by the door. She began taking the rest of the supper up, and presently Nute Whipple came in to make his usual, "Supper smells good enough to eat, durned if it don't."

Outside, Will called. "Hey, Hallie! Look's like there's company coming!"

Supper was left to sit on the table while they all rushed to meet the wagons pulling up by the well. Danjel and his folks had arrived. Hallie, following the others at a slower pace, felt another of those sharp back pains as she mentally assessed her supper menu. I must hurry them all inside before the rain hits. Reheat supper. There's plenty of meat and beans...enough biscuits to start with. I'll make a big pan of gravy. Children like gravy and there is bread when the biscuits run out. Hallie felt assured of enough supper for everyone as she reached the wagons and began to welcome her new neighbors.

As it happened, the population of McCain Valley grew to the count of thirteen on that night in early June. Not only did the nine Andreasons come to stay, but it was also the night little William McCain chose to make his appearance. For by the time the last of the supper's dishes had been washed, Hallie could hide her discomfort no longer.

Charlotte Andreason said she had been suspecting as much and had urged Hallie more than once to "rest a bit". Finally, Hallie had to admit it was "her time". Perhaps not the ideal time, but time, nonetheless.

Hallie undressed in the bedroom assisted by the older daughter, Hulda, who discreetly turned her head as she helped her hostess into her nightgown. Hallie's teeth chattered with nervousness and her fingers fumbled at the buttons.

In Missouri the birth of a baby was a very private matter with only women and the family doctor in attendance. Even the husband was banished from the scene, and certainly no children were allowed on the premises.

Children, as Hallie recalled from experience, were shuttled off to neighbors or family until the doctor had left with his little black bag that the well-informed Melrose children knew the doctor used to carry a new baby. Certainly, women were not brought to bed for the birth of their first child while rain poured down on a roof threatening to leak over a house bulging with visitors!

"Don't you worry none. Mama is good vith getting babies here," Hulda assured.

And Charlotte confirmed that she had indeed served as a midwife many times back in her native Sweden. It did seem unnecessary to call Ethel Hartwell out to make the ride in the rain.

"I reckon babies come the same in Sweden as they do here," Will had said to Hallie, but quickly added that he would go get Mrs. Hartwell if Hallie would feel better about it. Hallie had known she would have been more at ease with someone she knew, but didn't want to offend Charlotte. She told Will Charlotte Andreason would be fine.

Charlotte prooved quite capable in such proceedings Hallie would discover as the night progressed. Though worn out from her trip, she took charge and ran the whole affair with tact and efficiency. Always, Hallie would be grateful to her dear friend, for dear friend, Charlotte would become.

Despite her difficulty with the language, Charlotte managed to convey both sympathy and encouragement to the young novice being initiated by painful rite into the sisterhood of mothers. "It is best yu valk," Charlotte directed. "Valking helps much." And she walked beside Hallie, an arm around her, stopping to steady her when a pain came. Back and forth the length of the bed and four steps beyond then turn at the wall and back again. When the pains became hard, twisting jolts coming with steady consistency, Hallie was allowed to take to her bed.

The pain racked hours of the night drug on. The rain fell steadily making the new sod roof soggy. A trickle of water found its way through a crack between the sod blocks to slither under the tarpaper then dribble onto the bed. Charlotte simply sent Hulda for the table oilcloth and spread it over the bed covers. When the time came at last for the actual birth, she tucked one end of the oilcloth behind the head of the brass bedstead and Hulda held the other.

Hallie gave birth to her child and heard his first gasping cry from beneath this tent, rain dripping off the oilcloth to the dirt floor. Later, when the rain had stopped, Charlotte laid the baby, all clean and wrapped in soft flannel, into the tired, but eager arms of his mother. The eyes of the two women met sharing that mutual, mysterious something only mothers know.

A clear dawn was breaking when Will tiptoed in. His expression was a mixture of smiles and graveness as though he was undecided which was appropriate for such a momentous moment. The smile won for though his wife appeared tired, she wore a smile and was cuddling their son to her breast. The morning sun, still partially hidden behind the ridge, sent out its first timid rays to scout the valley. As they penetrated downward, they discovered the soddy on the knoll and momentarily bathed it in light. A bit of this brightness reflected through the small, back window where the new parents inspected their child. The elfin cap of delicate red fuzz on the tiny head was tinged with gold light. Will knelt and gently touched the hair, soft as peach down, with one rough callused finger.

"Do you mind, Hallie? Can you put up with another redhead?"

"I've always been a little partial to red-headed men," she murmured.

Will, disregarding Hulda who had entered carrying Hallie's breakfast, kissed his wife on her lips then smiling at Hulda went from the room.

Hulda smiled widely at Hallie. "Youst must be very happy. Such a fine husban', such a fine son."

And Hallie, still pink from her husband's display of affection, chuckled. "Yes, I suppose I am." Then teasingly, she added. "With all those calf eyes Rueben and Nute were casting your way at supper last night, I'd think there might be a good chance you will find a 'fine husband' yourself one of these days. There are an awfully lot of unattached men out here in the sandhills."

Her teasing brought an answering pinkness to the pretty blond girl's cheeks. She gave a merry giggle. "Oh, those two! They yust never see Svede girl before."

Hallie thoroughly enjoyed Hulda. It was almost like having one of her sisters with her. In fact, all the Andreasons were to become practically "family". While Hallie convalesced, Charlotte took over the management of the soddy leaving Hulda to care for Hallie and the baby.

Kristina at sixteen was equally as pretty as Hulda. She was assigned the task of looking after her younger brothers and sisters. These were Isaac who at twelve considered himself grown, happy-go-lucky Hilding who was eight, Inga, a blond angelic six year old, and eighteen month old Alfred. Alfred was a handful always on the verge of falling into a filled washtub or darting under horses' hooves.

The children were very solicitous of Hallie and baby William. They did their best to remember not to shout or bang about the house, though sometimes as children will, they forgot. They made amends by bringing offerings of wild flowers now blooming in abundance along the creek bed, bouquets of yellow, purple, blues and pinks.

While Hallie held court in the back room of the soddy, the outdoor work moved forward. Will and Rueben with their own crops planted, used their teams and plows to help the Andreasons turn the sod fields on their land. The seasons wait for no one and the arrival of the first killing frost in the fall had been known to come in late August. The sooner the Andreasons planted, the greater chance they had of a crop that coming fall.

When the pressing job of planting was finished, plans were made for the building of a home for the newcomers.

"Ve yust put up the one house," Oscar said. "Danjel can live vith us for now."

"That vill be fine in beginning, Papa. But law says I must have house on my own land."

Rueben said that was the law and he planned to put his own soddy up before long.

I heard of a family, an old couple and their widowed daughter that filed on adjoining claims," Will put in. "They satisfied the law with just one house. Built it so it sat on both sides of the boundary line."

"Vould dat vork, you tink?" Danjel was all eager interest.

"You could meet the requirements and still live under one roof. Danjel would be living on his claim and his parents on theirs. You shouldn't get any squawk from the government."

So that was how the Andreason's sod house was constructed. It was built in a matter of days with four men working and the older children helping. It had three rooms, a large central room with a bedroom at either end. The younger boys would share Danjel's bedroom, the girls would have the other one. The central room was large enough to provide the parent's double bed to be tucked back in a corner.

When the Andreasons had moved into their own house, Hallie found she missed the companionship and someone always handy to help with the baby, to give advice. It was nice though, to have the house to herself, to do her work at her own pace and in her own way. But, what a comfort it was to know Charlotte and the girls were only a good, brisk walk away. She need not long for female company ever again.

Chapter 26

There came a time in the latter part of June when Will felt he might spare a few days from his work. Since sighting wild horses or mustangs as they were often called, during the time he had ridden the range for the Hartwell Ranch he had longed to try his hand at catching some of the elusive animals. Ebee Whipple's tales of the mustangs had reinforced this desire.

"I sighted a band way off on some hills when I went to the lake the other day for cowchips," Will told Hallie one morning. "I reckon they moved in around there after the snow melted."

"I'm surprised they made it through the winter," Hallie replied.

"Horses can survive in deep snow better than cattle. They'll paw down to grass, and if they don't have water they'll eat snow."

"Maybe the band you saw has moved on," Hallie reasoned, hoping Will would drop the idea. She had listened to Ebee's stories and catching wild horses sounded dangerous to her.

"Doubt it. Plenty of grass and water right there." He grinned like a boy anticipating a fishing trip. "You and the baby would be all right for a few days with the Andreasons close by, wouldn't you, Hallie?"

Hallie said she would be, if he was set on going, but to be careful, for heaven's sake!"

Rueben and Danjel were as excited as Will at the prospect of chasing mustangs, and the three men began to make their plans. A trip must be made to the canyons with a team and wagon for a load of cedar posts. A stout corral had to built in case their chase was successful. A wild horse could not be picketed as the domestic were. It would fight the rope and either choke itself or break a leg, Will explained.

The corral, when finished, was circular with cedar post anchored firmly in the ground. Poles had been lashed lengthwise to the posts every foot or so, until the fence had reached a height of six feet. Oskar had helped with the corral construction but declined to accompany the younger men on the chase.

"I vill leave such tings to you young vons," he told them. "I'll vatch over tings in du valley vile yu is gone."

"We don't plan to take unnecessary chances,' Will assured anyone who expressed concern. "None of us can afford to be laid up with summer ahead of us."

Hallie was not all that reassured, but knew any female objections would not be appreciated at this point.

Armed with lariats and a supply of dried beef and rusks, a form of Swedish hardtack Charlotte had contributed, tucked in their saddlebags, the three left one morning at daybreak each astride a heavy-footed workhorse. Danjel rode bareback for he had no saddle. He was not an experienced rider but was determined to learn. The big horses snorted and tossed their heads as though anticipating an excursion with neither wagon nor plow at their heels.

Three days later, Hallie was drawing water from the well when she sighted the little cavalcade returning, riding in from the north. Rueben and Will were in the lead. Between them they led a small bay horse with lead ropes attached to both of their saddle horns. Danjel came just behind leading a sorrel-colored horse following with apparent docility. Hallie guessed it to be a mare for it was being trailed by a foal of undetermined hue.

Hallie could see, even at a distance, that Will's shirt was in tatters. As he rode nearer, it was apparent by the number of scrapes and bruises covering his face and the skin revealed by his ragged shirt, he had suffered an accident of some sort. His triumphant grin made it clear that whatever it may have been, it was considered trifling. They had caught horses! Horses with hooves smaller then "skillets"!

The riders had reached the pole corral and began maneuvering the nervous mustangs through the gate. The Andreasons could be seen filing along the trail that in only a few short weeks had been worn between the two homesteads.

Isaac arrived ahead of the others. "By gollies, ya got some!" he panted, eyes alight with admiration. "How did yu get'em?"

The horsecatchers were eager to do so, and as the others came to cluster around, the men told their tale.

Will, loosening the cinch on his saddle, started it out. "It was the first day we spotted horse sign about mid-morning." He tugged the saddle down from Pat's sweaty back and continued. "There was tracks in a big draw where the grass was good. You could see where horses had bedded down the night before and then moved off headed for water, we figured."

"We followed them tracks easy," Rueben said as he, too, worked at unsaddling his horse. "By the tracks we could see it was a small band, traveling slow, grazing as they went. It looked like there was some foals with them and maybe a few yearlings."

The story was delayed as the three work horses were watered from buckets the younger Andreasons had filled at the well.

"Shouldn't ve get vater for the vild ones?" young Hilding asked.

"I reckon it would be best if they settled down some," Will told the boy. The two mares and the foal were standing at the far side of the corral watching the humans with frightened eyes. "When there ain't so many around, I'll set some water in the corral for them."

It took little urging to get the men back at their story.

"Well, as I was telling you," Rueben, glancing over at Hulda, took up where he'd left off. "We was following them tracks, and we come on to their watering hole. There was horse signs thick all around, some fresh, others weeks old. They was using it regular like, we could see that."

"Vill, he got excited," Danjel spoke up. "Vill, you tell how ya figured it."

"Well, there was this rise back of the pond down at the south end of a little narrow draw." Will complied. "Behind the rise the draw pulled together just leaving a sort of passageway not more than eight feet wide. It had the makings of a natural trap."

Rueben and Danjel nodded. "And it was likely them horses would be coming in again for water the next day or two," Rueben added.

The men then told how they had camped out of sight of the watering hole, and waited until the next morning. They had then put the first part of their plan into action. They hid their horses in a gully they had selected deep in a tangle of chokecherry bushes that grew there. The two younger men were to stay there out of sight and to keep the horses quiet. Will took a short, sturdy branch and went to take the position he had chosen.

Several hours passed. Nothing disturbed the calm of the watering hole except for a pair of pintails that flew in, swam about for a while dunking their heads in search of feed then flew off.

All remained quiet, then came the soft thud of hooves from over on the other side of the ridge followed by the playful squeal of a foal romping along with the herd. An old mare, tall and bony, broke the skyline on the ridge then trotted down to water.

She was followed by perhaps twenty other mustangs. They were a ragged bunch, manes and tails long, and knotted with cockleburs. Patches of winter hair still clung to their coats. They were mostly mares and foals with a few yearlings pushed along by a shaggy-headed stallion.

The stallion was a bulky bay with a criss-cross of old scar tissue on his breast.

He'd snorted and stopped halfway down the hill. He'd pawed the ground restlessly as though he scented the intruders, then seemingly reassured, he'd trotted on down after the others.

According to plan, the horses were allowed to drink their fill. With full bellies they lazed around the pond, tails switching, foals nursing, taking their ease before going back out to graze.

"That was when we hit them!" Rueben's voice conveyed the tense excitement the men had felt as they turned this tranquil scene by the pond into bedlam. "We come a riding out of that gully for all we was worth, me and Danjel. Waving hats and yipping and yelling like a pair of lunatics. The herd broke and ran just trying to get distance between them and us."

The listeners were told of how the mares momentarily forgot their foals, even the stallion charged off, his role of protector abandoned in his fright. In their panic, as the men had hoped, the horses fled across the shallow water of the pond away from the oncoming danger. They crowded pell-mell into the narrow gorge to make their escape. The horses for a few crucial moments were almost at a stop as they crammed together pushing to get through the narrow opening.

"That was when I made my move," Will told the wide-eyed audience. "I'd been hunkered down behind a soapweed along the edge of that little gorge. Had my lariat ready, and when the horses was slowed up trying to get through, I stood up and tossed my loop. I saw I'd snagged one. I dallied my rope to the branch I'd twisted down into the dirt as far as it would go in among them soapweed roots."

Those listening were trying to visualize all this as the story unfolded by first one and then another of its participants. While Will was frantically dallying his lariat, Danjel and Rueben had reached the herd. The last of the horses broke through just as Rueben gave a desperate toss with his lariat loop. It settled over the head of a sorrel mare bringing up the rear.

164

"I was all set for a tussle," Rueben admitted. "But, instead of rearing and tearing around like Will's was doing, that old mare just whirled to face me standing stock still."

"A little horse…a baby, he stood off there vanting his mama to come," Danjel spoke proudly. "Dat's him in there. My horse, he is! He followed his mama home with us.

"Things had gone according to plan up until then," Will, leaning against the corral fence spoke, then winced as he shifted his position. "The rest of the herd except for the mare Rueben caught and her foal had taken off by then. I was doing my best to hang on to the mare I'd snagged. She was cutting all kinds of didoes at the end of my rope. I could see the branch was pulling up then it tore lose, and away we went! I was bouncing along on the end of the rope like a sack of oats."

Will shook his head and laughed. "My hands were slipping. I was hitting bunches of soapweed and cactus. Didn't figure I could hang on much longer when I took a bounce as she hit a trail at the top of the ridge. It threw me off to one side, out around a tough, old soapweed. You know how some of them have roots going down pert near to China." Will grinned widely at his listeners. "It was my only chance. I got my legs jerked up and planted my heels at the base of the soapweed, twisting the rope around one of those old dried nubbins at the base. It held. Yanked the mare backwards off her feet, and I got the rope wrapped around that soapweed in nothing flat!"

"You should have seen the durn fool," Rueben laughed. "There he was, his shirt near tore off, his belly and chest looking like a wild cat had had a hold of him. He had cactus stickers poking out of him. His hands were raw and bleeding, making the rope red where he was hanging on. And do you know what he said when Danjel here come a running up to help? 'Ain't she a beauty?' he says."

Rueben shook his head, "That little mare was up and a bucking at the end of his rope, and he says, 'Sure as shootin', she's with foal.'"

"And, I figure she is by the looks of her," Will joined in the laughter. "There'll be an increase in my horse herd before long."

That evening as Will soaked his aching, lacerated body in a tub of warm water, he continued to speak of horses. "Yes, sir! We got the makings of a horse herd, Rube. Those two mares are going to start us out."

Rueben who would take his bath after Will and Hallie had gone to bed, leaned back in his chair and puffed on his pipe. "You reckon we can get our mares bred to a good stud?"

"Won't be a problem. Hartwell's got a pretty fair one he'll let you bring your mares to for a fee."

Hallie, listening in the bedroom as she lay out clean garments for her husband, wondered how much such a fee would be, and if they would have it to pay.

There was the sound of Will sloshing water as he swabbed at his scraped skin. "Let a few years go by, and you and me will buy us a stud of our own. Maybe go back to Missouri and find a good one."

Hallie moved over to the window and gazed out into the moon-drenched night. The mustang mares and the foal walked the corral restlessly. The older one, the one that gave every indication of having been a domesticated animal that had strayed and joined the mustangs, stopped to stare at the lighted window, her tangled mane blowing in the wind. She had remembered to respect the loop of a rope…to lead. The men thought she was even broken to ride for a little patch of white hair on her back covered a scar from an old saddle sore.

The younger mare stalked the pole fence, her belly bulging under her shaggy coat. She wanted out of the confining corral, snorting with distaste at the buckets of water, ignoring the hay Will had put inside the gate.

How could Will think those two scrubby horses, one near to having a smooth mouth if Hallie was any judge, and the other one as wild as sin, could be the beginning of a horse herd?

"I'm ready for you to start working on me, Hallie," Will called. "I think I got the worst of the dirt off."

Hallie checked the baby sleeping in his bed that was a wooden crate lined with flannel and padded with a folded quilt. He looked so sweet and innocent. Would he someday go on such wild excursions…get such crazy notions? She smiled down at her sleeping son and knew the answer. After all, he was his father's son.

Armed with a needle from her sewing basket, Hallie came into the kitchen. Will was now seated in a chair by the table, a towel wrapped around his waist, a pair of small pliers on the table. He had moved the lamp over to the edge of the table so Hallie could see to extract the collection of cactus prongs in his skin. Rueben had offered, but said he feared his fingers were too big for such delicate work.

The task proved difficult for some of the thorns had broken off even with the skin and all were anchored with stubborn intensity.

"I'm afraid some of these are going to hurt," she warned.

"Don't fret about it. Just do your best to get them out. I feel like a blame pin cushion."

In an attempt to get their minds off the painful process, she asked about the foal. "Did I understand Danjel to say the colt is to be his?"

"We figured it that way. He don't know the first thing about riding a horse, but he was right in there doing all he could. We didn't want him to come away empty-handed. The foal maybe isn't much now, but time he's through growing, he'll be a dandy." He grinned and winced at the same time. "Yep, by golly! We all came home with a horse!"

Chapter 27

Summer came on in earnest. The men were working at plowing fireguards to protect their homes and fields. Grassfires were always a threat in the sandhills during the summer and fall months.

Hallie was in the garden as she often was in the mornings after finishing her morning house chores and the baby was down for his nap. She had quickly learned she must fit her work in around the demands of tiny William. The brim of her sunbonnet flapped in the breeze. A flock of sparrows chirped noisily in the plum thicket above the garden. In the distance, sheets made a white blur as they flapped on the Andreason's clothesline, and a figure, probably Hulda or Kristina, could be seen moving about in the Andreason garden.

One of the mares, the younger one that had produced a wobbly-legged foal just the previous week, nickered as she watched the teams at work. The men and horses could be seen plowing one behind the other, on the widening fireguard. A hawk flew above them, gliding, waiting. Suddenly, it dropped to grab some small prey frightened into the hawk's view. The hawk retuned to the sky, its prey dangling in its talons, carrying a meal, perhaps to a nest of young.

Hallie put down the hoe she had been using to chop weeds and bent to examine the row of bean plants. The first tender, green pods were ready for picking. She snipped off one of the pods using the nail of her thumb and nibbled it savoring the green crispness. It was such a treat to have fresh vegetables again. The purple-veined tops of the beets in the adjoining row thrust upward toward the sun in crowded growth. They were ready to be thinned. She was using her mother's method, waiting an extra few days to thin so the leafy tops might be big enough to be used for greens. When they were seasoned with vinegar and salt they made a pleasing dish to satisfy winter cravings.

The thought of the delectable abundance the garden would provide throughout the summer gave her a gratifying sense of security. They would need to dig a cellar to store garden harvest for the winter months.

The promise of this bounty was soon threatened, however, by the lack of rain.

Despite all the snow and the earlier rains, the surface soil that sustained the young plants both in the gardens and fields, was drying out. Hallie carried endless buckets of water to her wilting plants. Will and Rueben carried water in the evenings to the young apple tree seedlings. Isaac and Hilding came each evening with the team and wagon to fill barrels at the McCain well so that the Andreason garden might be watered, also.

Thank goodness, Hallie would think several times a day, there is at least one well in the valley. By late fall there should be three for both Rueben and the Andreasons had asked to be put on Ebee Whipple's waiting list.

Everyone had been so busy, there had been little neighboring. One Sunday the McNeils surprised them, driving over to see the new baby and to spend the day.

"Had to come see that new younun'!" Sam boomed as he climbed down from the wagon to hand Will a basket of food they'd brought along. He turned to assist Pearl who was holding baby Matilda. The men and children, however, upon hearing of the mustang hunt, took off immediately to inspect the horses in the corral.

Hallie, carrying the food basket Will had handed over, and Pearl with little Matilda in her arms, started on to the house. "A new baby can't compete with a new horse," Pearl chuckled. "Not with my bunch, anyway, but I can't wait to see him and your new house. I'm so glad it was completed before the baby came."

Pearl was suitably impressed by the soddy and by William. "He is a beautiful baby, Hallie. And would you look at that red hair! I'll bet Will is crazy over him."

Hallie admitted that he was, and that they were all spoiling him including his Uncle Rueben. Pearl gave Matilda a string of wooden spools with which to play, and after changing her diaper sat her on a quilt Hallie spread on the floor. The women started dinner preparations, visiting as they worked.

Pearl admired the geraniums Hallie had started in tins for the windowsills. She had gotten starts from Ethel Hartwell. Pearl was also eager to learn all about the Andreasons and was happy to hear what good neighbors they were. She reported another family had recently settled near them though she had seen little of them.

"They came from some eastern state according to Sam, sort of uppity. They have a son who used to teach school. He lives with them. Has bad lungs, Sam heard and came out here thinking it would be healthier."

Hallie was to learn that Sam was swamped with surveying jobs as more homesteaders found their way to the area. Also, the McNeils were making plans to turn their dugout over in its entirety to their farm animals and were going to put up a sod house at last.

"I'm going to insist on four rooms and a loft for the boys," Pearl stated firmly. "The children can't be brought up properly in that dugout, and Sam can afford it now with the extra surveying."

"I'm glad you've put your foot down," Hallie informed Pearl. "You've sacrificed so much, you should have a decent place to live."

A rather strange expression crossed Pearl's face, Hallie noted, and Pearl started to say something then seemed to change her mind. The conversation turned to another topic. Pearl bent to pick up William from his bed placed on two chairs near the table. She began cooing and cuddling him as one will a baby.

Little Matilda watched this with solemn eyes then began to fuss and rolled off her quilt onto the dirt floor. This action produced the desired affect for immediately Mama Pearl put the other baby down and came to brush off her own little one and reseat her on the quilt. The women exchanged knowing smiles.

The day of visiting went well. The Andreasons were invited over to meet the McNeils. Danjel was the only member of the family who had met them and that was when he went to ask Sam to survey their claims. It proved to be a congenial group with no end of things to talk about. While the children played, the adults spoke of land, crops, gardens, and the need of rain.

The afternoon sped by. The McNeils would have to start the drive home soon. Hallie made coffee and put out the plentiful leftovers from dinner along with the cake Pearl had brought and the huge pan of sweet rolls Charlotte had contributed. Charlotte had a special talent with light breads. Whatever she baked was fluffy and fine-textured.

Sam, Hallie noted, reached just as quickly for a second sweet roll as did the rest. A steady diet of Pearl's cooking must have finally weaned him from the heavier variety. She gave a silent chuckle as she recalled Sam's previous comments on "feathery bread".

The McNeil boys had made friends right off with Hilding and Isaac. The two little girls, Nancy and Inga, had spent every moment of the afternoon together playing house beneath the branches of the plum thicket. The pair shed tears when the time came for Nancy to be hoisted into the homebound wagon. The tears were wiped away, however, when they were informed they would be seeing one another at the Fourth of July celebration. This occasion would be held in Dry Bend in just one week's time.

It had been an enjoyable day from start to finish, but Hallie found when the last goodbye had been called from the doorway, she was exhausted. Such a Sunday might be restful for the men, but for the women, it was a day of labor.

Hallie groaned as she removed her shoes and lay down on the bed to nurse the baby. She lay reviewing the happenings and conversations of the day in her mind as she rested. There was no doubt that Rueben was attracted to Hulda who pretended indifference. In Hallie's opinion, it would not hurt Rueben to cool his heels a bit. He had been far too popular with the girls back home for his own good. And hadn't the children had a fine time? Her younger brothers would have fit right in. With these thoughts, her mind turned to the loved ones in Missouri, wondering how they might have spent the day. Had they gathered at one of the relatives for dinner? Had Emily been escorted home from church by George Brodee? How pretty Ida and Tom's little Lousia Marie must be.

She would soon be six months old. As the image of these faces came to mind, the ache of homesickness threatened. "No, little one. We won't allow that," she murmured gazing down at her small son. "It has been far too nice a day to let it end on an unhappy note."

The day of the Fourth was a scorcher. Despite the heat, few if any were deterred from attending the celebration. Many, such as Hallie, would have their first trip to the town. Word, as usual, had been passed over the prairie hills so even the most recent newcomers to the region were informed of the event.

Those who had not been to the little town in recent weeks would find changes taking place in its expanding boundaries. These changes, of course, were due to the influx of homesteaders and their demand for supplies and equipment. The enterprising Feeny Huebanks was in the process of enlarging his store. Henceforth, it would be known as Huebanks' Mercantile, a source of all wants from neck yokes to knitting needles.

Ebee Whipple was president of the school board. Under his leadership, a frame building was replacing the sod schoolhouse. There was talk of a church, a brick bank, and two buildings near the store were being built. One of these, it was said, was to house a newspaper and printing shop for a hopeful young printer from Chicago who was certain his destiny lay in the west.

The other building was to be a two-storied structure similar to the Huebanks' building. Its ground floor was to be rented out for offices or shops, the top floor would have sleeping rooms…a hotel of sorts.

There was an effort afoot to get a doctor to settle in the, up and coming, little town. And a fellow that freighted from Kearney out to Dry Bend was heard to say that if they were going to have a hotel they just as well get a decent place for a man to eat. Indeed, Dry Bend had prospects for the enterprising.

The businessmen of the town were in charge of the festivities. There was a water well near the picnic ground where cold water could be pumped and tubs of lemonade where a person could get his cup filled for a penny. Stronger drink was not yet sold in the town. If there was a jug or two passed around out behind the store, it was kept out of sight of the womenfolk. There were games and foot races for the children with prizes of tin whistles and balloons.

Jacob Hartwell had been asked to speak. He picked the proper hour…when everyone was sitting about in the late afternoon beneath the canvas canopy erected to supply shade. Even the children were tired enough to sit and listen, at least in part, to what he had to say.

His speech was quite stirring, Hallie thought as she shooed a fly away from the sleeping baby in her lap…all those patriotic phrases befitting the day of independence. Eloquent praise for Dry Bend and the county with land he depicted as being some of the finest in the state. It was a fine speech and was well received. Hallie heard more than one declare, "Now, there's a man could talk to those politician fellows down in the capital!"

When the speech was over people began to move about. Lemonade-sodden children as well as a good number of adults found their way to the makeshift "conveniences" that had been provided, camouflaged by canvases.

Men stood about in little knots, sharing plugs of tobacco and opinions. Children darted in and out among the clusters of adults making new friends, hunting for those they may have met at an earlier occasion...teasing...laughing...quarreling as children will.

Fistfights broke out occasionally among some of the boys. Not for any special reason, just "feeling their oats" like bantam roosters in a chicken yard. Bert McNeil and Isaac Andreason had such an encounter with another pair of boys though the women in the party were not to learn of it until suppertime. It had started over teasing, as is often the case. One of the two Jeston brothers east of town made fun of Isaac's brogue. Isaac took a poke at him and in a moment, all four boys were exchanging blows. Dust fogged above the heads of the group of children that quickly formed a circle to cheer or jeer, depending on whom they championed of the four dirt-smeared boys rolling about on the ground.

Nancy and Inga had wiggled through the legs of the older children to get a better view only to discover their brothers were involved. They scrambled out to run sobbing to their fathers, "Bert and Isaac were getting killed!"

The skirmish was halted and the participants made to shake hands. The boys were sent to the horse tank to wash before presenting themselves for supper. The two girls were told to say nothing of the incident to the women. "Fighting always upsets womenfolk."

A swollen eye and the unmistakable signs of a nosebleed did not go unnoted by the observant. The women exchanged glances, but said not a word. All was going smoothly until eight-year-old Hilding came in all out of breath from his play with some other Swedish children he'd met. He plunked down in the empty place on a blanket next to his brother, Isaac. The McNeils, McCains and Andreasons were eating together as they had at noon. Isaac, whose eye was now nearly swollen shut, was handed a plate of sandwiches. He took one and turned to pass the plate to his younger brother.

Hilding's hand stopped in mid-air as he looked up and saw Isaac's face. "Vot happened to you, Isaac? Did a bee bite ya?"

Everyone burst out laughing as the red-faced culprit grinned ruefully. "Ya, it was a bee all right. But, the bee, he don't look so gud neither."

Hilding's face showed his bafflement. Why was being stung by a bee funny? Grownups were hard to figure. He patted Isaac's arm in brotherly sympathy.

Chapter 28

Supper things were stowed away, and folks began to congregate for the dance. A good many of the young people were paired up for the evening. Hulda Andreason was going to the dance with Rueben who had gotten his bid in just a few minutes ahead of Nute Whipple.

Danjel had asked the older sister of Hilding's Swedish playmate, and two youthful cowhands from the Hartwell Ranch were to squire Kristina Andreason. The two had come rushing up to ask her, practically stumbling over one another. Kristina had arched an eyebrow and mischievously ansered, "Vi, boys. I yust can't decide vich vun of you to choose. I vill youst have to choose the both."

After the younger ones had gone off, Hallie sat nursing the baby in the shadowed security of the wagon. She could see the people strolling by on their way to the dance area. The sound of Carlotte crooning softly as she put little Alfred to sleep in the adjoining wagon could be heard. It felt good to sit still. It had been such a long day, starting before daylight. It was wonderful, though, to be away from the homestead with its endless chores and worries. Good to meet folks, laugh and visit. Everyone they'd met since coming to Nebraska was here today.

She wondered if anyone had stayed home from the celebration. Even the McNeil's neighbors, Rachel and Emmet Loomis, the couple that moved up from Kansas, and whose baby had been born in their wagon, had shown up. They had stayed pretty much to themselves today, but at least they'd ventured out. The Loomis baby was eight months old now...doted on by his parents. Just as we do, Hallie thought as she kissed the top of William's fuzzy head.

Oskar and Will waited for their wives, hunkered on their heels, talking quietly, as they smoked their pipes at the side of the McCain wagon. When William and Alfred were sleeping snugly, the men escorted their wives to the patch of ground where the dance was being held. A wagon had been pulled up to serve as a platform for the musicians. Lanterns were hung on poles to be lit when it grew dark. A lively polka was in progress when they arrived. Will grinned and winked at Oskar.

"Do you suppose these gals we brought can dance?"

Oskar grinned back and putting his arm around his wife's ample waist declared, "Ve better find out before ve buy dem lemonades." Laughing, Will grabbed Hallie and swung her out into the circling tide of couples skipping and stomping up dust in time to the music.

As Hallie had discovered at the Hartwell's dance, the men at these affairs outnumbered the women by almost half. Unless a female had a broken leg or two heads, she wouldn't be sitting out many dances. Partners came in all shapes and sizes, bashful toe-trodders, bold boot-stompers. And then there was Grover Ditmore smelling gamier than ever in the summer heat.

Peter Bergstrom, and Bandy Rodgers were much in evidence. Having lost out with Pearl, they were now vying for the attention of a widow woman who lived with her son and his family on a homestead south of town. Folks, it was said, were betting on Peter.

When a couple of hours had passed, the sweating musicians called for a break while they had a cool drink and caught their breath. Will and Hallie moved to the outer edge of the crowd where the air was a bit cooler. Inga and Nancy had gone to check on the babies and reported they were sleeping soundly. Reassured, Hallie noticed Rachel Loomis returning from no doubt having checked her own little one. Hallie had taken a few steps toward Rachel intending to start a conversation when a strange cowboy smelling of whisky pushed past her. He stopped directly in front of Rachel.

"Wall, I swan! It sure is Flo! I seen ya awhile ago and I says to myself, 'That there's got to be Flo.'"

Rachel's face had turned dead white...a hunted, trapped expression frozen there.

"I couldn't hardly believe my eyes. How'd you get clear out here from Topeka, honey girl? Don't tell me Ma Beaker's opened up a business here in this little berg."

Rachel called out desperately to her husband attracting the attention of those close by. Emmett, visiting with Sam and Pearl, heard his name, looked up startled and saw the man confronting his wife. He began pushing his way through to her. Meanwhile, Rachel was trying to pull her arm free as the befuddled cowboy coaxed, "Come on, honey. Come have a little drink with me."

The Loomis wagon was parked not many yards from the dance area. Rachel appeared intent upon reaching its safety, the tipsy cowboy stumbling in her wake. "Wait up for me, Flo, honey. Don't be mad at me."

Emmett was out of the crowd by then and with a few swift strides reached the wagon a step ahead of his wife's tormentor. Making a long reach over the wagon's side, he drew a rifle from beneath the seat. Rachel was slumped against the wagon as though the strength had left her legs. Hallie and Will were near enough to observe the quick glance he gave his wife and to hear his terse words, "I'll handle this."

Rachel put out a hand as though to stop her husband, then dropped it to her side with a futile gesture. The baby in the wagon began to wail.

The cowboy lurched up with a silly grin on his face. He shook a finger at Emmett. "Hey, fella! I seen her first. She's my girl tonight!"

"Shut your mouth! Emmett warned grimly. This is my wife you're talking about."

By now, a crowd had gathered by the Loomis wagon, those in back shouldering and craning necks for a better view. The cowboy had come to an uncertain halt, the gun barrel pointing at his belly.

"Aw, now, fella. I don't want no trouble. I was just wantin' a little fun. Les go have us a lil drink. Come on. Flo, you come, too." He took an unsteady step forward.

`Sam nodded to Will, and the two men closed in. Sam came from behind Emmett wrapping his arms around the angry man, pushing his gun barrel so it pointed toward the ground. Will was using similar tactics on the cowboy, hustling him off into the gathering darkness. A couple of his buddies appeared and promised to take him off to sober up.

When the rifle was safely out of Emmettt's hands, Sam encouraged everyone to go back to dancing. "This here was just a little misundertandin' brought by too much licker," Sam assured folks as they turned away mumbling speculations among themselves.

"What was it that fellow said to her?"

"He called her Flo. I thought her name was Rhoda or Rosa, something like that." Hallie heard these remarks. "Well, it was a funny business if you ask me," one woman answered.

Hallie didn't know what she should do. The Loomis baby was crying lustily now, and Rachel still clung to the wagon's side, her face pressed to the rough wood, her shoulders trembling. Hallie climbed into the wagon and picked up the baby, quieting him as best she could. At last, Emmett collected himself and moved with tired steps over to his wife's side.

"Come on, Rachel. Don't cry. Let's just go home."

Sam hastily began hitching the team that had been munching hay at the back of the wagon. Will was back by then and he pitched in to help. Emmett boosted Rachel into the wagon. Hallie handed her the baby. "We didn't get to visit today. You folks will have to come over with Sam and Pearl one of these first Sundays for dinner," Hallie invited. "That way they can show you the way to our place."

Rachel Loomis struggled to smile, and nodded, wiping at a tear. Will held up his arms to lift Hallie down as Emmett climbed into the wagon and clucked to the horses. The wagon moved off disappearing into the darkness.

Looking after the departing wagon Hallie pondered the cowboy's words...what they implied. Could Rachel truly have been "that kind" of woman? "Well, what if she had been?" Hallie asked herself. "Hadn't Jesus told the woman at the well, to go and sin no more?" And she slipped her arm through Will's and they made their way back to the prairie ballroom.

The sun was coming up when the grays breasted the final ridge the next morning. Will pulled them to a stop and waited for the Andreason wagon to pull up along side. The two wagons, silhouetted against the early morning sky, their tired passengers assaying the valley below. The various colored fields could be distinguished glimmering with dew in the morning coolness. Here and there, a wisp of fog drifted low like shreds of gray smoke, gliding silently on the air.

A tinge of gold in the ripening oat field looked like a quilt block appliquéd to the greenish-beige background of the valley floor. The pale greenness of Rueben's oats planted later and not yet at the ripening stage was another, the darker green of corn and potato plants, the brown of Andreason's fields striped with green rows of late planted corn. A giant quilt in the making, Hallie mused looking down and remembering what Will had prophesied that first day about the settling of the valley.

Would the quilt ever be complete? Would blocks of fields and meadows outlined by fence and road some day cover its floor?

Houses? Barns? A school? Church? The wagon moved forward carrying its passengers down into the valley where the answer lay.

Chapter 29

The month of July was typically a hot one. Only small amounts of rain had fallen in recent weeks. Will walked his fields fretting over the suffering cornstalks as a mother might over a feverish child. The corn leaves hung listlessly during the day beneath the onslaught of heat, their roots thirsty for moisture. He and the others in the valley were extending their strips of plowed fireguards as the chance of fire in the drying summer grasses was an ever-present fear.

Rueben, with the help of the other men, had a soddy now on his claim. A bunk bed and some shelves had been installed and Rueben slept in his little house thus meeting the government's requirements. He continued, by invitation, to take his meals with Will and Hallie. Hallie also insisted upon doing her brother-in-law's washing and ironing. Rueben, in return, was always quick to carry the wash water or to lend a hand with the supper dishes, and when grocery supplies were purchased, Rueben paid his share. The brothers often shared fieldwork as they had when they were boys at home.

One particularly hot afternoon, Rueben and Will had taken a break from hoeing weeds in the cornfield. They were in the house, having coffee and some of Hallie's oatmeal cookies. Hallie was snapping string beans she had picked that morning. The baby was lying in his box bed beside her chair. The little box bed was easily moved to wherever she was working, indoors or out. William was waving his hands with the jerky motions of an infant, cooing happily. Bread was baking in the oven and Hallie, going to check on the browning loaves, paused at the window.

"There's a team and wagon coming," she said.

The men got up and went outside to see who might be driving in from the north. Few had settled out in the north hills by the summer of '81.

The heavily-laden wagon that came to a halt by the well was drawn by a tired, mismatched team. The smaller of the two horses was a pretty chestnut, obviously saddle stock, while its larger mate had been bred for heavy labor. The corner of an iron bedstead pushed out above the bulky heap of items in the wagon, a crate of nervous chickens squawked at the rear.

A bearded man who appeared to be in his early thirties, stepped down leaving a woman of like age on the seat, a small, fretful child on her lap. Two little, pigtailed heads belonging to a couple of towheaded girls of about seven and eight, protruded from among the piled belongings. The man favored an arm that was bandaged and held in a sling.

"The name's Adams. Could we water our horses and fill our water jugs?" The man held out his good hand to shake the one Will was offering.

"Help yourselves. There's plenty," Will assured him. "Have your wife and young ones hop down and come in. We're just having a cup of coffee.

Hallie, who had come up beside Will with the baby in her arms, seconded the invitation that was gratefully accepted. Later, after the horses had been watered and the visitors were seated around the McCain's table munching on slices of fresh bread, their story was told.

"We're on our way down to Grand Island. My wife's folks farm there, and we used to live there when I was working at the lumber yard," Ed Adams began. "Early this spring, we came out here and filed on some land. We figured to get a foothold and start up ranching. That's why we took land on north where there would be room to expand in the years ahead." He shook his head. "We figured wrong."

The wife, Hallie never did learn her first name, was a bundle of nerves. She began to shed tears as the story was told in a strained, halting voice by her husband.

"We filed on a quarter of land about twenty-five miles north of here. It had a fine spring of water that fed a lake down in one corner of our claim. We built a dugout, planted some corn and fenced off a piece of pasture around the spring. We'd brought ten head of cows and a bull with us besides a saddle horse and a team." The man looked over at his wife who was wiping tears.

"We didn't have any neighbors, but with the youngsters and all we had to do, we didn't get lonesome. Once in awhile, we'd see a horsebacker off at a distance, but they never stopped by to say howdy. Not until awhile back, that is, did they come. Then six or seven came riding up. They were wearing guns. Ordered us to take down our fence. Said they didn't allow barbed wire on their range. THEIR RANGE! I'd filed on my land legal. I told them so, said I wasn't taking down my fence! They left, but they made it plain the matter wasn't closed."

He took a swallow of coffee and shook his head when Hallie offered him another slice of bread. "Thank you, no, ma'am. We didn't stop here to eat you out of house and home."

"I reckon they came back," Rueben said.

"You reckoned right. They were back that very night. We were sleeping when the dog woke us up barking. We could hear horses running. It was too dark to see what was going on, but when daylight came, we could. The fence had been jerked out and was all cut and tangled up. The cattle and horses were gone. The dog was dead."

"Couldn't you get the law after them?" Hallie demanded in angry indignation.

"Wasn't any law out there, not for miles, anyhow. We just patched the wire and put the fence back up the best we could. We weren't going to give up that easy. The horses had come wandering back and I located four of our cows."

"Them bad men come again though, didn't they, Daddy?' the oldest of the little girls piped up.

"Yes, two nights ago. We woke up hearing stampeding cattle, men yelling and gunfire. Like to scared the wife and kids to death. They ran a herd of cattle straight over the top of the dugout. Dirt was falling, the kids were screaming. The roof caved in, and a critter with it. We couldn't see it in the dark, but it was lunging around breaking up everything. I'd pushed the family back into the far corner when the roof started coming down so the critter hadn't hit us yet. He would have in short order. The dugout wasn't any bigger than half this room," he indicated the kitchen they were sitting in.

"It hit Daddy!" The daughter spoke again. "Didn't it, Daddy?"

"Yes. I'd made a dive for the door hoping it hadn't gotten jammed. It hadn't and I yanked it open. That steer...I could see it in the moonlight, was a big, long horned steer, saw the light from the open door. He made a lunge for it and one of his horns caught my arm before I could get out of the way." He patted the bandaged arm.

"We didn't have enough light to see what damage he had done to my arm. It was numb, but I could feel blood with my other hand. I just took off my shirt and wrapped it up. We sat there and waited till daylight."

Ed Adams looked over at his wife, again. "Come morning, we'd already decided. We couldn't fight what we were up against alone. Maybe, someday when things change some and the children are older. Maybe, we'll try again."

Hallie sat out a pan of warm water and clean cloths so Mrs. Adams might clean and re-bandage her husband's wound. It was an ugly sight, swollen and inflamed. It was obvious a doctor should see to it as soon as possible. Hallie brought out the bottle of carbolic acid they kept on hand. When mixed with water this would disinfect cuts and scratches. Hallie hoped it would be helpful in clearing up the infection in the injured arm.

It was a long drive to Grand Island, a town far to the southeast. It was decided Rueben should take off the time to accompany the Adams the rest of the way. If the condition of Ed Adam's arm should worsen or they had a breakdown, they would need help. Rueben saddled up and left with the Adam's family.

Watching from the open doorway, Hallie looked after the wagon as it climbed the ridge. What a harrowing experience they had undergone. What an ugly ending to their homesteading venture. But…the thought prodded, they are going home.

Guiltily, she turned from the door and picked up the baby. Such a thought was disloyal to Will. After all, they had a home here, now…neighbors. The crops were growing. If they got a good rain or two, they would have something to harvest. With this optimistic thinking, she said to her small son, "It is past your feeding time, young man."

And she carried him over to the rocking chair.

The Adams had left their crate of chickens behind. "They'd likely die before we got them back home, anyway," had been the reasoning when Will had protested. "You folks can use them, and it's little enough what with your brother coming along to see us through." Will had then tucked a little sack of oats he'd been hoarding for the grays into the Adam's wagon over their objections.

"It might just be what those horses of yours need to speed them along," Will had insisted. So it was in this manner Hallie obtained ten hens and a rooster to add to her little flock of hatchlings in the old dugout.

"Might be a fellow could have an egg with his pancakes," Will commented with a grin the next day and warned Hallie to keep a sharp eye for coyotes and skunks. "They could clean you out of poultry in short order," he reminded though Hallie was well aware of the fact.

The hens were a blessing to Hallie for despite their having been shuttled about, hens are touchy about that, they continued laying a nice gathering of eggs each day. She fairly gloated over the half dozen or so, big, white eggs she would find in the nests Will built along the east wall of the dugout. It was such a treat to have eggs for breakfast or to use in recipes seldom used since her arrival in Nebraska. If only they had milk and butter, she could set a real table.

The chickens did not lack for care. Their water pan was always filled to the brim, and they were free to roam about filling their craws with grasshoppers and bugs throughout the day. Every night after they had gone to roost in the dugout, the door was carefully closed.

One morning about a week after Rueben had returned from escorting the Adam family to Grand Island, Hallie heard a loud squawking down toward the dugout. The men had already left for the field. Rushing to the door, Hallie was just in time to see a coyote dashing off with one of her young chickens dangling from his mouth. The rest of the flock was running about madly, cackling their heads off. Hallie quickly drug a chair over to the door, climbed up and grabbed the loaded rifle kept on pegs above the door. With a quick glance at the baby sleeping in his bed, she ran outside.

True to the vow she had made that first lonely night on the homestead, Hallie had learned to load and fire the rifle. She had learned to balance the barrel on something sturdy, to aim and fire. Will had not taken it too seriously, chalking it up to one of the fancies women get, but Hallie had not forgotten what she had learned.

The coyote was entering the plum thicket above the dugout as Hallie ran out the door carrying the rifle. She climbed cautiously up the dirt trail that led past the thicket. The coyote's haunches were visible where he had stopped and was now intent upon tearing the feathers from his breakfast.

Hallie crept closer. Judging herself near enough, she lifted the rifle to her shoulder and then struggled with its weight as she aimed and pressed the trigger.

The sharp crack of the rifle brought the men from the field at a run. They arrived at the scene to find Hallie standing triumphantly above the dead coyote lying spread-eagle over his ill-gotten gain.

"I got him! I got him!" Hallie cried. "I shot a COYOTE!

Will, out of breath from his dash from the field, gathered his rifle from the sandy trail and admitted with a chuckle that is sure looked that way. "Woman, you like to of scared us to death when we heard shooting up here." And noticing his wife rubbing her shoulder, he remarked, "I warned you this rifle has a kick if it's not braced on a fence or something. It's too big for a woman."

"Maybe it is," Hallie answered him. "But, I don't care. I'll shoot it again if I need to."

"I reckon you've got you a regular Daniel Boone in the making," Rueben joked as they went to inspect Hallie's "kill".

This was only the beginning of the good-natured kidding to be directed at the "hunter" during the next few days. Of course, the Andreasons who had heard the shot, were told of her exploit, also. But, this distraction from the daily routine was short-lived.

The long, hot days wore on filled with summer work. The McCain's oats were ripening and would soon be ready for harvesting though the lack of moisture these last weeks would cut the yield, Will predicted.

One scorcher of an afternoon, Oskar and Danjel drove their horses over as they did twice a day so the animals might be watered without having to haul it to them. They had brought water barrels in a wagon to fill for house and garden use. Isaac had ridden along commissioned to deliver a great loaf of Swedish limpa bread still warm from the oven.

"I'll put the coffee on," Hallie called from the door. There wasn't a sign of a breeze, she noticed as she turned back into the kitchen. It was too hot for coffee, but the men never seemed to think so. They needed an afternoon break from work and often chose to take it when the Andreasons came for water.

William gave a fussy cry from his bed. Isaac who had come in, asked if he should pick him up.

"Go ahead," Hallie said as she went about getting the breadboard to slice some of the fragrant bread. He's got heat rash, poor little thing." She smiled as Isaac hoisted the baby to rest against his shoulder with the ease of one accustomed to helping with younger siblings.

The men were coming up the path to the house and Hallie could hear their conversation through the open door.

"You could roast a goose in this heat." It was Rueben speaking in a grumpy voice.

"Crops are sure hurting," Will spoke. "Wish that little bank of clouds off in the west would bring some rain."

The men paused in front of the soddy and studied the clouds huddled timidly on the horizon. "Don't look like much, I don't tink," Oskar commented and the men after rinsing off the dust at the wash bench, came inside.

By the time the men had finished lunching and were taking the last swallows of their cooling coffee, a faint rumble of thunder was detected. Chairs were hastily shoved back, and the men went out to inspect the sky.

"By golly, she's built up and a moving this way," Will exclaimed gleefully.

Hallie, with the baby in her arms came to stand with the men and eye the sky. Sure enough, a huge cliff-like thunderhead was moving rapidly their way. There was more thunder and a flash of distant lightning. Dare they hope?

The giant cloud continued to move their way. The cloud was directly overhead by the time the Andreasons had filled their barrels and were preparing to start home. They all grinned jubilantly at one another as the first big drops of rain fell. The drops felt icy to their skin. Then...the first pellets of hail came...clinking as they glanced off an upturned bucket by the well.

There were only a few of the gaily-bouncing white marbles at first...just threatening. Then the wind hit, driving the now thickly falling hailstones with an added force. They had retreated to stand in the doorway of the soddy, watching the ground become white with hail. The air, once so sultry, was now cold. The hail stopped abruptly after an assault of perhaps fifteen minutes. Then the rain came, soaking the thirsty fields where the crops lay battered to the ground.

Helplessly, they looked out through the falling rain at the pulverized remains of the oat field, knowing that in all likelihood the other fields in the valley were in similar condition. All the hours of work, the hopes had been for naught. As though by mutual agreement, the heavy-hearted men avoided one another's eyes and the naked hurt mirrored there.

Oskar cleared his throat and spoke to Isaac whose young eyes held tears. Hard years of experience influenced his words. "Du Lord, He gives, und du Lord, He takes. Ve vill yust have tu try some more."

Chapter 30

The men, Will, Rueben, Oskar, and Danjel, left the following week. When Rueben had accompanied the Adams family to Grand Island earlier, he had heard that extra workers were often hired for the construction work of the railroad spur being built some fifty miles southeast of McCain Valley. The men were going to see if they could find employment there for without crops to harvest they must earn money to see them all through the winter. The women and children were left behind to manage the homesteads.

At least this time I am not alone in the valley, Hallie consoled herself remembering those times Will had been on the roundups with the Hartwell crew. Will and the others had left at daybreak and Hallie had walked down to the well to get a bucket of water. As she pulled the brimming bucket of cold water to the top of the well, she gave thanks for the double blessing of both neighbors and water.

Though the two households provided morale support for one another, they did not spend a great deal of time together. They were simply too busy. Despite the ruined crops, there was plenty of work to be done. The hail-damaged gardens must somehow be coaxed back to life. Root crops such as potatoes, turnips and carrots might still produce though they would be late. The tender melon vines were gone as were the beans. Some of the hardy squash and pumpkin vines looked as though they might be getting new leaves. If frost held off into the fall, there should be some vegetables to put away for winter.

There were the chickens to watch over. Following Pearl's example, Hallie had loaned a couple of her hens to Charlotte when they began to show signs of being broody, so that she too, might start a poultry flock.

The mustangs were now gentle enough that they could be turned into the fenced pasture. The job of watering them had been allotted to Isaac who proudly saw to the task.

Oskar had left his team behind so his family could haul water and to provide transportation if and when needed. The other three had taken their teams for Rueben had been told that teams were also needed.

A task that was shared and they all actually came to enjoy was the gathering and hauling of cowchips. A trip to the lake for a load of chips was considered a holiday. A picnic dinner was packed and little William's bed taken along. Inga was usually given the job of keeping track of rambunctious Alfred who darted about through the chip-gathers like a frisky puppy. Hallie could not help but laugh at the little fellow's antics, grateful William had not yet reached that stage.

These trips to the lake were a welcome change from the routine work at home. The chip gathering was done at a leisurely pace with a generous amount of teasing and playing by the young ones.

On one of these excursions, the boys were in a particular teasing mood. "Here's a gud vun for ya Kristina! It's a nice big vun." Isaac was pointing to a big, wet fresh pile left by a cow that very morning when she had come in for a drink.

Wisely, his sister called back from where she bent down for the last dry chip needed to complete her armload. "Thank you, no. I got all I can carry." Kristina had placed the last chip on those already in her arms and was holding the dry, odorless object in place with her chin.

This maneuver caught Isaac's notice and recalling how sensitive his sisters had been in the beginning about handling the dried cow dung, he made a side remark to Hilding. "Don't ya vunder vat dem fella's that cum hangin' round our place on Sundays vud say if dey cud see dem girls cuddlin' up to dem chips?"

Though her cheeks were pink, Kristina ignored her now giggling brothers. It was true several young men as well as a few not so young, had come calling since the pretty Andreason daughters had been discovered at the Fourth of July doings in Dry Bend. Nute Whipple was pursuing his interest in golden-haired Hulda taking advantage of the fact his chief rival was away working on the railroad spur.

Another of the hopeful suitors who came calling was an older bachelor homesteading north of the Mitchell place. He had a ripe aroma, a straggly beard stained by tobacco juice and a tendency to stutter. Isaac and Hilding were in their element after a visit from this fellow, and to provoke their sisters, began to mimic him now. Having divested themselves of their own armload of chips, they hooked their thumbs under their suspenders to give them a hitch, gave a spit off to the side and then stuttered out imaginary compliments. "Y-y-yu s-s-sure is a purdy g-g-gurl. Vud y-y-ya marry m-m-me?"

The chips Hulda and Kristina were carrying were dropped at this point and a wild chase around the wagon and across the lakeshore ensued with shrieking girls in pursuit of whooping boys.

Hallie smiled the next day remembering the teasing and fun of the day before. She was hanging out wash on the line. Certainly, the older Andreason girls did not lack for admirers…some quite nice looking in fact. But out here it would only lead to a life in a soddy or worse…a dugout among some lonely hills. She tucked a strand of windblown hair back beneath her sunbonnet as she stooped to take another freshly laundered diaper from the pail at her feet. She gave it a quick shake then took a couple of wooden clothespins from her apron pocket. She couldn't help feeling sorry for the girls despite the attention they were receiving. They were missing so many of the things she and her sisters had taken for granted…parties, pretty dresses, church socials, shopping, the gaiety and frivolity she had enjoyed.

Hallie's hands, pinning up the wet square of flannel, were red and wrinkled from the soaking they'd received in the hot, lye-soaped washtub. She gave them a rueful look. A girl should have those few carefree years. She heard the baby's demanding cry from the open door of the soddy where his box bed sat. Carrying the now empty pail she hurried toward the house.

"Mommy's coming!" she called in a placating voice and stepped up on the wooden doorstoop. A scream locked in her throat as her eyes met the flat unblinking ones of the rattler sunning full length on the floor in the square of sunshine inside the doorway.

The baby cried in his bed placed near the door so Hallie could hear him if he fussed while she was outside washing. Rigid, Hallie cautioned herself, "Keep calm! Think!" The snake had his eyes on her, but for how long? William's tiny fists waved angrily above the edge of the box as he cried his displeasure at being kept waiting. What if the snake noticed those moving fists…struck at one? The empty bucket, completely forgotten slid from her fingers and plunked down on the stoop. The snake struck at the bucket hitting the hard, metal surface with a "ping".

Hallie jumped backward more from reflex than thought into the yard. She looked wildly about for a weapon. The garden hoe was tilted against the soddy wall. Grabbing the hoe, Hallie went back to the doorway. The snake, now coiled, lay by the bucket that had rolled inside the doorway, his ugly head reared and tail vibrating a constant buzz. Hallie lifted the hoe high and brought it down with all her strength. Crippled, the snake writhed and struck at the hoe blade. Again and again, Hallie lifted the hoe and brought it down until all that was left of the snake were bloody remains and broken dirt clods where she had chopped the floor.

Hallie dropped the hoe and lifted the now screaming infant from his gore-spattered bed. She ran from the house with the baby in her arms. Her knees weak and trembling, she walked up and down, tears of fright on her cheeks. The baby had quieted and was asleep before she could force herself to re-enter the soddy and the mess awaiting her.

When the baby was tucked safely on the big bed in the back room Hallie faced the task of disposing of the dead snake. Using the hoe, she scraped the oozy heap and bloody dirt out the door. A hole was dug and the mess buried. Fresh dirt was sprinkled over the floor and packed down smoothly. The baby's bed was wiped clean with a wet, soapy cloth. All evidence of the incident was gone. All that remained was a gnawing premonition. Sooner or later, an encounter with a rattlesnake would not end as fortunately as it had that day.

Chapter 31

Darkness was settling in. The heat from the early September day clung heavily upon the valley. Hallie sat by the table reading a copy of Clyde DeWitt's latest efforts at his newly established "Dry Bend Tribune". Ethel Hartwell saved their copy to pass on to Hallie. Isaac had dropped it off on his way back from the ranch where he had ridden to check on the mail.

A feeble breeze crept in through the open door pestering the lamp flame, making the shadow caper on the clay walls. A few fat, lazy flies bumbled and buzzed about the room hoping to discover some uncovered edible. A coyote on the ridge rendered a sudden, sharp falsetto yap. Startled, Hallie jarred the table and made the oil in the lamp sway drunkenly in it's glass base. The flame sputtered sending up a frail spiral of black smoke to streak the freshly cleaned chimney.

Hallie put the paper aside and went to listen at the door. She hated these dark, lonely nights with Will away. During the day she was kept busy, but the nights.... The coyote, it sounded like a young one, was really getting wound up. He punctuated each disjointed bark with experimental howls that cracked and wavered on the high notes. Hallie smiled listening to his inept rendition. It sounded as though he suffered from a bad case of adolescent voice change. The coyote gave up. All was quiet again except for the buzz of the sleepy flies and the soft lulling night songs of the friendly katydids outside in the grass. Hallie peeked in the back room. William was sleeping soundly, his small arms up by his head, the tiny fingers curled into miniature fists beside plump, baby cheeks.

Back at the table, she sat down and resumed reading. There was a smattering of political news, details on the progress of the railroads and a column of social activities such as they were. There was an article describing the soon to be finished brick bank and one announcing the cancellation of the evangelistic meetings to have been held by Reverend Sorenson. It seemed the unfortunate gentleman was laid up with a broken leg he'd obtained when his horse had fallen with him recently.

Near the bottom of page one, (there were only two pages to an issue), there was an advertisement. It offered a reward for information leading to the capture of the cattle thieves known to be operating in the region. Her eyes skipped on to the adjoining advertisement detailing a yard goods sale at Huebanks' Mercantile. She scoured the list of sale items with interest. How nice it would be to be able to afford such purchases. Her fingers fairly itched to be sewing. Perhaps there would be enough money from Will's earnings for material to make Will a couple of nice shirts and a length of dress goods. The baby was growing out of the little garments she had made for him earlier, also.

Hallie, elbows on the open newspaper, her chin resting on cupped hands, drifted off into a tantalizing daydream...she was entering Huebanks' Mercantile, dressed very fashionably, of course, as befitted the wife of one of the county's established ranchers. An eager clerk steps forward, but Mr. Huebanks motions him aside preferring to wait upon such a distinguished customer himself. Escorted by the proprietor, she saunters over to the yard goods department and delicately fingers the displayed fabrics. She chooses pretty ginghams, soft wools, and flannels, enough to keep her sewing for months. Hallie could almost smell the newly dyed cloth and the satisfaction of cutting into new material with sharp scissors.

The lamplight shed a complimentary glow upon Hallie's face, the blue eyes staring, lost in the fantasy being entertained in her mind.

"Ma'am." A man's voice spoke from the darkness outside the door. "Can you help me?"

The daydream splintered into fragments. A startled Hallie sprang to her feet knocking her chair backwards to the floor with a thud. The outline of a man's figure could be discerned dimly just beyond the reach of the light. Hallie edged back toward the corner where the stove sat, keeping her eye on the door. She felt for the handle of the skillet she'd left to dry upturned on the cooling stovetop. Gripping the handle tightly, she gathered enough courage to ask in a voice she hopped held a note of authority, "Who's out there?"

The figure moved forward and stood swaying in the doorway. "Don't be afraid, ma'am. I'm just hurt, is all."

The man was obviously too weak to be dangerous, Hallie realized and released her grip on the skillet. Perhaps the stranger sensed he had reached refuge for having held to what must have been his last remnant of strength, he allowed himself to crumple into a heap inside the door.

Hallie went to kneel beside the unconscious man. She managed to turn him so she could examine his chest. The front of his shirt was caked with dried blood and dirt. His fall had started the bleeding again for fresh blood was beginning to ooze around the dried stain. She unbuttoned his shirt and worked it gently back from the bleeding shoulder. Hallie sucked in her breath as she saw the small, round, blue-edged hole.

"That's got to be a bullet hole!" Hallie spoke in an awed whisper.

Thus began an experience Hallie never spoke of, not to a living soul…not until she was a great grandmother and a widow of many years.

On that night in the fall of 1881, Hallie discovered as she further examined the wound that another hole dribbled blood on his back. The bullet must have entered the right side of his chest and came out his back, she concluded. The path of the bullet was far enough to the side of his body that the bullet had perhaps only grazed the lung, or so she hoped as she anxiously scanned the pages of the doctor book a few minutes later. She learned as she read the pages devoted to the treatment of such wounds, how fortunate a patient was if the bullet passed through rather than lodging in the body. Numerous difficulties could result in such cases, all of them beyond her capabilities. As it was, the book advised little more than to clean the wound, provide the patient with rest and nourishment and let nature take its course.

Hallie made a pallet from a folded quilt and by tugging and lifting, managed to shift her patient on to it. She removed the filthy shirt, and with soapy water began to do what she could to clean away the blood and grime. He was a nice looking young man. Under his deep tan, his face though tired and drawn, appeared amicable with a mouth edged at the corners by "smile lines". Dark lashes lay spent upon the sun-browned cheeks now ashen from loss of blood. It was apparent he had kept himself clean-shaven in the past though whisker stubbles now covered the lower portion of his face. Hair, a rich chestnut and curly, was dusty and tangled above a wide forehead.

He must have lost his hat, Hallie thought pushing the hair back from the pale forehead with a wet cloth. She contemplated the face for a moment as she rinsed the cloth in the pan of water setting beside her on the floor. Who was he? Homesteader? Cowboy?" Bank robber?? "Don't be silly!" She told herself. "He's probably just a hapless cowboy who got shot by some hothead during a quarrel."

The bandaging was in progress when her patient began to moan and his eyes flickered open. "Who are you?" Hallie asked softly. "What is your name?"

The gray eyes attempted to focus. "J-Jake," he managed.

"You've been shot." It was more of a question than a statement.

The eyes found hers, debated and then, "Hunting. It was a hunting accident," he whispered.

Hallie was almost certain that this was not the truth, but for reasons she could not then or later have explained, she did not consider betraying the trust he had bestowed upon her.

Propped against a folded pillow, Jake, that was the only name he would give, managed to swallow several spoonfuls of warm broth from supper's left over stew. He grew drowsy as soon as he'd eaten, and Hallie thought he had dozed off when he spoke again.

"Could you water my horse, ma'am?"

She assured him that she would. When she stood up to go do so, he called weakly. "Don't tell anybody I'm here."

For five days Hallie hid both Jake and his horse. She had kept her promise and had not even divulged his presence to any members of the Andreason family who came for water or to care for the mustangs. During the day, Jake lay on his pallet in the back room hidden from view by the bed in case one of the Abdreasons should happen to glance behind the curtain that hung across the bedroom doorway.

The jaded horse had been led through the dark that first night to a draw over the ridge where he was tethered to graze. The saddle and bridle were hidden in some brush, and each night Hallie carried water to the horse and re-staked his rope to a new patch of grass.

None of the Andreasons appeared to suspect anything unusual at their neighbor's though Hallie knew Hulda was disappointed when she turned down a supper invitation.

"I'll come another time." Hallie had hunted for an excuse. "William's cutting a tooth and sort of fussy." At least that wasn't a fib. Hallie consoled herself as Hulda accepting this reply said to remember to send word with Isaac if she should need anything. William truly was cutting a tooth.

As Jake grew stronger he never spoke of recent times. He talked instead of his parents and their place back in Virginia. The war had changed it all, he said. His father had been killed, his older brother had lost an arm in the fighting. Taxes and poor prices had taken the farm after the war. Their mother had died...a broken heart...Jake figured. He and his brother had come west. And that was where his story always ended. What they had none since, he never said. Hallie was wise enough not to ask.

Jake had been well brought up. Hallie could tell. He was courteous to the extreme, speaking in his soft, southern drawl and always quick with his ma'am's when addressing her. He encouraged Hallie to tell of her family in Missouri, her childhood, the orchard, the friends she'd known there. He marveled at the carefree childhood years she'd enjoyed comparing them no doubt with his own during and following the Civil War. They laughed together as Hallie described her Aunt Susie's hats and how Hallie and her cousin, Emily, had vowed to wear trousers when they were grown up. Hallie had blinked back tears when Jake spoke of his mother and his memories of her. How she had made him promise when she knew she was dying to remember God's commandments and to stay close to his brother as they would be all that remained of the family.

As Jake grew stronger, they talked for hours on end, sharing their thoughts and ideas about life and people in general. Hallie had never confided in anyone, not even Emily, as she found herself doing with Jake. For instance, she might ask a question such as, "Have you ever noticed how men and cows always reach for the grass on the other side of the fence, always certain it must be greener or tastier on the other side? And how women and horses are content with the grass close at hand?"

Jake had chuckled. "I'll not argue with you on that. I reckon you have us critters pretty well pegged. Men want to search out new places, and women want to build a nest and stay put. My mother used to say she pitied the women having to go west with their men, but she envied them, too. And, she said if she'd had better health, she would have taken us boys after the war and headed west." He shook his head. "I've often wondered how things would have been if she had lived. I think Matt would have seen things differently."

By the third day, Jake was able to get up and walk a bit. In the evenings when it had grown dark, they would sit on the stoop and talk. Jake liked to study the stars and point them out. He knew the names of many of the constellations. He confided that as a child, he had dreamed of becoming an astronomer. They would locate the "Big Dipper" in the sky and Jake told of how his father had used it to

195

predict rain. If it was tipped so the "water could run out" it was supposed to rain. "It worked sometimes," Jake chuckled.

Jake was so easy to talk to, such a good listener, Hallie found. When she and Will talked it was Hallie who listened…if and when Will was in the mood to talk. Hallie had never told anyone how much she had dreaded the move to Nebraska. Now, she found herself confiding it all…the secret hope Will would change his mind and move back to Missouri. Telling these things to Jake did not seem like disloyalty to Will, but simply an exchange of thoughts and feelings with a kindred spirit.

Five days passed then on the evening of the fifth day when supper was over, Jake told Hallie he would be leaving as soon as it was dark.

"You're not strong enough to travel," she found herself protesting. "Wait another day."

"I wish I could, ma'am. I surely do, but Matt, he'll be thinking the worst if I don't show up soon."

And Hallie had known he was right. Sooner or later, Isaac or someone would discover either Jake or his horse.

Hallie had carried the baby and walked with Jake to where she had hidden his horse and saddle. Jake offered to carry the baby, but she had refused knowing even William's slight weight was more than Jake should attempt to carry up the ridge. She did hand the baby to him to hold while she saddled the horse. There was nothing left then but to say goodbye. Jake took her hand and raised it to his lips. He placed a gentle kiss on her fingertips.

"Goodbye, ma'am. I'll be beholden to you for as long as I live."

It was an effort for Jake to mount, but he accomplished it. He looked down at Hallie by the faint light of the narrowed moon. With a somber smile he reached down and gently tweaked a curl on her forehead. "Goodbye, Hallie."

He nudged his horse with a boot heel and it moved off slowly. Jake was looking back over his shoulder, but Hallie could not see his face clearly…the words that floated back to her, however, were. Through the quiet night came, "I love you, Hallie."

Hallie caught her breath. A lump rose in her throat. The soft plunk, plunk of the horse's hooves grew fainter…faded away. Jake was gone as he had come. A feeling of profound deprivation enveloped her…something was gone she had never had before and would never have again.

The baby shifted in her arms. Hallie tucked the blanket more closely about him, and started the walk back to the soddy. In the sky the Big Dipper twinkled, its seven stars distant beacons in the night.

Chapter 32

Will and the others came home for a short visit over one weekend. He hugged Hallie close and declared, "I've missed you like the dickens, honey! And you, young fella, you're growing like a weed," he'd said to the baby and chucked him under the chin.

William promptly puckered up and cried, frightened by this loud, male voice he'd forgotten. Hallie could tell Will felt hurt by his tiny son's reaction, and assured, "You've just startled him. He'll be back to being Daddy's boy by suppertime."

"I reckon so," Will agreed. "It's not good, having to be away like this. Can't blame the little fella if he forgets me."

The baby watched his father with big eyes as Will explained how they had gotten a few days off...a delayed rail shipment. "All kinds of men working there. They come from way off, some of them. But, there's plenty just like us...homesteaders trying to earn enough to tide them over for one reason or another." And Will continued to describe his job and the men he worked with.

Hallie put the baby back into his bed and went about preparing a meal. I'm back to being the listener, she thought as she began to peel potatoes. Will hasn't even asked what's been happening here. "Are all husbands like that or is it just Will?" she asked herself as she sliced a potato into a kettle. "Would Jake become like that if he married someday?"

On Sunday, the men were planning to leave in the early afternoon. They all gathered at the Andreason's for dinner. Geoffrey and the twins showed up, and Nute Whipple rode in as he was apt to do most Sundays. His grin, Hallie noticed, appeared a bit forced when he discovered Rueben helping Hulda set up a plank table in the yard.

Charlotte had just called dinner when one of the men spotted some hazy, gray clouds hovering above the hills to the northwest. Geoffrey gave his grim opinion. "I reckon that's smoke we see off up there."

It was smoke, rising ominously from the burning prairie. Rueben had jumped on his horse and ridden to the top of a hill. He returned to report the fire, a big one, pushed by the wind was coming their way. How it had started would remain a mystery. Lightning? Campfire? Sparks from a stovepipe on some grass-covered dugout?

The fire came on toward the valley pushed by an intensifying wind, its vanguard widening every mile. The smoke had already reached the valley, and the air grew thick with it as the men used teams and wagons to haul water barrels out to the plowed fireguards. With the wind blowing the fire was apt to jump the bare ground of the fireguards.

The women and children went inside the house to escape the smoke, closing the windows and doors. From the windows, they could see the fire sweeping down the flat land on the western edge of the valley. The hungry flames greedily devoured the dry, brittle fall grasses, never satiated, bent on destruction.

The head of the fire had now angled across toward Danjel's quarter. Thwarted by the plowed guard strips yet goaded by the wind, it spit bits of burning grass across the band of bare ground then swerved south. The fire now stretched from Andreason's borders to the west edge of the valley, up onto the west ridge and beyond into the hills. It was far too large a fire for a few fighters to extinguish. All they could do was hope to keep it from jumping their fireguards and if it did to fight those smaller areas.

The men and older boys spread out along the west boarders of both Danjel's and Oskar's land, watching for those smoldering missiles the wind was sending across the fireguards. They carried buckets containing wet gunnysacks to beat out any flames that sprang up on their side. The smoke became so dense that in order to breathe they were forced to tie wet handkerchiefs over their noses and mouths as they watched and fought these outbreaks of fire.

The fire passed on cutting through the hills to the southwest. The valley homesteads were safe unless the wind changed directions. The tired group returned to the Andreasons to rest and eat the dinner that had been kept warm for them.

The men decided not to leave as planned but to lay over another day. There was danger some smoldering tuft of grass or a cowchip might re-ignite if stirred by a breeze. Will and the others would take turns watching through the night, make certain the danger of fire was over before they left.

Hallie, carrying William, went home to check on Daisy and the chickens. The smell of smoke was still strong enough to make her eyes smart so she kept the blanket over the baby's face protecting him as much as she could from the acrid air. Thank the dear Lord, the men and the fireguards had stopped the fire! What would we have done if the men had been away? Hallie wondered. "The whole valley would have burned, most likely," she answered herself with silent certainty.

As Hallie walked she stopped and turned to look back. All was black from the fireguards in the valley to as far as she could see into the west hills. In the gathering dusk all was black where the fire had passed except for the occasional red cherry glow in the ashes of a soapweed root or a cowchip. Far off in the hills to the south, she could see the molten ruby line of the fire as it moved on. She thought of others who might live in its path. All any of them could do was what those in the valley had done…rely on precaution, and prayer. And Hallie thought of how Charlotte had had them all kneel and bow their heads to ask the Lord's guidance and protection for the men as they had waited out the fire.

Later, they would learn that all had not been as fortunate as those in the valley. The fire had burnt a wide swath that had angled in such a way it missed the ranch buildings at the Hartwell Ranch, but caught the haystacks on their open meadow several miles south, burning a good portion.

Word trickled back, a homesteader had lost his corn crop and a sow with a litter of pigs. The man and his family had been spared by their staying in their dugout as the fire swept over its grassy roof. Another homesteader had been overcome by smoke as he fought the fire at the edge of his corn patch. His charred remains were found where he had fallen. The fire slowed and then died out when at last it reached the river some thirty miles to the south of McCain Valley.

At four o'clock on the Tuesday morning following the fire, the men started back to their jobs. Once again the women and children were left alone in the valley to fend for themselves. As before, they would have little time for idleness. Preparations for winter must be made. More cowchips had to be hauled. The potatoes had to be dug and stored as would the other root crops. The lovely, balmy days of fall would be put to good use.

The wild plums were late that fall and not plentiful, but they searched out thickets in low areas where runoff from the rains had supplied extra moisture. These thickets produced a good supply for jams and jellies to be made up for winter. Charlotte and Hallie had experimented and found that pitted plums dried well. These could be used for sauce or pies later on. Picking the fruit was more like play than work. They all gorged themselves on the fruit as they picked, relishing the taste of fresh fruit.

On one such day, Hallie sat William in his box in the shade of a plum bush where she was picking. She knew from past experience he would lie in his bed entertained by the birds and the floating clouds. He's a good baby, she thought proudly. Already, he shows promise of self-reliance and having an independent spirit. Little Alfred had similar qualities she had to concede as she watched the little fellow scamper happily about in pursuit of a wily ground squirrel. His attention was diverted at that moment by a fat, sluggish bumblebee. Before Hallie could call a warning, he had received a sting on his inquisitive fist. His cry of outrage brought his scattered, fruit-picking family on the run.

Hallie advised Hulda to get the water jug from under the wagon where it sat in the shade. They made a handful of mud to hold against the swelling bump on the little hand. The cooling poultice eased the hurt and would bring down the swelling, Hallie assured. A temporarily subdued Alfred went to curl up in the shade by the baby. He gave some sound advice to the now drowsing William. "No touch bad bug! Bad bugs bite!"

Hallie dropping plums into her pail, smiled as she listened. Warnings never seemed to do much good. For some reason it generally took the real thing to truly make an impression. William would undoubtedly have to take his lumps just like Alfred and the rest of the world. She paused in her picking to look over at the two handsome youngsters. Oh, if one could only shield them from all hurt! But...she knew it couldn't be. Regretfully, it seemed, everyone had to learn for themselves.

Numerous trips were made to the lake for chips to be stacked on the south side of the soddies so they would be sheltered from the wet snows that were bound to come. Hallie even stacked a supply in one end of the chicken dugout to insure added dryness for at least part of her fuel. She remembered the difficulty in burning chips coated with snow.

Hallie fretted about the lack of a root cellar. She doubted Will would be home in time to get one dug before the ground froze. It was Charlotte who suggested they dig a pit in the floor of their soddies.

She said she had seen it done in the old country. Though not ideal, it would protect such things as potatoes, carrots and turnips.

Charlotte had Isaac and Hilding dig a pit at the end of one of their bedrooms. The root vegetables were harvested and placed in the pit. The pit was then filled with sand until it was level with the floor. It was not ideal, but as Hallie said when the same procedure was done at her house, "It would be handy in cold weather."

Isaac and Hilding had helped Hallie dig not only her vegetables, but they dug a pit for her to store them at the far end of her bedroom. In fact, all the Andreasons pitched in to help at times during the process.

"It would have taken me forever if I'd had to do it by myself," Hallie told them gratefully. "I don't know how to thank you."

Charlotte pooh-poohed her thanks aside.

"Vell, ve yust help vun another. Ve are neighbors!"

For Charlotte, that settled it. But Hallie knew how fortunate she was to have the kind, helpful family nearby.

Chapter 33

There was a killing frost in late September. Hallie and the Andreasons had sensed its coming and picked their sparse pumpkin and squash yield from the damaged vines to stack in the back rooms of their soddies. Overnight the foliage of the few garden flowers that had somehow survived the hail, turned black. The last of their blossoms withered. Hallie hated to see them go.

"Why is ugliness often so durable? Beauty so fragile?" Hallie asked herself these questions as she returned from viewing the dead flowers. As she walked she looked out across the valley to where the fire had burnt. That charred unsightliness would be with them until the growth of new grass next spring or the white camouflage of snow.

At the thought of winter Hallie gave an involuntary shudder. Fall would seen be gone and the confinement of the cold, snow-laden season would be upon them. All summer the expectation of "visiting come fall" had dangled before her like the proverbial carrot on a stick. Now, with Will working away, such plans had of course, been put aside. It would have been nice though, to have at least gotten over to see Pearl and the rest of the McNeils, Hallie pondered regretfully. And they'd not been able to issue invitations with Will gone. They had never had the promised Sunday with the Loomis family coming over with the McNeils.

She was at the well filling the pail she had left there on her way to the garden when the inspiration struck her. Maybe Charlotte and all of them would like to go visiting the McNeils. They could use the Andreason wagon. Hallie could fix food to take.

"Vy, not?" Charlotte exclaimed when Hallie broached the subject. "It vud be gud for us and the young vuns, too."

Sunday proved a pleasant, sunny day…ideal for the long drive ahead. An abundance of food was packed, and with everyone dressed for visiting, and Isaac driving, they set forth.

"Let's circle by to see if der is any mail," Hulda suggested, and her brothers had to tease. They knew she was hoping for a letter from Rueben. Their mother, however, put a damper on the teasing.

"Dat vud be a good idea. There might be letter from Papa or Mr. McCain," she said firmly. "Ve vill go by, don't ya think so, Hallie?"

So a stop was made at the Hartwell Ranch. Ethel was delighted to see them and insisted they all come in for a cup of coffee. Coffee as always, meant more than it implied. There were fresh cookies to pass around the table and milk for the smaller children. All this was served with bits of news from the ranch and community at large.

Hallie had never seen Ethel Hartwell happier. Jonny sat in his highchair as bright and chipper as could be. "Daddy will come today," he chirped. "Terry and Teddy, too."

He isn't forgetting his father or brothers, Hallie could see, but also noted the glow in her friend's eyes when the little fellow said a few minutes later, "Mama, more milk," and held up his cup.

Jonny thinks of Ethel as his mother, and…what of Ethel? Is she facing reality? After all, Jonny is growing. By next year, Geoffrey will likely be able to keep him at home with the older boys. Will Ethel be prepared to give up the child that is filling the emptiness left by her own lost children?

Hallie had her answer just as they were getting ready to leave. Jonny, down from his chair, spied his father and the twins riding up. The door was open and he was off like a shot. "Daddy! Daddy!" he called. Hallie caught the flicker of pain that darted across the older woman's face. It was only for an instant, and then she had stepped out on the porch to wave and smile at the new arrivals. But…the pain had been there. Hallie was certain of that, just as she felt certain more heartache lay ahead for Ethel Hartwell.

The McNeils were living in the new sod house. Will had planned on helping Sam with the building, but the hailstorm had changed those plans, too. It looked as though Sam and his sons had managed quite well on their own, Hallie thought as they were shown around. The new house was not as large as that of the Hartwells, but it had four good-sized rooms and a loft. And like the Hartwell's, it had wooden floors throughout. Each room had two windows that Pearl had curtained with brightly dyed and ruffled flour sacking. The furnishings were meager, but Sam confided to Hallie when Pearl was out of hearing, "I got a settee ordered at Huebanks'. "It's going' to be Pearl's surprise at Christmas!" Sam's eyes sparkled as he whispered his secret.

"You'd almost think…no it couldn't be that…Sam just want's to show his appreciation for Pearl's sacrifice. And it's the least he can do," Hallie told herself.

The McNeil children and the younger Andreasons had eyed one another shyly. It was after all, a number of weeks since they had seen one another. Then…"Any of ya want to go see the new puppy we got?" The ice was broken. The whole passel of youngsters trooped off happily.

The changes Pearl had made in the McNeil clan seemed to have no end, Hallie marveled as the visit progressed. Cleanliness, manners, orderly meals…no dog under the table! One would never believe it to be the same family of less than a year ago. What a pity Mattie had never been able to manage a household, Hallie mused sadly. She had put so much effort into it with only "muddles" as a result. Despite her failings, she had been loved. There had never been any doubt of that.

"And now, the children she left behind will turn out well, thanks to Pearl." And perhaps for the hundreth time, Hallie said to herself, "Pearl is such a remarkable woman…practically a saint!"

The time with the McNeils passed all too swiftly. The boys were called from the "outlaw hideout" the McNeil boys had in a washout over the ridge. Nancy and Inga came reluctantly from the shady side of the house where they had spent the precious hours together playing house. The women and the older girls had had a grand visit after dinner while Sam fell asleep over the newspaper he had started to read. But, the sun sets its course and makes no allowances for days folks wish were longer.

'Ve vill have to go if we gets home before the dark," Charlotte reminded the children. Hallie agreed. There were chores waiting. They must get started. Sam went to fetch the team. "I'll be with you in a minute," Hallie called as she went back into Pearl's bedroom to get the little bundle of diapers he had brought along for William. She bent to pick up a bib that had been dropped on the floor. And there…staring her straight in the face from beneath the hem of the coverlet on Pearl's bed was one of Sam's dress boots! The toe of its mate was visible in the shadows behind it.

As though mesmerized, Hallie remained bent over, the bib in her hand. Those boots hadn't gotten under Pearl's neatly made bed by accident…not in this well-ordered house!

Pearl spoke from the doorway, "Did you lose something, Hallie?" Hallie jerked upright as though stung. She felt as guilty as though she'd been caught rifling through one of the dresser drawers.

"Y-Yes, but I've found it," and she held up the bib and then poked it into the baby's bag.

The two women hurried out to where the others were climbing into the wagon.

Isaac 'Giddy upped", and the wagon rolled off amid a chorus of goodbyes. Hallie turned to look back over her shoulder. Sam and Pearl stood side by side, surrounded by children, little Matilda in Pearl's arms.

Pearl! Sensitive...educated. How could she bring herself to sleep with a man she didn't love? These thoughts whirled in Hallie's mind as she turned to catch something Hulda was saying. At the same time another thought was nudging its way into her troubled mind. "How do you know?" it asked. "How do you know Pearl does not love Sam? Perhaps loved him for a long time."

"It would explain a lot of things," Hallie had to admit to the nudging thought. And she lifted her face to the placid September sky. "I take it back. Pearl is a remarkable woman...and a good woman, I don't say different, but...she is not a candidate for sainthood!"

September passed into October, one day following another with little variation. The weather remained mild after the first frost for nearly three weeks. The nights and early mornings were cool, but the afternoons were like summer.

Will wrote to say he and the others would be coming home to stay by the first of November. Hallie was to make a list of things she would need for the winter and send it to him. He would bring the supplies home when he came. Will had also written that he might buy some coal. It would be a luxury to have coal to hold a fire at night now that they had the baby.

It was difficult to make out the list to send Will. Hallie did her best to keep it short, yet it grew lengthy. There were such staples as flour, molasses, salt, soda, vinegar, sugar, cornmeal, and dried beans, kerosene. She hesitated then added raisins. There were still coffee beans to list and they were dear. Her shoes were badly worn. They'd have to do, she decided. At least she had her good shoes to wear when they went somewhere. Two pairs of wool stockings were put on the list and two pair for Will.

There was little William. Not so little anymore. She must order several yards of flannel to make new shirts and nightgowns for him.

She would not order anything else. Will's wages would have to stretch over the winter. And maybe, just maybe, there would be enough money to buy a milk cow! That would be a birthday present indeed!

Isaac took the letter and a similar one addressed to his father from Charlotte, to the Hartwell post office. On his way back, as was his custom, he stopped by to chat with Hallie and leave her mail. Ethel Hartwell had sent the Dry Bend paper to Hallie. That day there was also a letter from Hallie's cousin, Emily.

Isaac didn't tarry as he did some times for he carried a letter from his maternal grandmother in Sweden. "Mama vill be so happy," he explained his eagerness to leave. "She vill cry." Then quickly he assured, "But it vill be happy tears."

Hallie understood exactly how it was. Precious words from home were apt to have such an effect on a person. They must be doubly precious if a whole ocean lay between you and that special loved one writing. She tucked her own letter in her apron pocket. It would be something to look forward to this evening. She would save it until after supper, savor each word of news from home. For now, she would read the Dry Bend paper and see what earth-shattering news it held.

The little paper was often hard-pressed for items of interest. This week's addition had a dull, pompous article reprinted from the Lincoln paper concerning the railroads. Beneath this was a small article bearing the heading, "Justice Carried Out!" The details of a speedy trial and a double hanging that had taken place in an adjoining county were given.

Hallie shifted her bottom on the stoop where she sat, and listened a moment for she thought she'd heard a sound from the bedroom. Satisfied the baby was still sleeping, she resumed her reading. The men brought to justice had been a pair of cattle rustlers caught red-handed. The law had been on their trail for months. They had cornered them once in a canyon a few weeks back. The rustlers had made a daring escape in which the youngest of the pair was wounded.

Hallie continued to read, a feeling of dread filling her heart. The names and descriptions of the now notorious brothers, were given. One-armed, Matthew Roten, age 36, blond and blue-eyed. Jacob Roten, age 25, brown hair, gray eyes, a bullet scar on right shoulder. "JAKE!" The article was describing Jake and his brother, Matt! A wave of nausea washed over Hallie. Jake was dead! Hung by a rope! The paper fell from her lap and fluttered away in the wind. Tears trickled down Hallie's cheeks. The words came back to her that he had spoken when he'd thanked her as he had said goodbye, "I'll be beholden to you for as long as I live."

Dear Jake. He wouldn't be beholden anymore. Nor, would he ever love again. Hallie got up stiffly and went into the house.

Chapter 34

The absent men did not wait until November to return home. They were called back in mid-October and stayed.

This period of October was a blur to Hallie as she looked back on it. First there had been the news in the paper about Jake and then the nights that followed filled with a series of bad dreams. Nightmares in which Hallie would see Jake's face as the hangman's noose was placed over his head, the eyes sad and pleading…then his body hanging limp, swaying in the wind. Time and again, she awoke in a cold sweat from such a dream. She would fight sleep fearing the dream would return if she closed her eyes. She would face a new day with taut nerves and tired body knowing another night would come.

It was after one of these particularly trying nights Kristina appeared at the door with an invitation. "Mama vants to know if yu vant to come make soap vith us?"

"There is nothing I'd like better," Hallie declared and quickly gathered up a few things for the baby and the crock of dripping she had been saving for this purpose. "I could use some good company, today," she told Kristina as they started out. "I've had enough of my own."

Charlotte met then at the door. "Gud, you come. Isaac said you been looking peaked, like."

"Oh, has he?" Hallie laughed. "Well, I'm just fine and ready to get at this soap making."

"Dat ve vill, but first ve got to have coffee." Charlotte shooed her toward the table. A spread of cookies and fresh sweet buns were in readiness. Cups waited to be filled from the pot bubbling on the stove. Hallie took a chair by the table with a feeling of contentment. Having coffee at Charlotte's was much like sitting down with her family in Missouri.

When coffee time was over the preparations for the soap making began. Hilding and Inga rode off on their stick horses to play while Isaac made his escape from "Voman work" to do some mending on a fence. That was what he said, but Hulda said it was most likely to go and play with Danjel's colt.

Little Alfred talked to the baby for a while then trotted off in search of Hilding and Inga. The women had finished melting down the congealed "drippings" and were ready to strain them through a cloth when Alfred let out a shriek from outside.

"Vut, now?" Charlotte, chuckled, half exasperated and started for the door to see what predicament her youngest had gotten into. Kristina had already darted out the door, however.

"I'll see to him, Mama," she called back.

But it was Hilding who was there before any of them. And it was eight-year-old Hilding who used his stick horse to beat the rattler to death that had bitten his little brother on his small chubby, bare foot.

Time is of the essence, this much they knew, in the treating of snakebite. The older girls and Isaac chased in the team. Hallie loaded everyone into the wagon along with a feather tick while Isaac harnessed the team. Within minutes they were started on the six miles that stretched between them and the Hartwell Ranch where hopefully help could be found.

The jouncing wagon had drawn even with her own soddy when Hallie's frantic thoughts recalled something Ebee Whipple had told them in one of his stories concerning snakebite.

"Isaac, stop!" she cried out as she handed William to Hulda. Isaac jerked at the lines as Hallie leaped over the side of the wagon and ran to the dugout at the base of the ridge. In seconds, she dashed back carrying a squawking hen she'd found on the nest.

Those in the wagon must have thought she had lost her mind as she ran up with the chicken. Isaac reached down a hand, to help her back up. The wagon lurched forward. Hallie closed her eyes and with gritted teeth, took a grip with either hand on the soft underside of the hen. She pulled with all her strength, ripping the hen open, exposing the pulsating heart and warm entrails.

Inga screamed. Pairs of incredulous eyes stared. Charlotte drew Alfred closer as Hallie held out the dripping body toward them. Hallie doing her best not to vomit, said, "It's to draw out the poison. Ebee Whipple said it helps."

Charlotte gave a shocked nod, but offered no further resistance. She held out the dusty little leg. Already it was beginning to swell. A purplish-red was spreading from the area of the tiny wounds made by the fangs of the snake. Quickly, the foot was pushed into the warm mass and held firmly.

The drive to the ranch holding the bloody chicken around Alfred's foot seemed endless. When at last they pulled into the yard, Ethel Hartwell with Jonny, was at the gate to meet them. "I saw you coming from the window. I guessed from the way you were driving there was trouble," she explained as those in the wagon gave her details in fear stricken voices. "Snakebite! Well, thank the dear Lord, I just saw Jacob and some of the men ride in. He's had more experience with that than I have."

Jacob Hartwell and a couple of cowboys had not stopped at the barn but came on to the yard. They must have spotted the hurrying wagon as well, and suspected it brought bad news of some sort. The dust hadn't settled around the Andreason's winded team before the Hartwell had taken the drowsy, whimpering child from its mother's arms and stretched him out on the grass of the yard.

"Mrs. Andreason, we need to open this up some and try to suck the poison out. Sometimes, that helps."

Charlotte nodded numbly. "Vot ever is best."

Ethel came running back from the house where she had gone for a pan of hot water. Her husband would need to wash the sharp knife he used for medical purposes. Alfred's bloody foot and the knife were cleaned then Ethel knelt alongside Charlotte. Together they held the little boy while the wound was enlarged.

Charlotte turned white as the knife drew bright blood, but she continued to hold the leg of her son, speaking words of comfort all the while in a soft, Swedish croon. As quickly as the opening was made, Jacob Hartwell bent and placed his lips over it. The procedure of sucking and spitting out the blood from the wound help draw out the venom, they explained.

"The sooner the better, I've heard, Ethel told them. "You folks putting that chicken on his foot like you did probably kept the poison from spreading."

When the task was finished the exhausted, whimpering child was carried into the house. He was placed in the big bed in the room off the dining room. Odorous poultices were concocted out in the kitchen and applied, one after another, through the long hours that followed. Little else could be done other than attempting to keep the child comfortable...pray and wait.

"I sent two men off riding good horses," Jacob Hartwell told Hallie who would relay the information to the tense family gathered in the bedroom. "One of them will take word to that child's daddy, and the other one is going to ride to Hankville. You know that's in the county east of us. Somebody said the other day, they'd heard a doctor had set up practice there. If he's there maybe he'll come and look to the boy."

The older man gave Hallie a straight look. "It's twenty miles I reckon, and like I said, I don't know if there's a doctor there or not. I figure we'd better try what we can. The boy is in bad shape. That's a lot of poison in a body that size."

The hope that had kindled in Hallie's breast at the word, "doctor", flickered out. "You don't think there is much chance for him, do you?"

Jacob Hartwell, shook his head sadly. "The Lord knows I hope I'm wrong."

Oskar and Danjel arrived at the ranch just before sunup the next morning behind a team that had been pushed too hard over too many miles. Danjel's team would never be much use after that trip. Will and Rueben planned to follow as soon as they had settled up with the crew boss and drew what wages were coming to each of the four valley men. Perhaps, they realized they would not be returning to their jobs. Not that fall, anyway.

Less than an hour had passed from the arrival of the Andreason men when a weary cowboy riding a horse he'd borrowed after his gave out, guided a saddlesore young doctor up to the ranch house door. Little Alfred's condition had worsened. His leg was enormous, a feverish dark color. The doctor took one look and shook his head.

Charlotte who had clung to the hope a doctor would be able to perform a miracle of some sort, slumped in her chair by the bed. The tears she'd held back spilled over as she held the small, hot hand. Alfred was oblivious to all this. He lay quietly now, his breath labored. When he opened his eyes, now and again, they were glassy with fever. It had been several hours since he had been aware of those about him.

The doctor made a poultice from something he had in his bag and administered some fever medicine. He admitted honestly that he didn't think it would help. "The child is so young, and obviously it was a large amount of venom."

"Is der nothing?" Oskar pleaded, his voice cracking.

"If he were older, perhaps the poison could be counteracted with a last ditch remedy of arsenic. But, that is apt to kill an adult. I can't try it on a child. It would kill quicker than the venom in one so young."

Such was the sad verdict.

All that sorrowful day, they waited. Will and Rueben got there shortly before noon to stand about helpless with the rest of them. The cowboys went about their chores down by the corrals with hushed voices. They too, were waiting for the inevitable word to come down from the house.

Just as the sun tipped the west hills, spilling vivid hues of flaming pink and gold across the sky, the word was passed. "The little one was gone."

Silently, the cowboys came. They gathered in a cluster outside the house, holding dusty, wide-brimmed hats in their hands. They fumbled the worn felt, embarrassed by unfamiliar emotions. These rough, capable men, Hallie knew, were not strangers to injury and death...far from it. They lived with these adversaries, day by day. They knew the rules of the life they lived, exulted in its challenges. But, they seemed bewildered now. Why should death take the life of a child who didn't even know the rules? And so they stood, confused and saddened, wishing to convey their sympathy in this humble way.

It was from this group that Jacob Hartwell sent out riders to carry the word. Another funeral was to be held. This one would not be at the ranch, however. It would be in McCain Valley for the mother had requested that her son be taken back to his home. Little Alfred would be laid to rest on Andreason land.

Chapter 35

Dawn saw a slow procession consisting of the Andreason's two wagons along with Rueben's and Will's starting the mournful journey back to the valley. When the wagons lumbered slowly down the last ridge, Hallie looked out over the valley from her seat beside Will. It had changed little since the first time she'd seen it not much more than a year ago. The only discernible difference was the dusty little patches of plowed ground and the gray cubes of the soddies.

The prairie fire and its black path have left more of an impression than we humans, Hallie thought as she stared at the emptiness spread before her. Once, I found a sort of beauty here, but no more. "I hate every inch of it!" she told herself as she envisioned the tiny, still form being brought back to the valley to be buried. All this country does is take! It never gives the poor fools who come here anything but empty promises. And she drew little William closer.

"We're home," Will said when he pulled the horses to a stop by the well. "I'll get to the chores. We'll go over to the Andreason's soon as I'm done."

Geoffrey and the twins came riding in while Hallie was making a fire to boil coffee. They had gotten word and had come for the funeral that would be that afternoon. Will sent them in to share coffee and the ginger cookies Hallie sat out. She felt to emotionally drained to make conversation and excusing herself went into the bedroom where she could nurse the baby. Hallie heard Will come in, and later the Mitchells leave. "I should get up," she told herself, but she felt listless and old…just a lump on the bed where she lay.

How can I face the funeral? Poor Charlotte! Poor Oskar…poor all of them!

Hallie clutched William to her breast, fresh tears falling to dampen his fuzz of hair. Dear Lord why? Why did that dear, sweet, little boy have to die?

"Hallie, don't be crying." It was Will. "You've got to be strong."

"I'm tired of being strong!" was Hallie's rebellious answer. "I'm tired of people dying!"

"I reckon we all are, but we've got to deal with what comes."

"Yes, I know." Hallie lay there for a few more moments, then...seemingly resigned, she put the baby down and sat up. "Would you bring in a pan of warm water. I and the baby need to wash up before we dress."

Will went for the water, and Hallie opened the lid of the chest to take out his suit. It should have been aired for it smelled of camphor, but then so will everyone's, Hallie reasoned. These funerals gave little time for niceties.

On the short drive to the Andreasons, Will filled Hallie in on some news Geoffrey had confided. "He and Elva Whipple are getting married. That will be a good thing, don't you think? He can bring Jonny home to live and have all his boys together."

"I know how you felt about Sam and Pearl marrying so soon, but like I've tried to explain, it's different out here. A man with young ones has to have a wife."

Hallie understood this, but she thought of all those who would be affected by the marriage. Ethel Hartwell would have to part with Jonny. The boys would have a new mother. Another woman would be taking Catherine's place...using her things. And Hallie thought of the big, awkward girl expected to fill the roll of wife and mother left vacant by the lovely, gentle-voiced Catherine.

Hallie couldn't help but feel sorry for Elva, Ebee and Angel Whipple's eldest daughter. Would Geoffrey learn to love her? Or will he simply see her primarily as nursemaid and housekeeper? She doubted this marriage of necessity would turn out as well as Pearl's and Sam's. These thoughts were depressing and only added to Hallie's melancholy.

The day proceeded as such days will. By noon, several wagons and a dozen or so horsebackers had arrived. There were the Hartwells, McNeils, Whipples, McCains, and some other area homesteaders. The bachelor whose visits plagued Hulda and Kristina, came. Several cowboys from the Hartwell Ranch rode in. The women all brought food to leave the bereaved family so they need not be troubled with food preparation for a few days.

The turnout for the funeral filled the Andreason soddy. There was not nearly enough seats so many of the men stood, leaving the chairs for the women and family. The coffin, hastily built, sat on a bench by the west wall. Each one as they entered filed respectfully past to view the little child "sleeping" there. There was no minister. Jacob Hartwell would lead the service once again.

Hallie tried to shut out the sound of muffled sobbing as the beautiful words of the Twenty-third Psalm so filled with promise and comfort were read. She closed her eyes shutting out the sight of Charlotte's and Oskar's white, stricken faces. She prayed, "Oh, dear God, be with them. Give them the strength to live through this day…" Hallie's prayer floundered as answerless questions filled her mind. "But, what about tomorrow, and the next, and the next? What about the next child that dies? Will it be another of theirs? Will it be a McNeil? One of Geoffrey's? William?"

A hymn was being sung, "The Old Rugged Cross" with its familiar words. A mammoth lump rose in Hallie's throat. She bit down on her lip to keep from sobbing aloud. Would this never end?

It was over. They were driving to the spot Oskar had designated for the grave. It was a gentle rolling rise of ground just at the northwest corner of the homestead. During the night he and Charlotte had decided. In a choked voice Oskar had explained his intentions to Will and Hallie. "I vill give land. Some day ve vill make a church dere for the valley, you and us."

"That we will, Oskar. That we will. The day'll come when your little boy will be resting in a proper churchyard," Will had assured.

The last prayer was said. Charlotte was led away by Oskar and her remaining children. Hallie, holding William, thought to follow and then changed her mind. It was best for her sorrowing friend to be with her family, now. They will comfort one another.

Folks began to speak of getting home before dark and of chores to do. One by one, the wagons drove off. Hallie, with the baby in her arms, climbed into their wagon.

Hallie waited. The task of filling in the grave had been left to Will and Rueben. The sound of the dirt hitting the coffin lid carried clearly to the wagon where Hallie sat. Each soft thud made something inside of her tighten…tighten and tighten…and then it snapped!

"I've had enough!" Hallie didn't know she had spoken aloud. Her back stiffened, and she sat up straight with her chin lifted. In that instant, Hallie made up her mind. She was going home! Home to Missouri!

Supper was a dismal meal. Neither of the men nor Hallie had any appetite. Rueben went back to his soddy. Hallie stacked the dirty dishes in the dishpan to wait until morning. Her decision to leave had not wavered.

There is no point in putting it off. I'll tell Will now. Maybe, if he realizes I'm serious, that I won't be talked out of it, he'll come to his senses and come with us.

Instead of taking out his pipe and lighting it as he usually did after supper, Will took the baby from his bed to hold. He sat gazing down at his son's eyes sparkling in the lamplight. Hallie steeled herself against this scene and walked over to the window where she could see the faint glimmer of the Andreason's windows. Imagining the sorrow behind those windows strengthened her resolve. She turned to face her husband.

"I'm going home, Will. This is no place to raise William. Come with us!" Hallie went to kneel by her husband's chair. "We've tried it here. It's just not worth what it costs. Let's go home together."

"Hallie, don't ask that. Don't ask me to go back like a whipped pup with his tail between his legs. Can't you understand?"

"You wouldn't be the first to admit he was wrong about this country."

"I'm not wrong! It's good country. Maybe it's harder to claim than we figured, but a man can make it here. It'll take some doing, but it can be done!" Will touched her cheek with his fingers. "Stick it out with me, Hallie."

If the memory of that child-size coffin being buried in the ground had not been so fresh, Hallie might have weakened. As it was, she stood up and took a few steps back. "I'm sorry, Will. I hate to hurt you, but I'm going. I know we're short on money so I'll write to my father. He will send me money to come home."

"I reckon he would, but there's no need of that. I can still manage to send my wife home on a visit to her family without asking them to pay for it."

And that is how they spoke of it after that. Hallie was going to take William back to show him off to his grandparents. It was easier to explain it that way to Rueben and the Andreasons. The upcoming visit was spoken of quite casually in front of Rueben, but Will realized she had no intentions of returning to the little soddy.

Will walked dejectedly through his empty, ragged fields while up at the soddy Hallie cleaned and packed, readying to leave. What Will's thoughts were, Hallie did not know. She knew what her own were. They held the images of loved faces, welcoming arms, the glad greetings of home. Home! She was going home! Will? She would not think of Will.

Chapter 36

Most folks wanting to reach the train depot at Prairie Rose caught a ride on whatever conveyance was headed in that direction. Hallie, not wanting to make anymore demands on Will, insisted on using this method of reaching the depot.

"There is no need of you driving all those miles. I'll catch a ride with someone from Dry Bend." Hallie had been adamant about this, and Will had flared, "You can't get shut of me quick enough, can you?" He had stomped off when Hallie tried to explain that wasn't it at all.

Will went to Dry Bend ahead of time to line up this ride Hallie would need to Prairie Rose. He returned with arrangements made. He had discovered when he'd inquired at the mercantile store that the Huebanks were planning a buying trip to Omaha in a few days. "They said they'd be glad to take you and the baby with them to the depot. Said I should bring you in the night before. You can spend the night with them and you can all get an early start the next morning."

And that is how Hallie came to bid Will goodbye in the Huebanks' living quarters above the store.

Hallie found supper with the Huebanks was a talkative affair. She was filled in on all the happenings of the small town in no time. "The new saloon is causing a lot of controversy," Mrs. Huebanks confided "A lot of people think it is the last thing we need," she said as she passed the dinner rolls. "Anyway, we've finally got the solid citizens of the town to do more than talk about putting up a church. They are raising the funds and ordering the lumber."

"High time, too!" Feeny Huebanks declared. "Any self-respecting town needs a church."

"The Reverend Sorenson has agreed to pastor the church full time when it's finished." Mrs. Huebanks passed the platter of fried pork chops to Hallie. He's getting too old for that circuit riding."

"A doctor is needed badly," Hallie said. "Do you think one will ever move here?"

"Yes, indeed, there is talk of a fellow from Lincoln coming in a few months," her host assured. "Dry Bend is growing. No two ways about it!"

Hallie had volunteered to do the dishes while the Huebanks went below to do some last minute inventory. When the dishes were finished, Hallie faced the empty apartment. The baby had been fed and was down for the night. There were books in a bookcase in the living room, but after selecting one, Hallie found she couldn't concentrate on the pages. She could feel the slight scratching beneath the pleating of her blouse where she had pinned the fifty dollars Will had insisted she take with her. She felt guilty about it. Twenty-five dollars would have purchased her ticket and seen her through to Missouri. Will could have used the other twenty-five to purchase a milk cow or the coal he'd planned on.

Hallie wandered aimlessly about the room. She stopped at the window overlooking the dusky street. There was little activity. A lone horse stood at the rail of the new saloon. A faint, tinny tinkle of a piano could be heard. A half-grown, bony pup sat forlornly in a square of light made by one of the store windows. Poor thing. He looked as though he were starving.

There were the table scraps. She would take them down to him. Carrying her offering, Hallie descended the steep stairway that was built on the outside of the store to the street. The skinny pup cringed toward her on his belly, begging for affection obviously more accustomed to a kick or curse. He sniffed timidly at the scraps then reassured by Hallie's voice, began to eat hungrily. She stroked his short, rough coat. Good bones and intelligent eyes. He'd make someone a good dog if given the chance.

It was a warm evening, and Hallie sat on the bottom step leaning her back against the banister post. The pup was happily crunching at his meat bones. The stars were beginning to scatter across the deep ebony of the sky. The prairie sky did have a sort of mystical beauty. Had the sky been like that back in Missouri? She couldn't remember.

It seemed such a long time since she'd been there. Had it changed? The orchard? The creek? Her mother's smile? Were they looking older...her mother and father? Had they missed her as much as she had missed them? Of course they had. But, they'd not write and tell her so. They'd not want to worry her. Instead, they had sent letters of encouragement; how proud they were of their daughter and Will, how fine it must be to build a place up from scratch like they were doing. Even in the beginning they'd not said, "Don't go."

Hallie remembered her wedding day so well. How her father had answered in a strong, sure voice when the pastor asked, "Who giveth this woman?" "Her mother and I," he'd said and placed Hallie's hand gently but firmly into Will's.

She thought back to how she had felt during the ceremony. How she had realized she was truly leaving her parents and childhood, starting a new life. How grownup she had felt standing there beside Will, repeating her vows. Some of the words came back to her as she sat quietly in the moonlight, the now content pup asleep at her feet.

"To love and to cherish...for better or for worse," she murmured the words. They had sounded so purposeful and grand. But...how was she to know, standing there in her white dress on that lovely June day there would be such an abundance of "worse"? No one had warned her about becoming a homestead bride in Nebraska!

Hallie tilted her head back and looked up at the stars once again. "It's been hard, Lord. You know it has. And I've tried. No one can say I haven't tied."

Softly the night wind blew, tenderly touching her cheeks, drying at the beginning of tears, whispering as it passed. "Has it been all bad, Hallie?" Hasn't there been a goodly share of 'better'?"

Hallie thought of little William sleeping upstairs, of the Andreasons, Pearl, all the others. Her little sod house. And Will...what of Will? She still loved Will. Was love enough?

The wings of the hawk barely moved as he rode the wind, leisurely drifting over the tiny town that had invaded his territory. The morning sun washed the prairie world with its glorious colors, gilding the feathers of the flying hawk, flooding over the endless grass, turning the dewdrops to beads of gold.

The harshness of the town itself was softened, as the sun painted bare boards with a creamish tint, hiding the dusty streets with yellow sunbeams, dancing on the window fronts...starting a new day.

There was movement in the town, not much at this early hour, but some. A team and buggy drove up in front of the Huebanks' Mercantile. An older woman came out carrying a satchel to be assisted in by the driver who then climbed back into the seat beside her. They drove off toward the edge of town where they took the trail leading to Prairie Rose. A small dog rose from his dust bed at the foot of the store stairs, stretched and shook the dirt from his coat.

The hawk continued his circling, swooping lower, more intent on the earth below, his hunger growing. A foolish prairie chicken poked its head around a clump of tall grass at the edge of town. It pecked at some fallen seeds. The movement caught the eye of the hunter. A feathered missile shot from the sky to claim its breakfast.

Midmorning. The hawk floated again overhead, hunger satisfied, lazily watching the comings and goings of those below. A pair of riders came up the trail from the east. A woman hung freshly washed sheets on the line back of the new hotel. A man came out of his shop, looked up and down the street, scratched his sandy hair with an ink-stained hand then went back inside.

The Whipple wagon loaded with well digging equipment, could be seen leaving town. Ebee and Nute rode on the board seat with a woman between them holding a blanket–wrapped child. A spotted cow was tied to the tailgate of the wagon, a lean pup trailing at her heels. The sun shone down with friendly warmth on the little caravan. A gentle breeze pushed encouragingly at the backs of the travelers pushing them west…over the rolling hills, following the trail leading in the direction of McCain Valley.

About the Author

One of the fifth generations of her family to call the Sandhills of Nebraska home, Maxine writes of the land and people she knows. She fits her writing in between the demands of being an active farm/ranch, wife/mother/grandmother. Always fascinated by the history and stories past down by her forebears, she has taken the liberty of using this material to create works of fiction that are not only entertaining but have that special ring of authenticity we all search for when choosing a book.

Maxine has had numerous short stories and articles published in various magazines, and in a variety of anthology publications. In 1998, she won the literary category of the Nebraska Mother's Creative Arts Competition.

Printed in the United States
15996LVS00004B/190-270

9 781403 386519